In a single motion Raymond drew off his nightshirt and Susanna buried her face in the thick soft fur of his chest while he fumbled at the fastenings of her clothing. She did not fight him when he slowly pulled her dress over her head. She felt as though her limbs had melted into an incredibly soft sweetness, and she was utterly at his command. He removed her underclothing, and she lay naked beside him, her soft, peach-tinted skin exposed to his exploring hands. Embarrassed, she tried to press herself to him.

He pushed her away. "No, I want to look at you," he murmured in a low voice hoarse with desire. . . .

Fawcett Gold Medal Books
by Katherine Sargent:

CAJUN LOVER

LOVESPELL

OUTCASTS FROM EDEN

LOVESPELL

Katherine Sargent

FAWCETT GOLD MEDAL • NEW YORK

A Fawcett Gold Medal Book
Published by Ballantine Books
Copyright © 1987 by Katherine Sargent

Library of Congress Catalog Card Number: 86-91388

ISBN 0-449-12949-7

Manufactured in the United States of America

First Edition: April 1987

FOR STEVE STANSBURY

1

I⊤ WAS ON A BURNISHED, BLUE-SKYED AUTUMN DAY THAT
Susanna met Raymond Galt. The scent of woodsmoke
hung heavy in the air, and brilliant leaves colored russet
and gold and orange skittered this way and that in the
sharp, clean breeze. It would have been a shame to waste
such a day cooped up indoors, and so it was that Susanna
was working in the herb garden behind her cottage when
the thunderous pounding commenced on her door.

"I'm coming!" she called as she stood up and wiped
the dirt from her hands on her overskirt.

Apparently, whoever was there did not hear her, for
after a brief pause the pounding began again. "Yo, Mistress Collins!" a man's voice bellowed. "Be ye home?"

Susanna walked around the small house to see a group
of four men who had obviously been hunting, as they were
carrying muskets and pouches for ammunition. One of the
hunters, a giant of a man with a head of reddish-brown

curls, was slumped forward, his arms slung over the shoulders of two of the others. The fourth member of the party, a stout gray-haired man with a round, low-slung belly, was hammering on her door with one clenched meaty fist. In his other hand he held a brace of pheasant, upside down.

"No need to bash the door in, Simon Hastings," she said, taking in the situation at a glance.

"I'm sorry, Mistress Collins, but Geoffrey and Raymond and I were out hunting and Raymond . . ." Simon jerked a fleshy thumb toward the man in the middle . . . "was shot in the shoulder."

"I did it," said the fourth man, William Fitzsimmons. "It was an accident, of course."

"It's a pretty bad wound, and you were the nearest person who knew aught of healing, so we carried him here," Simon added.

"Yes, yes, I can see what's happening easily enough. Bring him inside." She lifted the latchstring and pushed open the door, letting the men precede her, half-carrying and half-dragging the victim.

"Lay him out beside the fire," she said as she removed the overskirt that protected her dress of blue linsey-woolsey from dirt.

"It's a good thing you were home, praise the Lord," said Simon. "When I saw your latchstring was out I said, 'Maybe she's gone to Ebenezer Akin's, or to tend someone else who's sick.' I'm right glad you were home, not only on account of the bullet being deep. 'Young though she be, there's no one can heal as well as Mistress Collins, like Goody Collins before her, bless her memory,' I said to the lads. 'She got the skill from her mother.' I told them that only last winter, when the goodwife took so ill with the coughing sickness we thought she would not live to see the spring, it was you who saved her, with your potions and poultices. She only got weaker after Dr. Griggs bled her, but now she's as good as new, praise be to God.''

"Open the shutters and stand out of my light," Susanna said shortly, as she washed her hands and then fetched her medicine chest. Simon Hastings was a good soul, but he would talk your head off if you let him.

The other two men, Geoffrey Able and William Fitz-simmons, Susanna knew from church. The victim was a stranger. She had only the impression of great size and strength, and a well-made body, before she knelt beside him on the hearth, unbuttoning his shirt and pulling it back from the bleeding wound. When she probed gently with her knife he stiffened, choking back a moan. His skin was very white up to the collar of his shirt, and above that it was brown from the sun. Surely he's a man who works out of doors, she thought. His chest and arms were knotted with muscles and covered with a thatch of thick, soft, reddish hair, a shade lighter than the hair on his head.

"It's far in all right, but the bullet didn't shatter any bone. He should mend fast once it's dug out. Geoffrey, fetch me a bottle of brandy." Geoffrey Able was a thin, slack-mouthed man with a large Adam's apple that bobbed up and down when he talked and a shock of dark hair that he was always brushing back out of his eyes. He looked dull-witted, but he was not. He moved at once in answer to Susanna's crisp command.

"Take a good deep drink," she said to the victim when Geoffrey handed her the bottle, "and bite down on this, hard." She put a piece of wood between the stranger's teeth. He was disconcertingly rugged and virile in appear-ance, and although she had seen many half-clothed men, the overwhelming masculinity of this one made Susanna feel ill at ease.

3

He took the wood between strong, flawless white teeth. "Are you ready?" she asked.

He nodded. She dug deep into the wound, working as swiftly and gently as possible. The man's face went white beneath his tan but he did not whimper. Susanna was forced to probe for some time before she found and removed the bullet, but the stranger did not move or make so much as a sound.

"You are brave," she said, smiling down at him and holding up the bullet. "I've never seen one embedded so deep."

Spitting out the piece of wood, which now bore the marks of his teeth, he spoke for the first time. "Do you know you're very pretty when you smile?" he said. "You looked so solemn when I first saw you."

"I'm surprised you take note of such things at a time like this," she answered dryly, although she was well pleased that he thought her pretty. "Most men would have their thoughts on their health, if not the state of their immortal souls. That bullet could have lodged in your head."

The stranger shrugged. "God will take me when He sees fit. There's naught I can do about it. You've the prettiest nut-brown hair I've ever seen, and eyes the same color. Has anyone ever told you that you've got streaks of sunlight in your eyes and hair?"

Geoffrey and William, a short man whose red nose attested to his fondness for the bottle, nudged each other, grinning. "He's not too sick to pay court to a pretty girl," William said.

"When that day comes, it really will be time for you three louts to dig my grave," the stranger replied, looking up at Susanna with such a cocky smile that she dropped her eyes in confusion.

4

"We're not through yet," she said, leaning over him to pick up a pair of tongs. She almost lost her balance, and the stranger grasped her about the waist to steady her. She looked down, flustered, and he gave her a broad wink with an extraordinary sapphire-blue eye. Susanna felt the warmth of his large hands seep through the cloth of her dress, and although she enjoyed the feeling, she did not smile when he exerted an unmistakable pressure on her slender waist.

She drew a red-hot coal from the fire and swiftly applied it to the wound. At this he finally moaned softly and closed his eyes, his lids fluttering. He went even whiter, and a fine film of perspiration sprang out on his face and body.

"That should do it," Susanna said. She wound a linen bandage around the wound and rebuttoned his shirt, trying to avoid the piercing blue eyes that had reopened and were scrutinizing her with unabashed interest.

As soon as she was finished she stood up and smoothed out her dress in a prim gesture. "Don't get up," she said hastily to her patient when he tried to follow her. "You lie quietly by the fire for a while."

He leaned back, easing his head onto the warm hearth-stones as if it were aching.

"Would you like some bread and cheese and beer?" she asked of the other men. "It's all I have to offer you at this hour."

They nodded eagerly. She bustled about, fetching food and wooden trenchers and placing them on the table her father had made. When she finished the three men attacked the simple food with relish. Susanna ate a bite or two to be sociable, although she was not hungry. She could not refrain from stealing a few glances at the man who covered almost the length of her fireplace. He had closed his eyes and seemed to have forgotten her. She noticed that the color had not returned to his face.

"Who is he?" she asked when her guests had taken the edge off their hunger.

"Who, him?" said Simon Hastings. "Raymond Galt. Pardon me, I didn't realize that the two of you had not met. Though why you should have, I don't know, as he hasn't been in Boston long. And bless me, the town is growing so fast, you can't be expected to know everyone any more. Not like the old days. Why, just the other night I was saying to the wife that Boston must have upward of nine, even ten thousand souls by now, what with the shipping business growing so fast, and new shiploads of folk from England more than glad to come over now that we've paved the way for 'em." Simon's barrel chest swelled with civic pride.

"What does he do?"

"Who? Oh, you mean Galt. He's a carpenter at the shipyard, although to hear him talk you'd think he owned the place."

"He means no harm with his boasting," Geoffrey said.

"No, no, I didn't mean that," Simon said hastily. "I like a man with ambition. Show me a man who doesn't dream, and I'll show you one who will never amount to much. It's just that most men don't noise their plans abroad as much as Raymond does. If that one realizes half of his schemes he'll own the whole of Boston one of these days."

The other two men laughed. "That he will," said William.

"First he talks of being the captain of a vessel, then of owning his own ship, then of owning a fleet of them, and then of owning his own shipyard," Simon continued.

"Nor is that the end of it. He has only to talk to any sailor at the harbor to get the most fanciful notions! First he says he'll be traveling to some country where women have three breasts, then he's going to sail a sea with precious gems instead of sand at the bottom, and next he's all for buying land in some outlandish place where the soil is so free of stones that a plow slides right through it!"

"Where is he from?"

"From the north, I think, from a settlement in Maine. Came here to work in the shipyard, as I said. And a proper one with the ladies he is, too! Here only a couple of years, and paying regular court to the Widow Harden. And if that weren't enough, half the young girls in town have been making eyes at him, to be sure! They say that he and the Widow Harden have an understanding, although the banns can't be read until she's out of mourning."

Susanna felt a sharp stab of disappointment to hear that he was as good as engaged, but she brushed the feeling aside. Raymond Galt meant nothing to her. She must not attach any importance to his words of flattery. They came too quickly and easily to his tongue, and he seemed to have them ready for any girl who caught his eye. The Widow Harden was rich, and would be a good match for an ambitious young man.

"She has a plump purse," William said, as if reading Susanna's thoughts.

"She's plump all over, to be sure, is Elizabeth Harden," said Simon. "I'll bet it's not just her purse he's after. She's still a comely woman, although not, it's true, in the first flush of youth. But who wants to tame a new wife? They improve with age and seasoning, if you ask me, like cider. It's like breaking in new soil—let another man do the spadework."

The other men laughed and exchanged knowing looks, but Simon glanced uneasily at Susanna, as if embarrassed that he had spoken in an unseemly manner before a young unmarried woman. "But we've taken up enough of your morning," he went on hastily. "Is it safe for him to move?"

"Does he live close to the shipyard?" she asked.

"Not far."

"He really should rest. That's a good walk back."

"We'll help him," the other two men said. "We got him this far, we can get him into town."

"And here's a brace of pheasant for you, and thanks for your trouble," said Simon, rising and holding out the birds.

"Oh no, you owe me nothing," she said hastily.

"It's not in payment of debt, but a gift," he said. "I never thanked you properly for tending Charity last winter."

"Well then, thank you. I'm much obliged." She took the birds. "I'll share them with Ebenezer and Goody Akin."

The other two men had gone to the hearth and pulled Raymond Galt to his feet. "Do you think you can walk?" asked Geoffrey Able.

"Of course I can walk. Leave me alone." Raymond shook off his would-be benefactors, took two tottering steps, and fell forward. Geoffrey and William grabbed him before he hit the floor.

"Leave me alone," Raymond said again, shaking them off. "It's just that it's so hot in here." His companions shot worried glances at each other. Susanna had barely kept her breakfast fire alive, and the room was comfortable.

Rising, Susanna hastened to Raymond's side and placed her hand on his forehead. It was burning hot. "He's got a fever," she said, just as his legs buckled beneath him

8

again, as if someone had hit him hard behind the knees. William and Geoffrey sprang forward and barely kept him from collapsing onto the floor.

"He's sick," Susanna said. "I'm afraid he'll have to stay here. He can't possibly be moved far. Here, you two, put him in bed." She pointed to the large bed in front of the fireplace.

"But Mistress Collins, it won't be proper . . . " Simon Hastings began.

"Of course I won't stay here myself," she replied. "I can spend the nights with Ebenezer and Goody Akin until he's well."

The two men had slipped their hands under Raymond's elbows, but they continued to look at her doubtfully, like a pair of dumb oxen.

"Be quick about it," she said. "Look at him—he's weak as a kitten. The man is too ill to be moved. Even if you could get him into town he'll need nursing, and who's to do it if he's a bachelor?"

No one could gainsay this argument, and so Geoffrey and William pulled back the bolster, blanket, and coverlet of Susanna's bed and poured Raymond Galt's giant frame on top of it. After his head rested on the pillows they removed his boots and pulled the bed clothes over his fully-clothed body.

"That's right," Susanna said. "Bundle him up nice and warm."

No sooner had they covered him than his teeth began chattering, and he pulled his knees up to his chest. "I'm c-cold."

"You three, run along now," she said briskly. "I've work to do. Never fear, I'll stay with the Akins. And Simon, thank you again for the pheasant."

After the three men had left she examined her unexpected guest more closely. Raymond Galt was asleep now, his face flushed and burning with fever, and Susanna found it far easier to look at him without his deep, bright eyes boring into her. She thought he was the comeliest man she had ever seen. She reached out tentatively and smoothed his thick, reddish-brown hair. It was surprisingly soft, and springy to the touch. His forehead was high and wide, and his jaw, which she traced with her finger, was firm and square. Touching him set off a strange quivering in her stomach.

She unbuttoned his shirt and removed it, marveling again at the whiteness of his skin where it was untouched by the sun. She ran her fingers lightly over his upper body. It was as smooth as marble, knotted with long ropes of muscle and covered thickly on the chest and lower arms with reddish hair. He stirred and mumbled in his sleep. Susanna withdrew her hand, embarrassed to be touching an unconscious man in such a manner.

She fetched one of her father's old nightshirts, which her mother had never given away, and pulled it over Raymond Galt's head. He was large—the largest man she had ever seen, standing well over six feet—with hands to match his size. His feet were short and broad but delicately molded. It took great effort for her to lift even the upper part of his body and to pull the nightshirt over it. Later, when he was better, he could remove his pants himself.

When she had made him as comfortable as she could Susanna took the brace of pheasant and walked a few hundred yards to the home of her nearest neighbors, Ebenezer and Hannah Akin. Her knock brought Hannah to the door.

"Susanna, we were just sitting down to eat. Come and

join us." The Akins' table was laid with a fine goose roasted with apples, beans, parsnips, and garden greens.

"Oh Ebenezer, look what Susanna's brought us!" cried Goodwife Akin, holding up the pheasant.

"Aye, and fine looking birds they are, too," he said, rising. "I'll hang them outside till they're gamy."

"Don't get up from your meal," Susanna said. "I'll do it."

"How did you come by such fine birds?" Ebenezer asked after she rejoined them. "A gift from a grateful patient?"

Susanna related the morning's events for the old man and his wife. His small, frosty blue eyes gleaming in his white-whiskered face, Ebenezer, who was hard of hearing, cupped his ear and leaned forward so as not to miss a word of her recital.

"So that's the way of it," he said slowly when she was finished. "Raymond Galt, eh? I've heard the name, but never met the man. He's a good worker, a good carpenter, says Enoch Burroughs from the shipyard. I know that much."

"Do you mind if I sleep upstairs until he's well?" Susanna asked.

"Nay, lass, you needn't even ask. You know you're always welcome here. Come to that, you can sleep in our bed and we'll stay upstairs," Ebenezer said. "The nights aren't cold enough for us to need a fire."

"I wouldn't dream of putting you out of your own bed," she protested. "I won't hear of it."

"We don't mind going upstairs for a few nights, but have it as you wish. You could have brought him here, you know. We'd not have turned a sick neighbor away, even one we don't know."

"I thought it would be easier to nurse him if he were

downstairs in my cottage. That way I won't have to run up and down all day. Besides, he needs to be by the fire. And while I'm doing my work I can keep an eye on him." Her heart was pounding, and she hoped this explanation sounded reasonable. She had really left Raymond in her own home because it was the only way she could see him alone.

"Aye, that makes sense," Ebenezer said, after he had considered it in his slow, methodical fashion.

After she moved a nightdress and the few things she would need into the upstairs room of the Akins' house Susanna returned to her cottage and examined her patient again. His chest was rising and falling in the even rhythm of sleep, and he was not having any trouble breathing.

"I will take good care of you, Raymond Galt," Susanna whispered, tracing his lips with her finger. It was the first time anyone but herself had slept in her house since her mother's death summer before last, and it was good to have company. The loneliness she had suffered living by herself had been almost as painful as a physical disease. She smoothed Raymond's soft, thick curls back from his forehead and he smiled in his sleep. "Yes, I think we shall get on together."

After she had settled him she set about fixing some arrowroot broth. She would try to force a few sips down his throat later. When she had that simmering on the fire, she went outside to finish tending her garden.

Her gardening trowel and other tools lay where she had dropped them. Only a short time had elapsed since that morning, but it seemed to Susanna that a great change had taken place in her life.

For days Raymond Galt drifted in and out of a fevered sleep. Susanna nursed him patiently, placing cool cloths on his forehead, getting him to sip arrowroot broth and a bit of claret when he was awake, sponging him off as far as decency allowed. Finally his fever broke and the day came when his forehead was cool. When she checked on him that morning he seemed to be in a normal sleep.

Susanna stood looking down at him, and thought with a pang that she would miss him sorely when he was gone. On an impulse she leaned over and brushed his lips lightly with her own. In an instant his arms shot out, locking themselves around her like steel bands, and the sapphire-blue eyes opened.

She struggled to wriggle out of his grasp, laughing and twisting, but her efforts were in vain. "Not until you finish what you started," he said.

"You tricked me," she said in protest. "You weren't asleep at all."

"I wanted to see what you've been doing to me while I lay here at your mercy. It's not fair to kiss me when I'm not awake to enjoy it."

Drawing her to him, his mouth covered hers and he kissed her, slowly and gently at first, and then, when she responded with a hunger that belied her outward calm, with increasing fervor, until his exploring tongue sent tiny shivers of desire racing through her.

For an instant a small warning voice in the back of her mind admonished her, but she silenced it as Raymond pulled her onto the bed beside him. Half pinning her down with his massive frame, he kissed her until she stopped fighting him. His hands stroked her slowly, following her supple lines until she felt the resistance flowing from her body. His mouth moved slowly to the hollow at the base of her throat, and she leaned back, closing her eyes and parting her lips, abandoning herself to the pleasurable sensations as his lips feather-touched her throat and tugged at her delicate earlobes with tantalizing persuasion. The tip of his tongue gently flicked the shell-like curve of her ear, sending messages of excitement along her nerve endings.

She felt her breasts swell and tighten as she lay crushed beneath the hardness of his chest, and she gasped when he rolled partly off her and moved his large hands upward to cover them, teasing their pointed tips beneath the thin fabric of her dress ever so lightly with his fingers until they hardened into tight, pulsating buds of pleasure.

Reaching up, he untied her cap. Then he undid her hair, letting it cascade in a golden-brown torrent down her back. "You're a strange one," he said. "On the surface so cool and distant, with a face as austere and haughty as the mistress of the manor when you want it to be."

He reached out and traced the curve of her lips with his finger. "It's your mouth that gives you away. It's too full for that remote expression you wear. And when your eyes melt you look like a different person."

He arranged her hair so that it tumbled loosely over her shoulders, and kissed handfuls of it. Then he stroked her scalp lightly with his fingers, kissing her until she felt powerless to resist him.

In a single motion Raymond drew off his nightshirt and Susanna buried her face in the thick soft fur of his chest while he fumbled at the fastenings of her clothing. She did not fight him when he slowly pulled her dress over her head. She felt as though her limbs had melted into an incredibly soft sweetness, and she was utterly at his command. He removed her underclothing, and she lay naked beside him, her soft, peach-tinted skin exposed to his exploring hands. Embarrassed, she tried to press herself to him.

He pushed her away. "No, I want to look at you," he murmured in a low voice hoarse with desire. He inhaled sharply as his eyes fixed on her full, perfect breasts, their pink tips blushing softly in the flickering firelight. "God, you're beautiful," he murmured, reaching out to cover her breasts with his large hands. They seemed to fit perfectly. Carefully he drew her toward him, as if she were infinitely fragile, and she flowed toward him irresistibly. A great shudder shook his body as her bare breasts brushed against his chest, which was heaving spasmodically with his ragged breathing. He held her at a slight distance from him for a moment letting the coarse mat of hair on his chest send thrills of excitement coursing through her tight, swollen breasts.

With strokes as light as a feather he teased her rosy peaks with his thumbs, until she moaned and lay back on the pillows, surrendering completely. Slowly bending his head to her breasts, he began a teasing arousal with his tongue, sending hot jolts of need rippling through her. His teeth joined in the playful torment, nibbling gently until she thought she would go mad. She clutched spasmodically at his shoulders, drawing him to her, begging him mutely to end this fiery torment of the senses.

"Yes, my proud haughty one," he whispered. "I like to see you begging me. I plan to drive you as mad as you have driven me since the moment I laid eyes on you." His hands stroking her slowly, languorously all the while, he drew back, forcing the raging in their bodies to subside for a moment. "I knew you could look this way—soft and lovely, your eyes like two warm melting pools. I've been dying to see you with your hair falling loosely around you, and your face with that look of total abandon."

His hands, which continued their leisurely exploration, had reached her silken belly. When he stroked it lightly she arched her back, sighing. Then his lips followed the path his hands had taken. When he nibbled softly at the skin of her belly, his hands stroking her inner thigh with the feather-light touch that drove her wild, she let out a low moan like that of an animal. Her thighs were suddenly hot and wet and trembling with need.

Suddenly he was beside her again, gathering her to him so that she felt his rigid, throbbing manhood pressed into her belly. "I can't wait any longer," he said. "I know it's your first time, and I planned to take forever, but I'm about to die."

"Yes," she whispered. "I am dying too. Do whatever it takes to end this torment."

She felt one hairy thigh part hers, and suddenly his hands and lips were rough, harsh and greedy and demanding. They seemed almost to punish her. Slowly he lowered his giant frame onto her as the passion pounded through her blood. She gasped in sweet agony as he pierced her delicate membrane, crying out for release as he eased himself into her. She moved with him, clumsily at first, until they found the tempo that welded their bodies into a single organism. The wild, spiraling tension mounted to breathless peaks of ecstasy. Their pleasure mounted until they exploded, in unison, into a thousand shooting stars.

Afterward, they lay drowned in a flood of contentment and peace. He kissed her moist forehead as she lay back, her eyes closed, feeling the throbbing of her body slowly subside. For a long while they lay in each other's arms, content to hold each other.

Susanna had no idea how much time had elapsed, but suddenly she was ravenously hungry.

"Are you hungry?" she asked him.

"Starving. I could eat a horse."

"I think I can do better than that." She put on her undershift and set about collecting food. Raymond lay in bed and watched her, and when she was through with the preparations she brought the food to bed and climbed in beside him. They feasted on smoked venison and sliced beef, the mixture of corn and beans the Indians called succotash, and her delicious crusty bread, all washed down with great quantities of beer. For dessert they had apple tarts and the remains of a pumpkin pie.

"I never ate so well in my life," Raymond said, leaning back in bed and crossing his hands behind his head. "I'm sure that's the best meal I've ever eaten."

When the dishes were cleared Susanna said, "Simon Hastings says you are from Maine." Now that the sudden, overwhelming craving of her body had been satisfied she realized she knew next to nothing about Raymond Galt.

"Aye," he said. "I grew up in Montsweag, on the coast."

"Then you were no stranger to the sea when you came to Boston."

"I should say not. I learned to swim as soon as I could walk, and was lobstering and fishing as far back as I can remember."

"Your father is a fisherman, then?"

"No—I mean, not for a living. He's a gunsmith. My older brothers are in business with him now."

She smiled. "But you were too restless to stay at home polishing flintlocks."

"That I was. I've always loved the sea. My father let me sign on as cabin boy for a voyage to Boston when I was twelve. That's how I learned to sail. I liked Boston right off. The first time I saw it I vowed to live here some day. When I got home I pestered my father until he let me sign on for another voyage, and then another. By the time I was eighteen I was a regular tarpaulin."

"Tarpaulin?" The word was new to her.

He laughed. "That's sailor's lingo for an experienced seaman."

"Why are you working as a carpenter, if you want to be a seafaring man?"

"So I can build ships as well as sail them. I like everything about the sea and trafficking on it, and I want to know every aspect of seafaring, from what cargoes make the best profits to how to build and navigate ships."

When he talked of the sea he had the enthusiasm of a boy, and his extraordinary blue eyes danced in his sun-bronzed face. "I served my carpentry apprenticeship at home. When I wasn't working I was usually down at the harbor, talking to sailors about the distant places they had seen. By the time I had finished my apprenticeship and was ready to move to Boston I could build as neat a sloop as you've ever seen. Since I've been here I've learned to build larger ships—frigates and brigantines and such. I'm a master carpenter now."

His chest swelled with pride in his achievement. "I've sailed on voyages since I moved here, too. I've been south, to Maryland and Virginia and the Carolinas." Raymond had never talked so openly to a woman about his life, and he was enjoying it. He told her of his family in Maine, and the things he and his large family of brothers and sisters had done together when he was growing up.

When the day was far advanced he looked outside at the position of the sun and uttered an exclamation. "I had no idea it was getting so late. If I'm well enough for this, I'm certainly well enough to work. We're very busy at the shipyard now."

She watched as he dressed. "Are you all right? Are you strong enough to get home alone?"

"Of course."

She got up and dressed hastily. "I've prepared some

18

arrowroot broth for you," she said, handing him the container. "It will help you regain your strength. Don't push yourself too hard at first."

"I'll be fine."

"You must rest for the remainder of the day. Don't try to work until tomorrow. You'll be weaker than you think."

"I'll remember." He leaned over and kissed her one last time. "I hate to leave you. Don't worry," he said in response to the unspoken question in her eyes. "I'll be back. I give you my word."

2

O<small>N HIS FIRST DAY BACK AT WORK</small> R<small>AYMOND</small> G<small>ALT CARRIED</small> around a heavy burden of responsibility for what he had done on the last day of his illness. The guilt gnawed at him all day like the pain from a bad tooth. Whenever thoughts of Susanna surfaced he felt terrible about injuring the girl. When he'd seen the question in her eyes upon his departure he had promised, in a moment of weakness, to visit her again. He would, but on what pretext? He decided that he would shoot a turkey and take it to her as a token of thanks for healing him. Surely he could not be faulted for that, even by Elizabeth Harden. And once in Susanna's house he would joke with her in the teasing manner women loved, and reassure himself that she was all right, that her life was going on as usual without him.

Since he had been initiated into the mysteries of love by a Pequot Indian girl when he was fourteen there had been many women in his life, but he had never felt guilty about one as he did now over Susanna. She should have saved her pent-up passion for a man who was free, a man who could return the love that she was so eager to give. He was, after all, going to marry Elizabeth Harden as soon as her period of mourning was over. He had long ago decided that it was just as easy to love a rich woman as a poor one, and Elizabeth suited him well. She was lusty, a good companion and housekeeper, and a shrewd businesswoman. The fact that she was older than he did not bother him, nor did the fact that she had borne four children, two of whom had lived past infancy. He enjoyed Patience and Felicity, her two young daughters, and looked forward to being a father to them.

Still, there was Susanna, tugging away at his thoughts whenever he stopped throughout the day to take a drink or wipe the sweat from his brow. Why couldn't he forget her, simply dismiss her from his mind?

When the workday ended Raymond returned to the room he rented, tidied himself by brushing the wood dust from his leather trousers and putting on his best jacket, and paid a visit to his betrothed. He felt some trepidation as he lifted the polished brass knocker on the door of her comfortable home facing the town commons, but when Elizabeth opened the door to him herself, her face wreathed in smiles, his fears evaporated. Her solid, well-fleshed body and merry, sensible face reassured him at once.

"Raymond!" she said, folding him in her ample arms and giving him a resounding smack on the lips. "You're home! You must tell me all about your adventures. Simon Hastings has noised it about town that you were at death's door."

"Nay, he exaggerates. The wound healed easily. I was sicker from the fever." Elizabeth's two daughters came running out when they heard Raymond's voice and embraced him, shrieking. The smaller one, Felicity, clambered up his giant frame and tugged at his curly hair.

"Leave the man alone, girls. You'll be the death of him," their mother scolded.

"Let them be, Elizabeth," he said, laughing at their antics. "They don't bother me."

She resumed her discussion of Raymond's accident. "Shot, were you, by that walleyed William Fitzsimmons? The man shouldn't be trusted with firearms. He's half-blind and drinks too much."

"It wasn't his fault, Lizzie. Many a man's shot hunting. I was lucky to get off so lightly."

She cast a hard look in Raymond's direction. "I hear you were well cared for."

"Aye, that I was, and a good thing too that we were close to someone who knew the art of healing."

As they sat down to one of Mistress Harden's ample suppers Raymond continued his tale, omitting, of course, his intimacy with Susanna.

"I can't believe that little strumpet kept you alone in her own home, without so much as a bundling board between you to protect her virtue!" his intended wife objected, her dark eyes flashing.

"She slept with Ebenezer and Goody Akin, Lizzie. Besides, I was out of my wits and weak as a kitten the whole time I had the fever. Even if I had the inclination and she was willing, I don't think I would have had the strength to wrong her." He hated to lie to Elizabeth, but she was a jealous woman and could be a terror when crossed. He had seen several samples of her violent temper and had no intention of inviting another display.

"Still, I say it isn't decent—a young girl like that, keeping you alone in her home! There's been talk enough about her and her kin. You'd think she'd want to protect

22

what's left of her reputation, after all that was said against her mother.''

"What was said against her family?"

Mistress Harden sucked in her round, red cheeks and cut her dark eyes in the direction of her young daughters, as if considering whether she should talk of such matters in front of them. After pausing for dramatic effect, she leaned forward and said in a voice that was low but heavy with insinuation, "It was whispered that her mother was a witch, and the young one's no better, if you ask me." She punctuated this pronouncement with a vigorous nod of her head. "I was afraid to visit you, for fear she'd put a spell on me."

"A witch? Susanna Collins?" Raymond threw back his head and laughed. Now that he was back in Lizzie Harden's home, eating her good food and warmed by her fire, with her two lively daughters on either side of him at the table, he felt entirely restored to his old good humor. He would stop feeling guilty. What he had done to Susanna Collins was no more than any red-blooded male would have done when tempted by such beauty.

"No, Lizzie, Susanna Collins is no witch. She's as sweet and pure a girl as you'll ever meet. What village gossip started such a tale? A woman jealous of Susanna's beauty, I'll trow."

"It was the mother who was most talked about, and it wasn't a woman who started it. It was none other than Doctor Griggs."

"Come now, Elizabeth—that old sawbones?"

"His word carries weight in this town, Raymond. He said that Goody Collins's healing was unnatural, that she consorted with the Dark One."

"Ha! Just because he kills half the people he tends, with his leeches and cups! I never knew Goody Collins, but if she taught her daughter the healing art, she must have been a damn sight better at it than Griggs. Do you know what Simon Hastings says of him? 'It's but a step from Griggs to the grave.' ''

Elizabeth rolled her dark eyes and snorted her disapproval. ''Simon Hastings says a great deal about everything, and much of it nonsense. It's naught to jest about, Raymond. When Extra Virtuous Morley was struck down with the quinsy, and Dr. Griggs had done all in his power to save him, Goody Collins brought him back from the very brink of death, I tell you. And she did the same for Mary Osborne when she had the throat distemper, and for Deliverance Bailey, and many more. And the babies she brought into this world all lived, aye, and most of the mothers too! Now can that be natural?''

''Lizzie! You'd damn the woman for saving lives?''

''Not for saving them, but for *how* she saved them. And that's not all. She consorted with Indians.''

''Surely you can't mean that!''

''No, I don't mean like Anne Marshall.'' Anne Marshall had slept with a brave from the Abenaki tribe and been sentenced to wear the figure of a red Indian sewn onto her sleeve as a punishment. ''Goody Collins was just friendly with them, and listened to their ways of healing,'' Elizabeth said.

''So? It stands to reason that Indians would know better than we what healing plants grow in the New World. They've been here a sight longer.''

''But what can a godless savage know of healing? And why would a Christian woman consort with devil-worshiping heathens? No self-respecting woman would lower herself to be instructed by them!''

''They aren't all bad. I had friends among the Pequots in Maine. Besides, if Dr. Griggs had evidence against

Goody Collins, why did he bring no charges against her? If there are witches among us, they should be hanged, for the good of the community and the health of our souls. Griggs must not have had any solid proof.''

"I still say, where there's smoke, there's fire." Elizabeth shot him a sly, knowing look. "And the girl's too pretty for her own good, if you ask me.''

"Well, let's not argue, not on my first day back. Tell me what happened while I was away.''

"I suppose the greatest news is that Samuel Coffin has bought the old Lawson shipyard, but I suppose you've heard that.''

"Coffin? Bought Lawson's? That is news! I wonder why no one told me of it at work today.'' Samuel Coffin was one of the richest men in Boston. He was an eccentric old bachelor who usually kept his purse strings tightly pulled, but he had a good head for business, and all his investments had prospered.

"There was talk of nothing else for several days, and then it all quieted down. I suppose everyone thought you'd heard.''

"Is he opening it up right away? He'll need men to run it.'' Raymond's mind was racing. Coffin might recognize his ability and give him a position of prominence. Perhaps he would invest in a ship for Raymond with the profits to be split. Perhaps . . .

"Better leave well enough alone. He's a hard master, and you're doing well where you are." Raymond suspected that Elizabeth did not want anyone more strong-willed than herself in his life, and that she intended to control him through her purse. However, when she married him her property would become his by law, and he planned to do the controlling. He knew there would be a struggle between them, but he was determined to gain the upper hand.

No need to force the issue now. He decided to change the subject. "Tell me, girls," he said, turning to Patience and Felicity, "what are you learning in the dame school?" The girls broke into an excited chatter, but while he talked to them Raymond continued to turn over in his mind the news that Samuel Coffin had gone into the shipping business and the ways in which this could be of use to him.

Later, after Elizabeth's slave girl Effie had cleared the table and the two girls had been tucked into their warm bed in a corner of the kitchen, Raymond and Lizzie retired to the parlor, where the best bed stood by a roaring fire. As soon as they were alone Lizzie took his face in both of her hands and showered him with quick, eager kisses. "I missed you," she said. "The Lord knows how I missed you."

"I missed you too," he replied.

Mistress Harden's hands were busy, pulling out his shirt and loosening her bodice. As soon as her clothing was loose Raymond thrust his hands into the top of her dress, grasping her heavy breasts with both hands. She closed her eyes and breathed a long sigh of contentment as his busy fingers found her large, thrusting nipples. Her hands grew bold, pressing his private parts through the fabric of his breeches.

"Aye, I have missed you," she repeated, her voice a low, husky murmur in her throat. They finished undressing each other, and as she folded back the bolster, blankets, and coverlet of her bed he could see her clearly, naked by the light of the fire. Elizabeth Harden was a handsome woman, and she was considered marvelously well-preserved for her age, but she looked better with her clothes on than off. Her large, pendulous breasts and round belly had stretch marks from bearing and nursing babies. Her legs were crisscrossed with raised, broken veins, and her thighs wobbled as she moved. When she leaned over to plump the pillows Raymond observed, as if for the first time, that the flesh of her behind was deeply dimpled and flabby. There flashed before his mind the picture of another body, supple and unblemished, with smooth, silky limbs and high, firm breasts, sweet-scented flesh, and round little buttocks.

"Come to bed," Elizabeth said, holding her heavy arms out to him. He finished undressing and slid in beside her.

"It's good to touch you again," she said, her hands busy on his body. "I've missed having a man in my bed. I mean, I've missed *you*."

Raymond closed his eyes and kissed her. She moaned with pleasure, pulling him closer.

Raymond waited for the excitement he usually felt in Elizabeth's bed to sweep over him, but he remained limp and cool. He continued caressing her body with his hands and lips. Nothing happened. He kept his eyes closed, and as a last resort consciously summoned up the vision of that other body. Thinking of Susanna, he felt himself stiffen, become aroused, but it did not last. After several minutes of vigorous encouragement on Elizabeth's part he lay back.

"It's no use," he said. "I guess I'm just tired."

"And since when have ye been too tired to roger me?" she demanded, sitting up and putting her fists on her ample hips.

"Since I was shot and fell ill of a fever," he snapped. "I'm sorry, I didn't mean to be cross," he said hastily, as her eyes flashed and she drew a deep breath, gathering her wits for an attack. When she opened her mouth he put his finger over her lips. "Don't," he said. "Whatever you were going to say, don't."

Suddenly all Raymond wanted was to be in his own room, in his own bed. He wanted to sleep alone. Elizabeth's dark, abundant hair, which had always seemed exciting and alive to him, now seemed frizzy and coarse. Her round, hard cheeks, full lips, and tilted nose gave her a porcine look. The longer he looked at her, the more she reminded him of a sow, fleshy and grunting over a trough of slops. "I'm sorry, Lizzie, I guess I just don't have my strength back yet."

"Very well," she said, punching her pillow angrily and turning over with a flounce. "I'm going to sleep. You may sleep here or go home, as you like. It's all the same to me."

She kept her back to him, stiff and unyielding, as he slipped out of bed, dressed silently, and left.

Susanna passed the next few days after Raymond's departure in a haze of misery, shame, loneliness, and remembered delight. She could not believe that she had given herself to a man who was as good as betrothed, a stranger she had never seen before. A young man named Michael Hale had been walking her home from church, dropping veiled hints about matrimony, and she planned to accept his offer when he asked her to marry him.

Why had she yielded to Galt's sweet words, words that apparently sprang readily to his tongue whenever a pretty girl was at hand! She had been told that he was a tease and a flirt, and that many of the girls in town had an eye for him. Why hadn't she been more cautious? What must he think of her? That she had given her favors lightly? Or perhaps that she found him irresistible? That would puff up his already considerable vanity! It was true that she found him more pleasing than any other man she had known. The worst part was that though she knew that what she had done was a great sin, there was nothing she desired so fervently as to do it again! Whenever memories of their time together rose—memories of his hands on her body, of his hungry mouth, of his strong arms around her—she would push them resolutely out of her mind only to find them springing up again, unbidden.

She was glad that it was a busy time of year. There was cider to be made from autumn apples, and beer to be put up, and slaughtering to be done. She and the Akins did their slaughtering together. After their pigs had been dis-emboweled, stripped of hair, and carved into sections, the larger cuts were submerged in brine to preserve them and stored in the dairy house to keep them cool, while the smaller cuts were turned into bacon. Each side of bacon stood in salt for several weeks before being hung from the chimney lug pole for smoking. Susanna was engaged in this household task when Raymond Galt appeared at her door one afternoon, bearing a large turkey he had just shot. Her heart jolted almost painfully when she saw him, and once again she wondered at the curious power he seemed to have over her.

"It's for you," he said, holding out the bird and wiping his feet before entered. "For taking care of me."

"Thank you." She hung the last of her flitches of bacon, and then fetched him a mug of beer from the cellar. "It's the last keg from last year," she said. "Good thing the time to put up more is upon us." She was dressed in a simple dress of brown homespun, with a white collar and cuffs. Her demeanor and dress were modest, but her full lower lip, broad cheekbones, and almond-shaped eyes gave her face a curiously passionate cast. The contrast was intriguing. The moment he looked at her the feelings for her that he had carefully suppressed flooded back.

"Has your strength returned?" she asked, to open the conversation, as he sipped his beer.

"Aye," he said, "although I was not as strong as I thought when I left you."

"I told you not to tax yourself too greatly at first."

"That you did." He gazed at her in silence. All the flippant witticisms that usually sprang so readily to his tongue in the presence of a pretty girl had fled. For once he was struck dumb. He felt as if his tongue were glued to the roof of his mouth. He had vowed to take her the bird, pay a short, proper visit, and depart, but once he gazed on her golden brown hair, gathered at the nape of her neck and tucked modestly under her cap, and the lovely eyes of the same color that had captivated him the moment he saw her, his resolution fled. Her willowy body conjured up remembered delights, and it required all the willpower he could muster not to crush her in his arms and smother her face in kisses.

Susanna managed to conceal the turmoil in her own heart as she sat facing him on the other side of the fire, her hands folded primly in her lap. He gave her a helpless look, as if he was at a loss for something to say next.

"Now that you've mastered shipbuilding I imagine Boston seems small to you, and you're restless for broader waters," she supplied.

He laughed, shaking his head. "How can you read me so well?"

"You're an ambitious man, your friends told me." She was smiling. He could not tell if she was impressed by his ambition or if she thought him foolish.

"I can't deny that I'm ambitious," he said, rubbing his chin thoughtfully, "but sometimes I believe I'm too restless for my own good. Often I think I'll never be able to settle down, that no amount of adventure will ever be enough for me.''

''Where would you sail, if you could go anywhere in the world?'' Susanna thought Raymond had a touch of lunacy, but despite herself she found his enthusiasm infectious.

''To the Bahamas,'' he said without a moment's hesitation. ''You'll find such wonders there as man has never seen. Wrecked Spanish galleons stuffed with treasure—bars of gold and silver, chests filled with coins and jewelry. And beautiful islands, where the air is warm and balmy all year long.''

''Air that is warm all year long! Even in the winter?'' She laughed and shook her head, clearly disbelieving him.

''It's true.''

''Who told you such a tale?''

''Sailors who've been there.''

''And they told you of these wondrous treasures? Bars of gold, and chests full of coins and jewels?'' Her tone was clearly skeptical. ''Do you believe every wild tale a sailor tells you?'' She remembered what Simon Hastings had told her—that Raymond talked of countries where women had three breasts, and of places where there were precious gems instead of sand on the floor of the ocean.

''I know it's true. The treasure's there, all right, in the Bahamas. The ships belonged to Spanish conquistadors. They were sunk in the last century when great gale winds drove them up on barrier reefs.''

''So you plan to buy or build your own ship, sail south, and find this sunken treasure?''

''Why not? Why not me instead of some other man?''

''It takes a lot of money to have your own ship.''

He laughed ruefully. ''That it does.''

"The Widow Harden's purse will help you there," she said quietly, looking him directly in the eye.

He squirmed in his chair. "Word travels fast." He suddenly regretted that he was engaged, and that she knew of it. "We haven't had the banns read yet. We can't till she's out of mourning. But yes, we plan to marry."

A heavy silence fell between them. "I'm sorry," he said at last, "about what happened between us. It was wrong of me. I mean, I'm not sorry that it happened, but sorry that I'm bespoken to another, and cannot make you an honorable offer."

"The responsibility lies with both of us. It was as much my fault as yours."

"Maybe what we did was wrong," he said, "but I couldn't help myself. I can't forget you. I haven't been able to drive you from my mind since I left. Susanna . . ."

Without warning he leaped to his feet and fell on his knees before her, grasping her about the neck and giving her a long kiss, which she was too astonished to resist.

She had known he would come again, would try to make love to her again. She had steeled herself against this moment. "No," she said, pushing him away. "We can't continue. It *is* wrong. It wouldn't have happened if I hadn't been alone so long." She shuddered, thinking how lonely she had been the previous winter, the first winter she had spent by herself since her mother's death. The very morning Raymond arrived wounded at her door she had been thinking that much as she loved autumn, it was the forerunner of another long, cold winter alone.

All her life Susanna had received physical affection. Her parents had been demonstrative, with each other and with her, and before her father died when she was five she could remember the three of them constantly touching and kissing one another. When she was a small child her father had loved to swoop her high up into the air and ride her about on his shoulders, and a dozen times throughout the day her mother would smooth back Susanna's hair, kiss her forehead, or straighten her petticoat—any excuse to touch her beloved child was a good one.

After her father's death her mother had been even more affectionate, as she'd had no one on whom to lavish her love except Susanna. After her mother had been buried and the edge wore off Susanna's grief, there settled on her a terrible and numbing sense of physical deprivation, a sensory craving that the adoption of an orphan kitten she could hug and cuddle had only partially satisfied.

Last winter, when the deep snows had kept her housebound for days at a time, Susanna had thought she would go mad. New England winters were a bad time for women under the best of circumstances. Men could hunt the year round, or cut a hole in the ice and fish. In the house, almost every man had some useful business to attend to—carpentry or home repairs, cobblery, carving wooden trays and trenchers. For women, beyond the necessary household chores there was little to do in the long cold months besides sew and spin and weave. That became weary work soon enough, if there was no one with whom one could talk.

"I want you," Raymond said, bringing her back to the present. "I want you as I've never wanted another woman." He was still kneeling at her feet, holding her hands.

"It's impossible," she said, trying unsuccessfully to pull her hands away. "You're promised to another."

"I know," he said. He studied her face. Her expression was strangely aloof, mysterious. He could not read what she was thinking.

"I love you," he blurted out. "I love you and I want to marry you." No one could have been more surprised by

33

these words than he was, for he hadn't the slightest idea that he was about to say them. But the moment they were out of his mouth he knew at once that they were true.

"Marry me! You've just told me that you're going to marry Elizabeth Harden, and now you want to marry me! You can't have two wives! I don't think you know your own mind."

"Yes, I do." He grasped both of her wrists, holding her more tightly than before. "I want to marry you."

"You'd be foolish to throw away the chance to marry a rich woman. All I have in the world is this cottage, a little livestock, and a bit of land."

"That doesn't matter. I'll find a way. I'll find someone to invest in me, to have faith in me. Samuel Coffin's bought the old Lawson shipyard. I'm going to talk to him."

She struggled to release her wrists, but the harder she struggled the tighter he held her. "You fancy me, I know you do," he said, the fear of losing her making him desperate. "You wouldn't have given yourself to me if you didn't."

She quit struggling, and spoke slowly and calmly. "Yes, I fancy you. There's no point in denying it. But I think you're crazy too, with your talk of sunken treasure and islands that are warm in winter. And you *must* be mad to tell me that you're going to marry another woman in one breath and ask me to marry you with the next."

When she stopped fighting him, and spoke to him so calmly, with a touch of scorn in her voice, he released her. Once free, she patted the smooth coil of hair at the nape of her neck and smoothed her dress.

"I do want to marry you, and my schemes aren't crazy. I'll prove myself to you. You'll see."

Susanna rose. "I think you'd better leave now," she said, opening her door.

"All right," he said when he was outside, "but I'll be back." It was the second time he had made that promise.

"No," she said, "I think it would be better if we didn't see each other again." She shut the door before he had time to say anything else.

After he had left she sat down slowly, trying to sort out her chaotic feelings. Even if he could break his engagement, Raymond Galt was not at all the kind of man she had decided to marry. In some ways he was like her father, who had also been an impractical dreamer, although not a loud, boastful one. Nicholas Collins had been a silent dreamer, a man who paused with his hand on the plow and looked off into the blue New England sky, seeing visions of distant places conjured up in his mind. People spoke of his dreaminess in a jesting manner, the same way the men who had brought Raymond Galt to Susanna had laughed at Raymond's wild tales. She would not marry a man at whom people laughed.

Nicholas Collins had worked hard, but he had not been cut out to be a farmer, and somehow things always went wrong for him. Then he'd died, and Susanna and her mother had eked out a living on their own, subsisting on gifts people gave her mother for delivering babies and healing the sick. There had been whispers about her mother, ugly whispers. Susanna knew there was no truth in the things people said about Abigail Collins, but she had made an easy target for people's frustrations because she was poor and powerless, a widow with no family and no man to protect her. Susanna wanted more than anything else to be accepted, to marry a man who would assure her a place in the community.

That night she ate supper with the Akins. "We saw

Raymond Galt at your door with a turkey,'' Ebenezer said. He spoke in a loud voice because he was going deaf.

"It was a token of thanks," she said. "It's a fine bird, but I'll never eat it by myself. You'll have to help me."

"He took long enough saying his thanks. He likes you," said Goody Akin with a gap-toothed smile. "I can tell he fancies you."

"Nay, you imagine it," she said. "Besides, he's not the kind of man I want."

"He has a handsome face," Goody Akin continued.

"But he talks wildly and brags, and has too high an opinion of himself," Susanna said. "I want a quiet man, someone sober and respectable. Besides," she added, "Raymond Galt is already promised to the Widow Harden."

"Michael Hale will surely speak as soon as he gets the courage," said Ebenezer. "He's almost worked off his indentures, and you could do a lot worse."

"How many times is it he's walked you home from church?" Goody Akin asked, her eyes gleaming.

"Oh, just a few," Susanna said modestly. Michael was frugal and industrious and well thought of. Slowly they would build a life together, have a family, and add to their store of worldly goods. She did want to marry Michael. Still, when Raymond Galt touched her she had lost all reason. She could not explain it.

"More like a dozen times, has young Hale walked you home. He'll be declaring himself soon, mark my words," said Goody Akin.

That night in his room Raymond experienced a turmoil he had never felt before. No sooner had he wooed and won a rich woman than he had proposed marriage to a mere slip of a girl with nothing but a cottage, a cow, and a few pigs—an orphan who lived on the outskirts of town and the outskirts of respectability!

Susanna must be right—he was mad! But the words he had spoken to her were true. He did love her, he did want to marry her. Elizabeth Harden would have a screaming fit if she ever found out that he had proposed marriage to another woman! He had had his life so neatly arranged, so satisfactorily planned, and then a chance encounter with a young girl had changed everything. Perhaps Elizabeth was right, perhaps Susanna was a witch. She certainly seemed to have cast a lovespell on him.

Throughout most of the night he lay tossing and turning, trying to determine what he should do. He had learned everything he could at the shipyard. The time had come for him to strike out on his own. He had something he had not told Susanna about, something he had told no one about. It was a map he had bought from a sailor, a map showing the exact location of a sunken Spanish treasure galleon. He would go see Samuel Coffin the next day when he finished work to see if Coffin would be willing to back him financially so he could get his own ship. He would share his secret with Samuel Coffin, show him the treasure map. With that thought Raymond was able to drift off to sleep and get a little rest before the next day's work.

3

O<small>N</small> S<small>UNDAY</small> M<small>ICHAEL</small> H<small>ALE</small> <small>ROSE AT FIRST LIGHT AND</small> dressed with extra care. He had decided that today was the day he would ask Susanna Collins to marry him. As he drew on his best woolen stockings he noticed ruefully that the right one was wearing thin in the toe. He would be glad when he was wed and had a wife to take care of him. Next he drew on his baggy leather breeches, and then his shoes. The night before he had cleaned the mud from them and polished their brass buckles until they gleamed. He had also brushed his best black jacket and his hat. He did not think it would be cold enough to need his cloak, but he'd brushed that as well.

When he was dressed he scrubbed his face and hands until they were red, paying particular attention to his ears. Then he wet his comb with water and combed his straight brown hair, looking in the mirror that hung over the washbasin in his small attic room. He peered at his face anxiously. He was certainly not handsome, but he did not think it was such a bad face.

Michael shook his head at the dark circles under his eyes. He had worked hard on Saturday, but still he had been too nervous and worried to sleep much the night before. Why he was frightened at the prospect of making an honorable proposal of marriage he could not say. It just seemed to him that his wits left him when he tried to talk to Susanna. He thought she was the most beautiful creature he had ever seen, and a wave of bashfulness swept over him whenever he looked at her. Because of their humble social standing they had both been assigned seats in the back of the church, and he thanked God that he had been seated directly behind her so that he could stare at the back of her head during services. On many a Sunday, during the long sermons, his mind was more on her than his devotions.

He dreamed of her, too, both sleeping and awake, often having to push from his mind sinful thoughts of her naked body and what it would be like to touch it. On many a night he woke from dreams of her to find his sheets a sticky mess. He washed the spots out as best he could so that Hope Walcott, the farmer's daughter who did the washing for the Burroughs, would not see them. He was sure he would die from shame and embarrassment if anyone ever noticed and remarked on the condition of his sheets.

Michael had thanked his Maker on more than one occasion that Susanna was poor, like him, so that his suit would not be presumptuous. If she had come from a more prominent family he would have had little hope of winning her. He could not marry until his seven-year indentureship was up, and he was in an agony lest someone else snap her up first. He would be free in March, and he estimated that it would be proper to begin courting her about eight months in advance. He had started walking her home from church in August.

The evening before, his master, George Burroughs, had noticed Michael's unusual sartorial preparations and commented on them. After supper Freeman Burroughs had been sitting before the fire in his kitchen, puffing comfortably on his pipe, while Michael used the light from the fire to brush his clothes and clean his shoes.

"Look at young Michael," he had said with a wink toward his wife. "What do you suppose the odds are he'll be paying court to Susanna Collins tomorrow?"

Michael turned beet red and ducked his head, earnestly polishing away.

"Are you ready to speak to her, lad?" he said.

"I've been ready, if I could only think of what to say."

"Just say what's on your mind. Come right out and tell her you want to make her your wife."

"But what do I *say* to her? I mean, how do I ask her?"

George Burroughs, who was a kind man, saw that the boy was genuinely frightened. "Leave us for a while," he said to his wife, who had settled down before the fire with her mending.

When they were alone he said, "Son, there's no reason to be so distressed. Susanna is willing, I tell you. She's more than willing. There's nothing a girl of marriageable age wants more than a husband."

"Sometimes I think that, too. But then again she can be cool and distant. I think she likes me, but I'm not sure."

"I had the same fears and misgivings when I proposed to the missus. When I walked to her house that day I wished that my feet would not move, and when I stood before her door I felt that my limbs had turned to water. I had courted her for months. Sometimes she was nice to me, and sometimes she acted so cold and indifferent I thought she did not care whether I lived or died. But when the time came to speak to her, I had no sooner stammered out a few words than she flung her arms about me and cried, 'Oh George, I thought you'd never ask!' '' He imitated his wife's voice in a high falsetto.

"If Susanna Collins did not want you she'd have discouraged your attentions long before this. Don't expect to understand her—you'll probably never do that. Women are strange creatures, and no one except the Almighty will ever figure out the way their minds work. They don't think in a straight line like you and me. Did I ever tell you the tale of Enoch Frale?''

"No sir, you did not.''

George Burroughs refilled his pipe, tapped it down, and lit it with an ember from the fire. There was nothing he loved more than to tell a good story. When his pipe was drawing well he began, "If a man reaches the age of thirty in these parts without marrying, everyone puts him down for a confirmed bachelor. Well, Enoch Frale had more than reached thirty and was still not wed, and it was accepted as a foregone conclusion that he'd never take a wife. Then, when he was about thirty-five, without a word of warning he up and married Sarah Warren, the worst shrew in town. I tell you, this woman had a tongue that could flay you alive. When his friends asked him why he married her when he could have married a sweet, obedient woman instead, he replied that he did it as a kind of penance. 'For years I led the carefree life of a bachelor,' said he. 'I enjoyed life so much I was afraid I would not go to heaven unless I suffered here on earth. I married Sarah so I would have a cross to bear.'

"Well, the village gossips started passing the tale about, as they will, and finally it got back to the bride. When Sarah heard it she flew into a rage. 'Does Enoch Frale expect to ride to heaven on my back?' she cried. 'We'll just see about that!' And then, just to spite him, she became the sweetest and most docile wife a man could ever hope for!''

They both had a good laugh at the tale. "Nay, lad, don't worry," George said, clapping Michael on the back. "You're a good man, and you've got good prospects. Any girl should be proud to have you for a husband. I was going to wait until later to tell you this, but I might as well do it now. When you and Susanna get married we'll give you a right proper wedding feast."

"Thank you, sir," Michael stammered, his eyes tearing. He thought that for an orphan boy who had emigrated from a London slum to the New World he was doing quite well for himself. "You've been like a father to me."

Michael had been considerably cheered after his talk with George Burroughs, but it had not kept him from lying awake half the night. If Susanna Collins would not marry him he knew he would die.

On Sunday Susanna walked to church in the company of the Akins. As she took her seat she nodded at Michael Hale, noting that he looked unusually pale this morning. After an hour-long prayer, followed by a psalm, Reverend Gilchrist ascended his high pulpit to deliver the first sermon of the day, which was directed against the vanity of women.

"Do not think it has passed my notice that many of you who are not married to gentlemen presume to dress above your station," said Reverend Gilchrist, looking sternly down at the congregation from his lofty stand. "Need I remind you that only the wives of freemen are permitted to wear lace or garments sewn with gold and silver thread? Have I not seen the wives of common goodmen dressed in gaudy colors, in silk hoods and scarves, slashed sleeves and embroidery? And have I not witnessed many of you, even the wives of freemen who should know better, wearing immoderately wide sleeves, wider even than the half an ell permitted by the law? And, in the summer months, have I not seen dresses cut immodestly low, revealing the tops of your bosoms, and short sleeves exposing your arms?''

Reverend Gilchrist's deep voice thundered so loudly that even Ebenezer Akin put down his ear trumpet. ''Your hair, which St. Paul commanded that you cover—have I not seen it riotously entwined with ribbons and dressed with that abomination—the curling iron!

''These wicked wiles, which you use to excite the lust of men, do not go unnoticed by the Almighty! You may adorn yourselves like the Jezebels and Delilahs you are, and walk about shamelessly like harlots and seductresses, but when you stand before your Maker on the day of judgment, you shall stand naked and ashamed! O whores of Babylon! He will not forget your unseemly conduct!''

Reverend Gilchrist's voice reached a crescendo of passion, and he grew red in the face. He had just begun warming to his theme, and spent several hours elaborating on the immodesty of women, the various forbidden parts of the body that he had seen them exposing to arouse prurient thoughts in men, and the exquisite torments awaiting them in hell.

As he described the writhing and moaning of women under Satan's tortures, and their screams and pleas for mercy, a dead hush fell on the congregation. It seemed to Susanna that she had never seen a sermon heeded with such rapt attention. She noticed many men in the congregation leaning forward, licking their lips with relish, their eyes glowing, eagerly awaiting his next words.

During lunch at the noon-house Michael Hale asked to sit with Susanna and offered to share his gingerbread with her. As he broke off a piece she noticed that his hands were trembling, and although he was as timid as a rabbit she thought once again that she would not mind spending her life with him. He was hardworking and honest, and not too bad to look at, although his skin was lightly pitted with smallpox scars and his left eye had an odd cast. He was poor, it was true, but it would be unrealistic of Susanna to think that she could marry a rich man. Many a young couple started out with less than they would have.

The morning's sermon was considered too indelicate for general discussion, so talk during the noon break was all of Indian trouble to the south. Relations with the Indians, which had always been tenuous at best, had been deteriorating steadily, and there had been sporadic raids here and there during the past year. Stories of defiled women and scalped men and children had drifted north until all the northern colonies had made financial provisions for arms and organized their men into militia units that drilled once a month against the Indian threat.

"They weren't organized enough to do much harm until now," said Simon Hastings, who had gained control of the discussion. "Tribal jealousies had the Indians at each other's throats, and they spent most of their time fighting each other instead of us. Until now no one seemed to be able to pull them all together."

Deliverance Bailey interrupted him. "Aye, but that was before. Everything's changed now, with this new leader of the Wamanoag tribe, this what's-his-name . . ." He snapped his fingers, searching his memory. "Metacom, that's it."

"King Philip they call him, when they speak English," George Burroughs inserted.

"Since Swanswea was attacked no one has felt safe,"

William Fitzsimmon said with a frown. The previous June a body of Indians had fallen upon the town of Swansea, on the eastern side of Naragansett Bay, and several people had been slain and wounded. Later in the summer there had been attacks on Rhode Island.

"King Philip is a clever devil, and seems to be able to get them all to sit and smoke the peace pipe together," Simon continued. "By all accounts he's a crafty warrior and a leader to be reckoned with. At least we can be thankful he hasn't persuaded the local Abenaki to join his confederacy. I won't rest easy in my bed at night if the Abenaki ever throw in with him."

"We can't count on their holding out forever," Geoffrey Able countered. "I've heard rumors that they're beginning to listen to Philip's appeals. And even without the Abenaki, King Philip's allies are growing in number every day. The Pennacooks threw in with him, and now the Nipmuks."

"The attack on Deerfield last month was one of the worst yet," interjected Deliverance Bailey. "And the trouble keeps spreading north. They're getting too close for comfort."

"Perhaps we should have two militia meetings a month instead of one," Geoffrey Able said, his prominent Adam's apple bobbing up and down in his excitement. "We've got to be ready should they keep pushing farther north."

Simon Hastings opened his mouth again, but just then the church bell rang and everyone prepared to return to church for the afternoon service.

After the service Michael Hale asked Susanna if he could walk her home. "I thought the afternoon sermon particularly good," he said to open the conversation.

"Very edifying," she murmured.

"In my opinion Reverend Gilchrist exceeded himself. I

have never heard him more eloquent, and his quotations, particularly those from St. Paul, were most apposite and to the point.''

''I thought so, too.''

They discussed the sermon in some detail, and then their conversation came around to the subject of Indians. ''It's not safe, living alone outside of town as you do,'' he said. ''You heard the talk at noon. The Wamanoag raids are getting closer every day.''

''I'm not really alone. The Akins are next door, and they've been like a family to me since I lost my mother.'' She was tired of hearing people talk about Indians.

''But they're old, and Goodman Akin is deaf. You're still by yourself in your cottage. You need a man to protect you.''

And where am I to find one of those? she started to ask. When they had reached her home she invited Michael to share her Sabbath supper of cold mutton, bread, cheese, and beer, then let the Akins know she had done so, for propriety's sake.

''My indentures will be worked off next March,'' Michael said when they had finished eating and were seated before the fire. ''I'll be a free man. Master Burroughs has asked me to stay on with him.'' George Burroughs had bought Michael's indentures by paying his passage from England. He was an expert silversmith, and also made pewter plates and tankards. Michael had done well and was now almost as skilled as his master.

''I've learned a good trade, and if I continue to do well I've got a secure future with Master Burroughs. He's got no sons to carry on the business when he's gone.''

He looked at Susanna hopefully. Well, it's coming at last, she thought. He's going to ask me to marry him.

''Master Burroughs has promised me the gift of a cow

when my service is up," he said tentatively, easing his way into the subject.

"That's very good of him," said Susanna.

"And Mistress Burroughs has promised me the gift of a suckling pig in the spring." Weak and limp with fear, he studied her face to read her reaction to his probing.

Get on with it, man, she thought. If you're going to ask me to marry you, go ahead and *ask* me.

"She's being more than generous," Susanna said.

"Oh, yes. They've both been as kind as parents to me." He felt rivulets of perspiration running down his armpits. "Added to your pigs and other livestock, and your household goods, it would not be a bad start."

"*My* pigs, *my* household goods?" she prodded gently. Again he looked at her as if hoping she could read his mind, without his speaking directly. When she remained silent, he said in a voice that was little more than a whisper, "I wouldn't be surprised if Mistress Burroughs were to throw in a couple of sheep."

"Indeed, that would be passing generous." Susanna shifted in her hard chair and tapped her foot with impatience.

Michael swallowed hard and folded his hands in his lap, to conceal their trembling. "I'm asking you to marry me," he said at last in a weak voice. "You have no father or I'd have spoken to him first."

"Oh." Susanna's heart sank. She had been looking forward to this for months, but when the long awaited proposal came, it was oddly anticlimactic. She couldn't understand why she didn't feel overwhelmed with joy.

"You don't need to answer me right away," he said, stumbling over his words and showering her with a spray of spit in his anxiety. "I can wait for an answer. We couldn't marry until next March anyway."

"Very well," she said. "I thank you for the offer, and I promise to give it my very serious consideration."

"Would you allow me to kiss you, that is, if you don't consider me too bold?" He had gone quite pale, and looked as if he were about to faint from shock.

"I suppose that would be permissible." He leaned over, took her face in both his sweaty, trembling hands, and kissed her lightly on the lips.

"Thank you," he said when this ritual had been completed.

"You're welcome," she said, trying not to laugh.

"Well, I'd best be going," he said. "I must be up by first light."

Susanna had planned to spend what remained of the day reading her Bible, but she was too restless after Michael had left, and too torn by her conflicting feelings about Raymond Galt, to sit still. Instead of reading she broke the Sabbath by baking. Baking was the hardest part of cooking, and she was good at it. She would make a number of loaves, and trade them with her neighbors for other things she needed. Carefully, she sifted wheat and rye flour from barrels in her cellar, removing the coarser pieces of grain and bran. Then she made her sponge, or dough formed of warm water, flour, and yeast. The yeast she obtained from a piece of dough she had saved from her last baking. She put her sponge where the warmth of the banked fire would raise it by the morning, when she would work more flour into it and knead it into finished dough.

On Monday, after she set the bread dough to rise one last time, Susanna made use of the beautiful fall day by going into the woods to collect some of the plants she used in making her simples and decoctions. Many of the ingredients in her medicines—sorrel, chervil, ground ivy, and pennyroyal—she grew in her own garden. Others grew wild in the woods. Tansy and elecamane grew everywhere. Along the banks of streams she plucked spearmint leaves. Next she stripped the bark of the elder tree, an ingredient in the poultice she used to treat throat distemper. Foxglove, or what the Indians called digitalis, was a remedy for heart trouble. Wherever she found them she collected snails and earthworms and put them into her basket. These she used to make snail water, which was useful for a variety of ills.

When the sun was directly overhead she sat down by a stream to eat the lunch she had brought with her. Her activity, the food, and the warm sun had made her drowsy, so after she'd eaten she put her cloak on the ground for a blanket and setting her herb basket beside her, lay down to take a short nap. She realized before she drifted off that she had walked a long way into the woods. She would have to start home shortly.

It seemed to Susanna that she had just fallen asleep when she wakened in alarm, aware of another presence. She looked up directly into the bright autumn sun. Outlined above her were two large, brown figures, whom she recognized at once as Indians. They had slipped up on her without making a noise.

When they saw her stir they were on their knees beside her in an instant. Susanna found herself looking directly into the face of a young Indian, dressed in fringed buckskin and moccasins. He had a fierce face with sharp, hawklike features, as rough as if hewn from granite, dark, reddish-brown skin, and jet black hair falling to his shoulders.

Susanna was too terrified to scream. The Indian tore off her cap, grasped her by the back of the head, and unpinned the knot of hair at the nape of her neck. Lifting his tomahawk high into the air, he pulled her head back until the veins stood out like cords in her throat. Susanna knew that he was about to murder and scalp her. She closed her eyes. Dear God, forgive my sins, she breathed, and tensed herself, waiting for the tomahawk to descend.

The second Indian spoke swiftly and unintelligibly, and knelt beside his companion, grasping handfuls of Susanna's hair, which fell in a rich, golden-brown tangle down her back. The first Indian relaxed his grip on Susanna's head.

She turned to the Indian who had spared her life. She could see that he was older. His skin was more brown than red, and deeply weathered. There were streaks of gray in his hair, and his face was not as fierce. The second Indian carried a musket, and she knew by the language he spoke that they belonged to the Wamanoag tribe, the leaders in the latest war being waged by the Indians against the settlers in New England. Her mother had communicated with several Indian tribes in their own tongues, and had passed a little of this knowledge on to Susanna.

"Please," she said, "if you let me go I won't tell anyone I saw you." She shaded her eyes against the sun and peered into the older Indian's face, trying to read his expression.

The Indians exchanged startled glances, and the one behind her lowered his tomahawk slowly—and, she thought, reluctantly. "How do you know our language?" he asked.

"I know a little of it, from my mother."

"Your mother?" The Indian looked at her fair skin and hair. "Your mother was not one of us."

"No," Susanna said. "But she was friendly with Indians."

Her two captors exchanged skeptical glances.

"Her name was Collins, Goodwife Collins. She was

good at . . ." Susanna paused, trying to remember the word for "healing." "She learned much from your people, about how to make sick people well."

"Ah," said the Indian who had spared her life. "A medicine woman."

"Yes, a medicine woman."

"Did you understand what I said before?" he asked her.

"No, you spoke too fast for me to follow you."

There was what appeared to be a short debate between the two Indians, again spoken too rapidly for her to comprehend.

"Get up," the older Indian said. The one who had almost scalped her was still behind her. He lifted her unceremoniously by the elbows while she struggled to her feet. The Indians allowed her to put her cloak about her shoulders. "Let me have my basket," she said, attempting to retrieve what she had gathered that morning.

"Leave it," the younger Indian said, kicking it over. He tied her wrists together with a leather thong, dashing any hopes she may have had of being released.

"Come," they said, motioning her to follow them into the woods. They moved toward the west, walking single file, with Susanna between them. She could tell that the Indians were prepared to travel a long distance, as each of them carried a long leather food bag tied to his back like a knapsack. As they walked she cursed herself for ignoring the admonitions she had heard only yesterday at church. If only she had not wandered alone so far from her home!

They walked for half an hour, finally arriving at a dense thicket where two horses stood tethered to spruce saplings. The horses were laden with sleeping skins, weapons, and ammunition.

The younger Indian grunted and signaled Susanna to mount his horse. Impeded by her bound wrists she required assistance to follow his order. Once she was safely aboard the two Indians untied the horses and slipped onto their backs with fluid motions, the young one riding behind her.

Clucking to their horses and nudging them with their heels, the Indians turned toward the west. As Susanna traveled farther and farther from her home, her panic mounted. Where was she being taken, and what would happen to her after she arrived there? Why had her life been spared? She was under no illusions that she had been spared because of her sex. She had heard many tales of women ravished and slain by Indians, and children, too.

It would be impossible to rescue her, even if anyone cared enough to make the attempt. She might not even be missed for a considerable time. The Akins would notice her absence first, but sometimes she and they went several days without seeing each other. Besides, what could they do—an old woman, growing feeble, and a deaf old man? No search party would come after her, of that she was sure. She was not important enough for men to risk their lives for her. She could not really count on Michael Hale or Raymond Galt coming to see her, and it was only Monday, so she would not be missed from church for a full week. Finally she decided to keep her wits about her and try to stop worrying.

The Indians traveled slowly and cautiously, skirting any signs of English settlers and giving towns a wide berth. Because it was autumn there were hunting parties about, and once they almost ran into one. Susanna could hear men speaking in English, and the report of a musket. She wanted with all her heart to scream as loudly as she could, but she knew that it would mean instant death.

She was able to observe her captors at leisure. One of them, the one who had almost scalped her, was truly ferocious looking, with stern features that looked as if they had been hewn roughly from stone, and hard, cold eyes. The older one was more confident and less hostile. Fortunately, the young man deferred to the older one.

Although they were traveling slowly, by late afternoon Susanna's body began to ache from the unaccustomed riding. At dusk, when the Indians finally stopped for the day and signaled for her to dismount, she was so tired that she would have literally fallen off the horse if the older one had not steadied her.

They had stopped by a swiftly flowing stream, which made a soothing noise as it rushed over stones, carrying brightly colored leaves swirling on its surface. When the Indians untied her Susanna revived herself somewhat by splashing cold water on her face. Then she rubbed her wrists, which had red, angry marks where the leather had cut into them, until feeling returned to them at last. The young Indian untied his knapsack, which Susanna knew held a food they called nocake or nookick. The nutritious substance was made by parching Indian corn in hot ashes and then beating it into a powder.

The young Indian fetched a bowl and mixed some of the nocake with water, then handed it to his elder. With his second and third fingers the older Indian scooped some of the mixture into his mouth, chewing slowly. After both of the Indians had eaten the younger one held the bowl out to Susanna. "Eat," he ordered. She had eaten two good meals already that day, and fatigue and anxiety had completely destroyed her appetite, but she was afraid to disobey. She found that the nocake had a pleasant taste and that a little of it was very filling. She knew that white men, who had learned to make nocake from the Indians, also carried it in pouches when they went on long journeys, and that it was considered to be the most nourishing food in condensed form.

After they had all eaten, and the younger Indian had rinsed the bowl, the older man threw Susanna a sleeping skin. She wrapped up in it warmly, her head nestled at the foot of a tree. After she was settled the older Indian retied her wrists and, choosing a tree about four feet from hers, settled down under his own skin for the night. Despite her worry Susanna was asleep almost at once.

4

THE MORNING AFTER HER ABDUCTION SUSANNA WAS SO sore she could hardly move, and only pride kept her from crying when she was forced to mount. The second day of riding was torture until her limbs gradually adjusted. The third day was not as bad, and by the fourth her soreness had disappeared.

Susanna could tell by the sun that they continued to travel due west. The Indians hardly ever addressed her, and when they spoke to each other it was too rapidly for her to follow. The Indian who had almost scalped her had cut the strings of her cap, and her hairpins had been scattered when he took her hair down. Since she had reached puberty Susanna had always coiled her hair at the nape of her neck and covered it modestly with a cap, and for a while she felt awkward letting it cascade freely down her back, but after their initial scrutiny the Indians paid little attention to her appearance and she gradually grew accustomed to it. As they traveled farther west signs of the English became fewer, until at last they disappeared entirely.

When the sun was directly overhead on the fourth day after her capture they arrived at what was obviously a semi-permanent Indian settlement beside a large lake, and Susanna was given the order to dismount. The Indians left their mounts in the care of a boy watching a pen full of horses, and pushed Susanna, still bound, before them as they walked through the camp.

Inside the encampment skins had been fastened over wooden frames to make a few tepees. From the large number of Indians it was obvious that many slept outdoors, using only sleeping skins against the relatively mild October nights. Children and a few dogs ran about, and women with infants strapped to their backs were occupied with scraping skins, smoking fish over small fires, or pounding corn with mortars and pestles. Susanna noticed that one woman was cooking the food the Indians called supawn, a thick porridge made of Indian corn pounded to a coarse powder and mixed with milk. As she and her captors walked by many of the women stopped their work to stare at Susanna with dark eyes set in broad, expressionless faces, and small children began following them.

On the western edge of the village a fire burned in front of the largest of the tepees. Susanna was motioned to stay while her two captors went in search of their leader.

After what seemed like an interminable wait, during which large-eyed Indian children continued to gather and gape at her, the older of Susanna's two companions returned with a man she suspected at once of being the one the Indians called Metacom, or King Philip.

Susanna was fearful, being the only white person in a camp of Indians, and her long wait to see their leader had not improved her spirits. When the dreaded Metacom, who had struck fear into the hearts of the men of Boston, appeared, she was truly frightened and lifted her eyes slowly, to try to take the measure of the man who held her fate in his hands.

Metacom was only of medium height, but he carried himself very erectly and with great pride. He was a handsome man, with cleanly molded features, reddish-brown skin, jet black eyes and long hair of the same color. His skin was smooth and unwrinkled, and Susanna was surprised that he was so young. She estimated that he was a little older than Raymond Galt. Only his eyes seemed old, sad, and bitter.

"Untie her," he ordered the older and gentler of her two captors, speaking in an abrupt, peremptory tone of command.

"Leave us," he said after Susanna was free. The older Indian slipped silently away. It was strange to see this man, who was so much older than his leader, meekly following orders, after Susanna had seen him in command for so long. The children also scattered, leaving them alone.

"I am Metacom. I am also called King Philip." He spoke in English, slowly and with dignity. Susanna did not know what to do. Should she curtsy? Address him as King Philip? He saw her discomfiture and smiled. The smile changed his face, lightening the expression in his eyes. "My men tell me you speak our language."

"Not very well—just a little."

"And that you are from Boston."

"Yes."

"Sit down," he said, motioning toward the ground. "I will sit with you. How are you called?" he asked when they were seated.

"My name is Susanna Collins."

"Who are your people?"

"My parents were Nicholas and Abigail Collins."

"Boston. Collins. I have heard that name. Yes, there was a woman from Boston named Collins, who had the gift of healing."

"She was my mother."

"So it is from her that you learned our tongue."

"What I know of it."

"I never met her, but I remember hearing people speak of her. She had more sense than most of your kind. The healing your medicine men brought from England kills more often than it heals. Our people were willing to teach, but most of you did not want to learn. Our medicines have healed us for hundreds of years. Savages, you call us, ignorant savages." Susanna was surprised that he spoke English so well.

"Your mother was different. Her eyes and mind were open. She learned much from our tribe, and from the Abenaki, about medicine. Why do your doctors drain your blood when you are ill? What could be more foolish? Draining the blood leads to death, not healing. A man needs his blood for strength. Disease comes most often from what you have eaten, not from bad blood. You should purge a man of food when he is ill. Give him ipecac to make him vomit. Then sweat him, and make him fast.

"Your people refuse to use the steam house. It is one of the best things for illness. Purge a man of the bad food he has eaten, then put him in the steam house. Heat stones over a very hot fire, pour cold water on them. Let him breathe in the steam. Then make him jump in the lake. The steam, and then the cold water, will flush the impurities from his body. Next make him fast for several days, to work everything bad out of his system. Then you give him medicine.

"Your doctors think that the more ingredients a medicine has the better it is. They surround everything they do in mystery, because it makes them look more important. Your medicine men don't like the simple medicines, but some of the simplest ones are also the best. Digitalis for a bad heart. Hellebore when the blood pounds too hard through the body. Golden seal for sores that won't heal. I am no medicine man, but I know these cures, and many more. They work. Look at my people. Healthy, strong. Who lives longer, our men or your men?"

"You don't need to convince me. I have heard all of this from my mother," Susanna said.

"She is dead now?"

"Yes, for about a year and a half."

"Too bad. She was not too swollen with her own importance to listen and learn. Devil-worshipers they call us, as if we do not worship our gods just as you worship yours."

"We worship only one God."

"But you worship a god who is father, and another god who is the first one's son, and a great spirit who is neither the father nor the son. That makes three gods, not one," Metacom said.

"Three persons, only one God."

"Explain this to me."

"I can't. No one can explain the mystery of the holy trinity."

"Not even your priests?"

"No, not even our priests. They say it is a mystery no one can understand."

"If no one can explain it, or even understand it, not even your wisest men, why do they expect anyone else to believe it?"

"I don't know. I can't explain these things. I am not wise."

"But you believe in this god who is three people and somehow at the same time one?"

"Yes, I do."

Metacom shrugged his shoulders. "Come," he said, rising gracefully to his feet. "We will walk by the water." She followed him to the edge of the lake, walking down a faint path worn in the grass. Women with downcast eyes went back and forth along the path, drawing water which they carried in earthenware pots on their heads. They moved gracefully, straight-backed, with heads high, their hips swaying slightly.

"Your people do not behave like this man Jesus they worship," Metacom said as they walked. He still spoke English, and the Indian women they passed seemed to understand nothing of what he said. "Your people like to speak of honor. They seem to attach great importance to it, but they keep their honor to themselves. They speak the truth among themselves, but not to us."

"They don't always speak the truth to each other either, I'm afraid," Susanna said.

"They think nothing of mocking us, or killing us," Metacom continued. They were walking along the lakeside now. "There are those of you who kill us for sport, or because you are afraid we will kill you first."

"Hardly an unfounded fear," said Susanna. "You have killed our people too—in Swansea, last June, and in Rehoboth, Taunton, and lots of other places. I didn't think the killing would reach as far north as Boston, but it has. I was never afraid of Indians, because of my mother. She taught me that if I were good to you you would be good to me, but your men almost killed me, too."

"Times have changed since your mother died. Yes, we have killed your people. And the killing has only started. Stop here," he commanded. He sat down by the edge of the lake and motioned her to do likewise.

"Your mother was a . . . ." he paused, searching for a word. "Her man was dead."

"You mean she was a widow."

"Yes, a widow. And now she is dead, too. So you are alone?"

"Yes, except for some relatives in England, some cousins of my mother's."

"No husband? No family of your own?"

"Not yet."

"And you? Are you like your mother? Do you also have the healing skill?"

"I do not think I am as skilled as my mother. But yes, there are those who think that I have the gift."

They were quite alone now. The lake was dark blue and tranquil, ruffled gently by the wind. Reflected on its surface were the trees that bordered it, hickory trees and maple, oak and spruce and ash. Only a few leaves still clung to their now nearly naked branches. In the distance, even farther to the west, mountains reached toward the clear blue autumn sky.

It was a beautiful sight, and Susanna found herself relaxing, despite her anxiety. Metacom did not seem so formidable, although he was clearly accustomed to being in command. He was obviously intelligent, and she was surprised that he was so interested in talking to her.

"You are young yet." As they spoke he was scrutinizing her, as if making some decision. "You have heard of me?" he asked.

"Oh yes. Everyone has heard of you."

He smiled, a bitter, mirthless smile. "I can imagine what is said."

Now that she was alone with the man who was to decide her fate, and he seemed reasonable and willing to talk to her, Susanna's anxiety overcame her better judgment. "Why have I been brought here?" she blurted out. "What is going to be done with me?"

Metacom only smiled. "That decision rests with me."

"Will you let me go home?"

"I can't. You know where our camp is."

"I promise not to tell anyone."

He looked away. "I know what English promises are worth."

"It looks as if you're accustomed to picking up and moving at a moment's notice anyway," she continued desperately.

"That's true, but we'll not find a better spot to spend the winter. We will need a base from which to fight. I'm sorry. If my men had known who you are, it is possible that they would have let you go, because of the affection my people bore for your mother. But now your release is impossible." The pungent smell of woodsmoke from Indian campfires drifted by. Susanna heard children calling out in play, and a dog barking. She panicked, thinking that she could be stuck here forever with these strangers.

"Am I expected to live here for the rest of my life?" There flashed through her mind the thought that she would never see Raymond Galt again, and she felt a shocking stab of pain that left her breathless.

He looked at her sharply, with anger. "You mean, will you be condemned to live with a band of ignorant savages?"

"I didn't say that."

"But you thought it. You're lucky to be alive at all. Why do you think you have been spared?"

"I don't know. I thought perhaps you wanted some kind of information from me, or to use me as an interpreter."

"Perhaps."

A young man walked by carrying a string of fish, and then they were alone again.

"I don't know anything you don't, and your English is excellent. Can't you just let me go? We only want to live in peace. Why do you persecute us?" Susanna asked.

His smile was slow and mirthless. "*I* persecute *you?* What a strange notion. We were friendly enough when the first ships came. We could easily have killed you all then. We didn't even have to kill you—without our help you would have died alone, of hunger and disease and cold. You knew nothing of this country. Your men had never even seen corn before! What would you have eaten without us? We gave you seed corn to plant, gave you food when your harvest died and skins to put on your backs. We tried to live in peace with you, but your leaders broke their promises. They take a little, then a little more, and they won't be satisfied until they have everything. We are being driven farther and farther west, and there will be no end to it unless we fight back. Finally I saw this, and I am the one who will make my people see it."

"But you gave us your land! We never fought you for it."

"We gave you permission to share it. Indian ownership is not . . . only for one man."

"Private."

"Yes, private. We Indians all own a lot of land. We own it together," he said.

"You mean your ownership is collective, territorial."

"Yes. You, white men, you measure out a piece of land and put a fence around it and say it is for you and no one else. To us this is stupid. We never thought that when you carved out a section for yourself it would mean that we would always be shut out of it." He looked over the lake, a look of profound melancholy on his face.

"But how can you stop us now? You can't stop the way we think, and you can't take back the land you let us have."

"No, but I can make life so uncomfortable for you that you will get in your big ships and sail back to England where you belong. A strike here, a raid there. You'll never know when we will attack next, or where."

"This is our land, too, now, as well as yours. At least that's the way we feel. If things become too bad soldiers will be sent from England to protect us. Professional soldiers," she said.

"I don't think so. If they were going to send someone from England to protect you, it would have happened by now. I think if things become too bad for you your chiefs in England will tell you to come home."

"What if we all decide to stay here anyway?" she persisted. "What if we're told to go home and refuse to? Massachusetts is the only home most of us have ever known. I think we will stay and fight. I don't think you can defeat us."

"If all our tribes join forces I think it is still possible to drive you out. But we must do it now, before more and more ships come. For too long the tribes fought among themselves, and that is why they were blind to the danger of the white man. Some of our leaders saw the peril, saw what had to be done, but they could not get the others to see it. Sessaquem tried to unite us all, and he failed. So did Sassacus, and Pumham and Uncas and Miantonomo. My own father, Massasoit, tried and failed to unite the tribes, and after him my brother Alexander. But now I am the chief of the Wamanoag, and I will succeed in drawing all the tribes together and ridding our land of the white man. I, Metacom, will succeed where others failed. The Nipmuks are already in league with us, and the Pequots, and the Pennacooks.'' The plaintive cry of a loon floated over the lake, piercing and eerie, shattering the quiet.

"Not the Abenaki," Susanna said.

"No, not the Abenaki, and not the Naragansetts. But the Saco and Androscoggin are ready to join us, and the others will follow me in the end. There is no other way."

"If you can join forces so can we. If we raise a great army we will kill you, and you will kill many of us, too, and there will be a great slaughter."

"I think that is what will happen. I suspect that before long your tribes—Massachusetts and Connecticut and the rest—will unite and declare war on us. Then there will be real battles instead of little skirmishes here and there, and, as you say, a great slaughter on both sides. I do not want the great slaughter, but I'm afraid that is what it will come to in the end."

He rose, motioning to her. "But I don't know why I speak to a woman of such things," he said abruptly. "It is permissible to speak to women of the gods, or of healing, but not of war. It is unseemly. Let us return before I forget myself further."

They walked back to the Indian camp in silence. Once there the older of Susanna's two captors appeared and shot Metacom a questioning look. He nodded his head, and with a sinking heart Susanna realized that a decision had been made; for better or worse her fate had been sealed.

The older Indian indicated with a jerk of his head that she was to follow him. He led her to one of the tepees they had passed on their way into the camp. With another nod he ordered her to stop outside, and while she waited for him he opened the flap of the tepee, went in, and re-emerged with a stout Indian woman whose braids had begun to show streaks of gray. He spoke to her rapidly for a few minutes. Several times during his speech she looked at Susanna with a nod of the head. Susanna searched the broad flat face for a clue to her fate, but the round black eyes were impassive, inscrutable. When the older Indian had finished speaking he left her in the care of the woman and departed.

"Follow me," the woman said in the Wamanoag tongue which was sounding more and more familiar to Susanna. Susanna followed her to another tepee, where a woman emerged with a large furry skin. They went from one tepee to another until there were six Indian women in their entourage, each with something in her hands.

The women surrounded Susanna and led her back down the path to the lake. They indicated, by words and gestures, that Susanna was to remove her clothing and get into the water. "I can't," she protested. "It's cold." For a moment the thought that they might drown her sent panic flooding through her. Then, as she had forced herself to do so often in the past few days, she willed the fear to recede. If she was going to be killed it would not happen this way.

The women continued to say "Come, come," and to gesture toward the water until, reluctantly, she shed her garments and waded in. Several women disrobed and followed her. There were small squeals from Susanna and a few grunts from the Indian women as the cold water hit their naked bodies. Susanna's breasts tightened and she saw her nipples tense and jut forth as goosebumps from the chill water puckered her fair skin.

One of the women opened a painted jar and removed a soft, strong-smelling white substance which she began to rub on Susanna's body and hair. It was a few moments before Susanna realized that it was a kind of soap. Another woman had removed a light, porous pumice stone from the bundle she carried and with this she began to rub Susanna's body vigorously. Another woman worked the soap into her scalp and her long, golden brown hair.

On land again, after Susanna's body and hair had been washed, she was wrapped in furs and rubbed until she was warm and dry. One woman's bundle proved to contain a beautiful fringed dress of light brown doeskin, decorated with elaborate colored beadwork; another had soft beaded moccasins and a comb carved of bone. When Susanna was dressed in her new clothes and her wet hair wrapped in a warm skin she was led by the Indian women back to their camp.

Susanna was told to sit down in front of the large fire. More women gathered, crowding around her, and gaping children watched as her hair was unwrapped and fell in a wet tangle down her back. Women fought for the comb, taking turns pulling the knots out of her long hair. For a long time they combed her hair, rubbing handfuls of it between their hands in front of the fire to dry it. By the time it was dry it was almost dark outside. One of her attendants took Susanna away and fed her a meal of succotash and vension, the first meat she had eaten since her abduction. Then she was led by the women back to the tent of Metacom at the western edge of the village.

Inside Susanna was placed on a sleeping skin. Her discarded dress and cloak were rolled into a bundle and placed to one side. The women withdrew silently, leaving her to her thoughts.

As soon as Susanna realized that she had not been led into the river to be drowned, and found herself being washed, groomed, and dressed by a crowd of Indian women instead, her fate had become obvious to her. She had heard of people who sacrificed human beings to their gods, but knew that these Indians did not do that. If they planned to use her as a slave she would not have been put through the elaborate washing and grooming ritual, or been dressed in fringed and beaded garments. She was to be offered to Metacom as a concubine. As she sat inside the dark tepee, waiting for her new master to come in, a stern resolve entered her heart. She would not submit to him; she would rather die instead.

After she had sat alone in the dark for what seemed like a long time, Susanna summoned enough courage to open the front flap of the tepee and peer out. A sentry stood guarding her to prevent escape. Beyond the silent brave the men of Metacom's inner circle sat around a fire, talking.

Susanna thought rapidly. The men were obviously in deep discussion, and their deliberations could last far into the night. She could catch a word here and there, enough to convince her that they were holding a council of war. They were too engrossed in their talk to be thinking about anything else, and any dalliance with her would certainly have to wait until the discussion was finished. If she were to make an escape attempt, the time to do it was now.

As long as the front flap was up, the large fire threw enough light into the tepee for her to be able to make out dim shapes around her. Quickly she rummaged through Metacom's possessions, feeling objects one by one, searching for anything that might be of use in an escape attempt.

She found a hunting knife in a sheath. When she lowered the flap once more, plunging the tepee into darkness, her guard outside only grunted.

Susanna's thoughts raced. The bottom skins of the tepee were secured by wooden pegs driven into the ground. If she could remove one of these pegs, there might be enough room for her to wriggle out of the back of the tepee. But how was she to loosen one of them, since it could only be done from the outside?

Susanna slipped the hunting knife down the front of her deerskin dress. It pressed uncomfortably against her breasts, and an observant person would notice it, but she would have to take the chance.

She stepped through the front flap of the tepee, her heart thudding so hard she was sure it could be heard. She was stopped at once by her guard. "No," he said in Wamanoag. "You must stay in the tent."

"I have to . . ." Susanna had no idea how to tell the man she wished to use the privy, especially as the Indians seemed to have none anyway. She gestured helplessly. "I have to go."

Apparently this meant the same in any tongue. The brave grunted. "Be back soon."

"I will," she said meekly.

Once behind the tepee her eyes were sufficiently adjusted to the darkness to see the peg she wanted at once, but as hard as she tugged she could not budge it. Removing the hunting knife from her clothing she began digging furiously at the earth around the peg, looking about from time to time to see if she was being observed.

She had the peg loosened so that it wobbled like a child's tooth that is about to fall out, but she could not remove it. Just when she had started to wonder how long she dared to stay out she saw the brave who had been set to guard her come around the corner of the tepee. She was so frightened she dropped her knife.

"What are you doing?" he asked suspiciously.

"Just wiping my hands on the grass," she replied lamely, struggling to keep her voice calm.

The man grunted, motioned. "Get back inside," he ordered.

Meekly she returned to the tepee, cursing herself for letting go of the knife. If only she'd had a few moments more. . . .

Inside she slipped her hand under the edge of the tepee at the approximate spot where she had been working on the peg. It was just loose enough for her to slip her hand outside. She groped around on the grass, her arm stretched as far as it would go. She groped farther and farther, gasping from the pain in her arm socket. Just when she was about to give up, her hand hit the cold blade of the knife.

She grasped the knife and slowly worked her arm back into her prison. She knew she must act rapidly now. She had much to do, and Metacom's council with his men couldn't last forever.

With the edge of the hunting knife she was able to cut a small hole in the skin at the bottom of the tepee nearest the peg she had loosened. When she had enough room to get her arm out, she dug frantically and blindly at the peg. She had almost despaired of success when, suddenly, her efforts were rewarded. She felt the sharp, dirt-covered tip of the peg in her hand and could have cried with joy.

Shooting one reluctant look in the direction of her dress and cape, which she knew she would have to leave behind, she pushed the hunting knife through the opening, and then slowly, as quietly as she could, burrowed her head under the narrow aperture and wriggled out an inch at a time, panting from the effort. There was barely enough room for her to squeeze through.

At last she was free. She rose, dusted herself off, and tucked the knife back into her dress. Now she had to get to the edge of the settlement, where the horses were penned. As soon as her absence was noticed she was sure she would be pursued on horseback. It would be futile for her to try to escape on foot. If she were to be pursued on horseback, she would have to have a mount, too. There was no other way—she would have to steal a horse from the pen.

First she had to avoid being detected by the Indians in the settlement. At first she'd been surprised that Metacom's tent was not in the center of the village. Now she realized that it was on the western edge because there it was farthest away from the white men. She was grateful now for its location. Although the men were engrossed in their talk, and the women and children had eaten and apparently retired for the night once darkness fell, she was sure there was no way she would have been able to escape from the center of the village without being detected by someone. Because she was on the western edge, she ran much less risk of being seen. She ran as hard and fast as she could into the woods, circling around the settlement, giving it as wide a berth as she could without wasting too much time. Once she stumbled into a young boy relieving himself beside a tree. She stopped and stared at him, her heart in her mouth. Would he tell anyone he had seen her? The boy only stared back at her with wide, solemn eyes.

She ran on until there was a stitch in her side and she was gasping for breath. Finally she reached the eastern edge of the village and drew closer. She could see the pen full of horses, still guarded by a young brave. She looked about for a weapon, and spotted a large rock. Slipping up behind him she cracked him over the head with it. He slid, unconscious, to the ground.

There was no time to waste. She searched the pen frantically, looking for the horse the older of the two Indians had ridden. She thought he was docile enough for her to handle, but he was in the center of the pack, not close enough for her to get to without raising a furor.

The horses, alarmed, began dancing and pawing restlessly, tossing their heads and rolling their eyes. She slipped up the bar holding the gate to the pen and ran inside. Putting her hand on the neck of the first horse she touched, she led him out of the pen and closed it swiftly behind her. She prayed silently that she had learned enough of the Indians' way of handling horses to make this one obey her.

Susanna climbed the rails of the horse pen and mounted the stolen horse. Nudging it with her knees and clucking softly, she went limp with relief when it obeyed her command, moving off at a slow walk. When they were far enough from the Indian camp so that the horses' hooves could not be heard, she kicked it with her heels, urging it on until it was moving at a brisk canter. She wanted to travel as rapidly as she could without exhausting her mount, so she stopped short of a gallop.

Susanna had to keep her wits about her to steer an easterly path through the untracked wilderness, but still she could not help looking back over her shoulder now and then to see if she was being pursued. Not until she had ridden for what seemed like an eternity did she stop worrying and concentrate on finding the first English settlement.

The Indians had made their camp far from the nearest white men, and Susanna rode for hours before she saw the smoke from chimneys rising into the clear, cold autumn night. She was afraid to stop. Even if she found shelter for the remainder of the night, no doubt she would have to travel on to Boston alone, and she was sure that a party of Indians would pursue her sooner or later. The more distance she put between herself and them the safer she would feel. She passed the first settlement, and then a second, before the sky turned from blue-black to gray, the stars faded, and birds began to make rustling noises in the trees around her. Finally, at the third white settlement she reached, she stopped, knowing that at first light its inhabitants would be rising.

5

Susanna had stopped at a small village, little more than a cluster of cabins in a clearing. At the first house she came to she slipped from her horse and began pounding on the door. It was opened by a man with a mop of tousled gray hair and sleep-swollen eyes. At the sight of a young white woman dressed in Indian clothing his eyes opened wide with surprise and he seemed to come awake at once.

"Please sir," she said, "I was abducted by Indians and I need your protection."

"Philip's men?" he asked.

"Yes. My name is Susanna Collins. They kidnapped me outside of Boston."

He nodded his head. "Some of our people have been killed, too. Come in, lass."

Inside two boys sat at a trestle table, eating cold turkey, cheese, and bread. Tankards of cider sat beside their wooden trenchers. "The wife is out back, milking," the man explained. "My name is Nehemiah Williams, and these are my boys, Jonathan and Makepeace. This is Susanna Collins, of Boston."

The two boys stared at Susanna, their mouths agape.

"What did the Indians do to you?" one of them asked.

"Where did they take you? How long were you held captive? Did they try to scalp you?" chimed in the other one.

"How did you get away? Is it true that the Indians are devil-worshipers? Is that your horse?" the first one broke in again.

"Boys, boys, hush and let the girl eat and have a bit of rest," their father ordered sharply. "Please sit down and have some breakfast," he said to Susanna.

She had been fearful of her reception, but as the fire warmed her bones and she ate her breakfast her trembling gradually ceased. She was just beginning to relax when a sturdy woman with high color came through the door. "Who was that on horseback at this hour?" she asked, then stood as if struck dumb at the sight of Susanna.

"This is my wife, Rebecca," Nehemiah said.

Warmed and fed, Susanna told the tale of her capture as briefly as she could. The boys asked a thousand questions and the man listened soberly, nodding, but the woman kept shooting hostile glances at Susanna as if she were somehow responsible for her own abduction. Rebecca Williams looked at Susanna's hair falling loose down her back and at her fringed Indian dress, as if to say that no respectable woman would dress that way. I'm glad she's not the one who opened the door, Susanna thought. I doubt I'd have been given as cordial a reception.

"Now my problem is how to get home," she said when her tale was finished. "I'm sure the Indians will send a party after me. King Philip said he couldn't let me go because I know the location of their camp."

"Aye," said Nehemiah, who had filled a pipe and was puffing on it reflectively. His wife was smoking one, too. "You're in a bit of luck there. There's a party setting out for Boston tomorrow. No one travels alone these days, for fear of the Indians. I'm sure they'd let you travel with them."

"Who is going there, please?"

"A man seeking employment in the shipyards, and another who has business with merchants that he wishes to conduct personally. They're traveling with a group from Emmett—that's five miles away—whose business I don't know."

Now that Susanna was safe and warm, she suddenly felt as if she might drop from fatigue. Goody Williams noticed her slumped shoulders and drooping eyelids. "You'll be wanting some rest," she said, her tone a shade less hostile. "You can have the boys' bed, upstairs."

As Susanna drifted off to sleep, all she could think of was that in a few days she would see Raymond Galt again. She knew now that she loved him. As soon as she got home she would have to tell Michael Hale that she could not marry him.

When Susanna saw her own small cottage once again she could have cried for joy. The party with which she had traveled from Winslow escorted her safely to her home, but she told them that she preferred to go in alone. She had looked forward eagerly to this moment, and had set her priorities: first, she must put on some decent clothing, then she'd inform the Akins that she was safe.

All of her plans were altered when she stepped into her house and was astonished to see Raymond Galt sitting on the settle beside her fireplace. "Raymond!" She had never been so glad to see anyone in her life.

"Susanna," he cried, leaping to his feet and crushing her in his arms so that she could hardly breathe. "My Susanna. I knew you weren't dead when I found your herb basket and your body wasn't with it."

"Body?"

"Indians only take the scalps. They leave the rest."

Tears came to Susanna's eyes as she looked about her small house. The ordinary household objects now seemed inexpressibly dear to her. She began telling him what had happened to her.

"You can tell me everything later. I've been staying here at night, waiting for you and taking care of your livestock. See, I kept your fire going."

"What does Elizabeth Harden have to say about that?"

"I told her I loved you and that I couldn't marry her. When you were stolen from me I realized I could never marry anyone else, and there was no point in prolonging the deception with her. Our engagement is broken. She had a screaming fit that could be heard clear on the other side of Boston, and threw a lot of crockery about, but it's all over now. But enough of that. Let me look at you."

He held her at arm's length, devouring her with his eyes. "By God, you're beautiful," he said, his voice husky with emotion. "Your hair—it's down." He gathered up a handful of her long hair and kissed it passionately.

"And what is this you're wearing?" he asked.

"Nothing decent." She looked down at the Indian dress. "It shows my legs. When I escaped I couldn't carry my clothes. This is what they put me in."

"I love it. It's so soft. Doeskin." He stroked her body, savoring the feel of her fringed Indian dress and the way it molded itself to her curves.

"I missed you so," he whispered, his sapphire eyes melting in the flickering glow of the fire. "I knew you'd come back to me, but I missed you."

"I missed you, too, Raymond. I would have given anything to see you." In the Indian camp, when faced with the prospect of never seeing Raymond again, she had realized that she loved him. She had not given herself to him simply because she was lonely and starved for affection. Despite his crazy schemes and reckless bragging, and the way men smiled at his boasting, she loved the man with all her heart. But shyness held her back from saying so.

Raymond pulled his shirt over his head, and then his trembling fingers found the fastenings of her dress, and in a moment it lay in a heap on the floor. She knew she should wait until they were wed, or at least formally betrothed, but once again she found herself unable to resist him. She was so glad to see him again that she threw caution to the winds, heedless of the consequences.

He drew in his breath sharply at the sight of her slim, perfect body. His eyes raked her greedily, up and down, and finally rested on her high, firm breasts, their pink rosettes blooming in the soft firelight.

"Raymond . . ." She wanted to tell him how much she cared for him, what he meant to her. It seemed to her that her whole life had been brown and gray until she met him, and now, suddenly, it was vivid, blooming with color.

He covered her lips with a finger. "Sh," he whispered. "Don't spoil it."

She felt the last of her resistance ebbing away as his hands reached out to cup her breasts. Her nipples tensed at the gentle, teasing caress of his hands, and then a great shudder shook his giant frame as he drew her to him. He held her close, so that her taut nipples pressed into his chest.

"My Susanna," he whispered. "You'll tease me beyond endurance." There was almost a note of pleading in his normally arrogant, boasting voice. His chest moved spasmodically with the force of his ragged breathing. How odd that she should sense it was he who was helpless and vulnerable, when it was she who was trembling and who felt as if her very bones had melted.

His hands made slow circles on her back, holding her lightly but firmly against him. Stopping only long enough to unbutton his trousers and let them fall from him, he drew her to him again, their bodies pressed naked against each other. She could feel his full erection pressing against her, sensitive and throbbing.

"I could devour you," he said, "one inch at a time." He crushed her in his arms so tightly that she almost stopped breathing. Then, drawing away from her, he drew the coverlet, bolster, and pillows from her bed and lay them on the floor before the fire.

"Come here," he said, holding out his arms to her, his bronzed face beautifully intense. "My wild Indian princess."

She lay down beside him, powerless to resist, and let him cover her face with small, soft kisses. When his white teeth tugged at her earlobe his breath, harsh and ragged, sounded in her ear like the roaring of the ocean. His head bent slowly to her breasts, and his tongue began teasing one nipple, sending a hot shudder through her body. His teeth joined in the exquisite torment, and the gentle nibbling at her engorged breasts caused her suddenly to clutch at his shoulders to bring him closer, a wild shudder shaking her frame.

As his tongue and teeth teased her rosy peaks until she thought she would die for need of him his hands traveled slowly down her frame. He stopped on her gently-rounded belly and began massaging her with a slow motion that caused her to arch helplessly against his electric touch. Each teasing bite at her senstive nipples was causing a fever that generated a molten ache in every limb. She began to pant and make little moaning sounds deep in her throat, and she bit her lower lip in frustration at the maddening slowness of his teasing arousal. Her hands clutched spasmodically at his broad, muscular back, her nails digging into him with the urgency of her need.

He drew back from her and laughed. "No wonder the Indians spared your life," he said. "If I had been Philip I would give a king's ransom to get you back." His fingers were stroking her inner thigh.

Susanna could bear no more. Raymond apparently intended to tease her until she went out of her mind. She decided that was a game two could play. Her teeth and tongue moved to his hard male nipples and gave them the same teasing attention that he'd accorded her. Then her head moved slowly down to his hard stomach, and she felt his muscles clench and release with tension as her lips brushed against him. When her tongue darted out to stroke his navel, he, too, decided that he had reached the limits of human endurance.

Lifting her as easily as he had her bedclothes, he lay her on her back. As prepared as she thought she was for him, she felt a quiver of fear at the almost painful thrust of his arousal as he slid into her with a pent-up hunger too long suppressed. But then she was lost in a rhythm so fiery she knew only its exultant throb. Raymond's rugged face, his piercing eyes, and head of thick russet curls loomed above her, all virile power and beautiful, naked aggression. Then she all but lost consciousness as the tension mounted and mounted until it broke, shattering in a moment of release that left them limp and gasping.

They lay collapsed in each other's arms, panting for breath and unable to speak. Suddenly the door to Susanna's house flew open. Silhouetted against the evening sky they could dimly make out a male figure.

"Susanna?" a voice called out. "I heard voices cry out. Are you in danger . . ."

Susanna and Raymond looked up from their pallet beside the fire, their naked, perspiring bodies still intertwined. Above them stood Michael Hale.

Susanna's eyes met Michael's. She opened her mouth, but nothing came out. Michael looked stricken, thunderstruck. "Susanna!" he cried in a wild, terrible voice. "Susanna, no!"

Before she could speak he was out of the door, running blindly. First he had heard that she had been kidnapped by Indians. Now here was his Susanna, whom he worshiped, groveling naked on the floor with another man, when the whole of Boston knew that they were as good as betrothed. He ran until he was panting and winded. A wave of nausea swept over him, so intense he thought he would faint. He stopped beside a tree, gagging in great convulsive heaves. Finally, relief came, and he was able to vomit. He retched until his sides ached, long after there was nothing left to come up. Then he sat down beside the tree, shaking, and cried like a child.

Elizabeth Harden was not one to give up her man without a fight. No slip of a girl, with nothing but a pretty face and slim figure to recommend her, would steal Elizabeth Harden's man right out from under her nose, not if she had anything to say about it!

The very day after Raymond Galt had told her he could

not marry her she'd begun organizing her campaign to win him back. That morning, after she had seen her daughters off to their lessons at the dame school, she executed the first part of her plan. First she dressed with special care. She spent some time choosing her gown and accessories, thinking it a pity that she was still in mourning and could not wear red, her favorite color. She decided instead on a dress of deep green velvet that had wide slashed sleeves with inserts of yellow silk, and yellow silk underskirts that rustled pleasantly when she walked. Yellow silk ribbons closed the slashed sleeves at her elbows, and matching ribbons lined the neck of the gown. She wore a starched double ruff of snowy white about her neck, and matching double cuffs on each wrist. She dressed her hair with special care, piling it on top of her head in a luxuriant mass and allowing a few tendrils to curl about her neck with apparent artlessness. She wore a single pearl on her forehead, attached to a headdress of gold filigree. Finally, she put on her favorite pearl earrings and studded her fingers with rings. Before her mirror she pinched her cheeks until they glowed a deep rose, and practiced a provocative pout.

Thus adorned, she paid a visit to Dr. Griggs, the self-proclaimed leader of Boston's medical establishment. The door was opened by a black slave who escorted her into the doctor's book-lined study. Elizabeth made a grand entrance, flouncing in with her silk petticoats rustling and her rings winking and flashing in the morning light. Dr. Griggs, a stout man with a florid complexion and an important manner, offered her a glass of wine and made polite small-talk with her before raising the question of the point of her visit.

"You are not ill, I hope?" he inquired politely, raking her with his eyes. It was well known that Dr. Griggs had an eye for the ladies. "You certainly appear to be the picture of health, the very picture of health, if I may take the liberty of saying so."

The Widow Harden lowered her eyes and acknowledged the compliment with a little simper. Apparently her toilette was having the desired effect. "No, thank you, doctor, it is not my own health, which has always been excellent, if I may say so, but a far more important matter, the health of our community, that brings me to you today. I have come to you not only because you are a doctor but because you are known to be a wise and judicious man, a man whose judgment is valued by the mighty and one whose counsel is sought in many matters not directly related to the practice of your profession. It is a matter of some delicacy, as you might imagine, sir," she said, rolling her large black eyes at him and allowing a husky note of intimacy to creep into her voice. "A matter requiring the utmost discretion."

"Madam," the doctor replied with a slight bow, "in my capacity as physician to the leading citizens of Boston I have been privy to the confidences of the mighty, and if I may say so, I hope that I have never betrayed that trust."

"I am glad we understand each other," she said. "The matter is a serious one, and I have struggled with my conscience and prayed many a night before deciding that it should be left to wiser heads than mine. Not to put too fine a point upon it, it is advice that I need, sir."

"I will do my very best to advise you, madam. My humble skills, such as they are, are completely at your disposal. Now, what is this matter that concerns you?"

"Well, sir, it is those people who endanger the community by attempting to usurp your authority. There are those who, with no qualifications whatsoever, presume to set themselves up as practitioners of the medical art."

"This has always been a matter of the gravest concern to me as well," the doctor replied. "I am, as you may know, a graduate of one of the finest medical schools in Europe." He waved his hand toward a wall adorned with sheepskin diplomas, written in Latin with a quill pen, each capital letter decorated with elaborate flourishes. "Unfortunately there are those who prey on the fears of the ignorant by promising miraculous cures and peddling outmoded nostrums which often do more harm than good."

"What a pity that they should find a receptive audience, when we are fortunate enough to have such expert counsel as yours at our disposal." The Widow Harden opened her eyes wide, batted her lashes, and beamed a look of undiluted admiration at the doctor.

Dr. Griggs received the compliment with a modest little bow. "The gullible, I fear, like the poor, will always be with us. These misguided women, with their ragbags of old wives' tales, no doubt mean well, and there was a time, no doubt, when their humble lore had its place. But now, dear madam, we have a science of healing, an organized system of medicine."

The doctor leaned forward, placing his finger to the side of his nose. "Galen, madam," he said in a confidential tone, as if he were revealing a secret. "Galen is the key to it all."

"Galen?" Elizabeth Harden said breathlessly, leaning forward as if she were hanging on his every word. "Galen, did you say, sir?"

"Aye, madam. Galen, and before him Hippocrates, are the cornerstones of the modern science of medicine. It was Hippocrates who taught us that the healthy body is one in which the four humors—blood, bile, phlegm, and choler—are balanced, and that illness, consequently, results from an imbalance in the humors." Dr. Griggs puffed out his chest, delighted to have such an appreciative audience before which he could parade his knowledge.

"Many centuries later," he continued, "Galen, enlarging upon the tenets of Hippocrates, evaluated all drugs in terms of the humors. He discovered that an imbalance in the humors can be corrected with the proper combination of drugs. There are purges for evacuation, for vomiting, to flush the body through perspiration, and, of course, the most important purge—that of letting blood, the excess of which is the cause of so many of the ailments that afflict mankind.

"The whole science of medicine is here, madam," he said, waving his hand at the rows of leather-bound medical books lining the shelves of his study, "written, of course, in Latin. It is, you will understand, a very complex science. Its mastery requires years of study, and, if you will forgive my saying so, mental powers far beyond those of the fair sex. But there are still those who continue to seek out unlettered women who know no more of the true science of healing than my servant Adam. Most of these poor women cannot even read English, let alone Latin! Their means of healing can hardly be compared to the scientific system of medicine which I have mastered."

"How fascinating it all is," breathed the widow, who looked as if she were thunderstruck at the doctor's revelations. "Of course, it is all completely beyond me. I'm sure I could never learn a tenth of what you know, were I to study ever so hard. How fortunate we are to have such a wise man in our midst! I would love to hear more about this sometime, but there is an important subject I have to discuss with you." She paused, building the doctor's anticipation.

"And what might that be?" he asked politely.

She rolled her eyes toward the door, to make certain that

it was shut and they were quite alone, and lowered her voice. "It is, unfortunately, not only the health of our bodies that is at stake. It has come to my attention that there may be one among us who practices the black art." This pronouncement was accompanied by an emphatic nod of her head.

"Ah. Indeed. Would you perhaps mean Susanna Collins?" As soon as the Widow Harden had dropped a hint as to the real nature of her mission, Dr. Griggs knew at once what she was up to. Everyone knew that the Widow Harden was as good as engaged to Raymond Galt. Simon Hastings had told everyone that William Fitzsimmons had shot Raymond Galt in a hunting accident, and that Susanna Collins had cared for him. It was also whispered that Raymond had been smitten with the young girl, and that he had been making nocturnal visits to Susanna's cottage since his recovery.

The Widow Harden must surely know that Susanna had long been a thorn in the doctor's side, as her mother had been before her. Not only did Abigail Collins, and her daughter after her, presume to heal the sick, infringing upon his territory, but there were many people who said openly that they preferred the ministrations of these women to those of any doctor. Worst of all, the number of patients whom the Collins women had restored to health was embarrassing. If the truth be known, their rate of cure was far higher than his own.

Elizabeth Harden clearly meant that it would be to their mutual advantage to have Susanna Collins out of the way.

"Susanna Collins!" the Widow Harden cried, as if she were astonished to hear the name. "How did you know it was she I wished to see you about? Have you heard the same tales I have heard?"

"I don't know of what tales you speak, but there were

86

ugly rumors about her mother, Goody Collins." He did not add that it was he himself who had started the rumors. "Since Susanna apparently learned what she knows from her mother, it would stand to reason that she follows the same practices. What is it specifically that you have heard?"

Mistress Harden wriggled her ample bottom, settling herself more comfortably in her chair. "Could I have another drop of this wine? An excellent Madeira it is." The doctor sprang to his feet and refilled her glass.

"Well, sir," she said, after taking a ladylike sip, "starting with the mother, you will recall that when Extra Virtuous Morley lay ill of a quinsy, you did all you could for him, and then Goody Collins nursed him, and brought him back from the very gates of death. Prudence Morley was so grateful that she gave Goody Collins a length of linen she had woven from her own flax. And Goody Collins was so pleased with the gift that she gave Prudence a poppet, and told her that if she would bury it in her garden it would prosper. And after that Prudence had a garden that was the envy of every woman in Boston— turnips the size of cabbages, cucumbers the size of melons, and such peas and beans and greens as you never saw! And Extra Virtuous's crops came in the same way. But his own twin brother, Righteous Morley, would have nothing to do with Goody Collins, and she put a curse on his crops, and they withered. And once Goody Collins . . ."

"That's all very well," the doctor interrupted her, "but that was the mother. What do you know against the daughter?"

"Oh, sir, it's the same story. Those Susanna Collins heals get well, and their affairs prosper, but if you cross her, she puts a curse on you, and your animals and crops die, and your children, too. And then there's the case of Endurance Sheldon."

The doctor pursed his lips and put his fingers together to make a steeple. Endurance Sheldon was a young girl given to hysterical outbursts, which nothing seemed to stop. The doctor had curbed them somewhat with a prescription of opium, castor, saffron, and maple seed. "Yes," he said, "what of Endurance Sheldon?"

"Well, when her mother, Dorcas Sheldon, was sick last winter with the throat distemper, and Susanna Collins was attending her, the little girl ran into the room where her mother lay ill, and suddenly there came upon her such a fit as you never saw!

"Endurance pointed to Susanna, and shouted, 'The Black Man is whispering to you!' Those in the house crowded around her, and could see nothing where she pointed. 'I see him, plain as day,' she insisted. 'It's the Black Man who tells Susanna Collins what to do. He goes with her wherever she goes, and whispers in her ear, and she does his bidding.' And there's ever so much more, sir. Why, only the other week . . ."

Just then Dr. Griggs's slave Adam knocked on the door and reminded the doctor that he was soon expected at a meeting of the town council.

The doctor rose. "What you have told me is most serious, Mistress Harden. I'm sure the matter should be looked into. Could you return another day, and give me the full particulars?"

"Oh, yes sir, I'd be more than happy to," said the widow, rising. The doctor helped her on with her cloak. "May I walk with you as far as the corner, since it's on my way?" she asked.

"I'd be honored, I'm sure."

Outside the doctor's house someone had pinned a sheet to his door. "What's this?" the doctor asked. On the paper someone had written the following rhyme:

"When patients sick to me apply,
I physicks, bleeds, and sweats 'em.
Then after, if they choose to die,
What's it to me?—I lets 'em!"

The doctor swore under his breath and tore the sheet from the door. "Yes, I think for the good of us all we must do something about Susanna Collins."

"I'm sure we understand each other perfectly, sir," said the Widow Harden, favoring him with her sweetest smile.

That very day news of Susanna's abduction had spread through the town. The Widow Harden thought with a sigh of relief that her problem had been solved, but still Raymond Galt had not resumed his visits to her.

For days after Susanna's return, her escape from the Indians was the most talked-about subject in town. Wherever she went she was required to repeat the tale. She was saddened to learn that others abducted at about the same time had not fared so well.

Shortly after her return Susanna made an inventory of her medicines, which she stored in one of the outbuildings behind her house. Here, in boxes, pots, and jars, were all the medicines her mother had taught her to make: tartar emetic for constipation, ipecac to induce vomiting, linseed oil for congestion, oil of juniper for pains in the chest. In one corner she kept her medicinal teas: alfalfa tea to ease the pains of arthritis, camomile tea for insomnia, calomel tea for indigestion, sassafras tea to reduce fever. She had lobelia for asthma, and a mixture of sulfur and lard to reduce itching. The sap of the pine tree soothed boils, decoctions of sumac, yellow root, and juniper berries were good diuretics. Her mother had invented her own cough syrup, which she made from a mixture of clover, mullein, wild cherry bark, and white pine twigs. A poultice for the relief of hemorrhoids she made by simmering the roots and leaves of cranesbill, privet, yarrow, and loosestrife. Besides digitalis, Susanna had other stimulants for the heart—horsemint, Virginia poke, Irish morning glory, and infusion of holly.

She was in her medicine shed when Hope Sheldon came knocking on her door. "Please, Susanna, come help us!"

"Is your mother's time upon her?" Dorcas Sheldon had had a baby almost every year for the past fifteen years.

"Oh yes. She's been in labor for two days, and we're so afraid she's going to die! It's a breach birth, and no one can turn the baby around!"

"I'm coming." Susanna hurried after the girl. A breach birth was a serious matter. If a baby came down the birth canal bottom first, a woman could not dilate enough to get it out. If no midwife or doctor could turn the baby around, the mother and baby usually died.

In the Sheldons' house the situation was just as Hope had described. In a corner of the fireplace sat the strange child Endurance, holding herself and rocking back and forth.

"What ails you, Endurance?" Susanna asked her.

"My sins lie heavy upon me!" the child cried in a terrible voice.

"Nonsense," Susanna said. "You're too young to have many sins. Now get out of the room and let me see to your mother."

Dorcas lay exhausted, her hair tangled about her head like a madwoman's. The attending midwife moved aside and let Susanna take her place. Susanna greased her small hands, slipped them under the sheets, and slowly began easing the baby around. It took her a full hour before she was able to slide the baby out, head first.

She held the infant up. "Look, Dorcas, you have another son." Dorcas, who was barely conscious, only moaned.

When Hope, Endurance, and other members of the family, who were waiting in another room, heard the baby's first cries, they rushed in. As soon as she entered, little Endurance stopped dead in her tracks and turned deadly pale. "Look," she shrieked, pointing at Susanna.

"What is it, child?" her sister Hope asked.

"It's the Black Man! He follows Susanna Collins wherever she goes!"

"Go on with your foolishness," said Susanna. "You and your tales of the Black Man! There is no Black Man following me! Be grateful your mother and brother are alive." She finished washing the baby, and handed it to his mother. Dorcas looked at the baby and gasped. On his forehead was a large strawberry-red birthmark.

Endurance looked at her baby brother and screamed. "It's the Black Man did it! He has the mark of the Black Man on his forehead!"

6

FOR DAYS MICHAEL HALE WALKED AROUND ENVELOPED in such a deep fog of misery that nothing could penetrate it. He went through life like a sleepwalker, doing his work mechanically, choking down a bit of food at night and then going straight to his room. He began forgetting things. He forgot to deliver a wedding present, a silver bowl for Silence Proctor, in time for her wedding. When George Burroughs found it he sent Michael to take it right to her, with apologies for its lateness. Then on the way back Michael forgot to stop and purchase etching acid as Burroughs had told him.

At first George Burroughs did not question Michael's behavior. The boy had been understandably miserable since the news of Susanna's abduction spread through town. He knew that Michael had walked to her house when she had been gone for about a week, to see that her livestock was being care for and that the house had not been ransacked.

He had come back in deeper gloom than before. Freeman Burroughs assumed that seeing the girl's house empty had upset Michael.

Two days later Supply Proctor, the father of Silence and the town baliff, came to Burroughs's shop to thank him for the bowl. "It's like miracle, isn't it, the Collins girl's escape from the savages!"

"Escape? Did you say the girl escaped?"

"You mean you haven't heard?" Supply Proctor was always one of the first people in town to hear and disseminate gossip. He immediately launched into the story of Susanna's abduction.

"Those heathens prepared the girl for a human sacrifice—stripped her of all her clothes, undid her hair, and dressed her in one of those ungodly short dresses their young women wear, the ones that cling to the body and display the limbs. That night they were going to cut her heart out and offer it up to their heathen gods."

Supply stopped to savor the attention everyone in Burroughs's shop was paying him. "The girl ran away. First she stole an Indian horse, and then she killed twelve bloodthirsty Indian braves—each larger and more ferocious than the last!" He had actually heard that she killed six Indians, but twelve sounded more impressive.

"How did she do that?" George Burroughs asked. He looked over at Michael Hale's workbench, and could not understand why the boy was not hanging on Proctor's words. Michael went about his work listlessly, without looking up.

"How could a young woman escape from Indians? I've never heard of anyone who did. And how could she kill all of those big men?" Burroughs said in wonder.

"I don't know how she did it. There are all kinds of stories about Michael, but the boy did not seem to be excited by his tale, or even paying particular attention to it. "Some say she made herself invisible, others that she cast a spell on the Indians and froze their limbs, so they could not move. I've heard it said she turned herself into an animal and ran on all fours through the forest."

Still Micheal did not so much as look up from his bench. "There are all kinds of rumors flying around about Susanna Collins," Supply said under his breath. "Since her return John Higgins has been taking statements from a number of people." John Higgins was the town magistrate. "It was Dr. Griggs who went to him first, and then Elizabeth Harden. Now many are coming forth, with tales of sorcery."

"Sorcery? Witchcraft? Surely not!" George Burroughs shot another look at Michael. "Come outside with me for a moment," he said to Supply Proctor in an undertone, jerking his head toward the door.

When they were outside Supply Proctor said, "That's what everyone is saying. Witchcraft. It makes sense to me, George. How else do you suppose she could have escaped?"

"I don't know. There were whispers against the mother, but I've never before heard aught against the girl."

"They are more than just whispers now," said Supply. "I wouldn't be surprised if the girl was soon brought up before Higgins."

"That must be why young Michael is so upset. He must have heard the rumors. I thought he'd be overjoyed when he heard of Susanna's return."

Later in the day, when George Burroughs tried to talk to Michael about Susanna, the young man said he didn't want to discuss her. When his spirits did not improve, George finally went up to Michael's room and insisted on having a word with him.

Burroughs found Michael face down on his bed, staring listlessly at the wall, still fully clothed.

"May I sit down?" Burroughs asked.

"If you like."

Burroughs sat on the floor beside Michael's bed. "We thought you'd be greatly cheered by the news of Susanna's return," he began.

Michael said nothing.

"Are you distressed over these rumors of witchcraft that are flying about? Don't worry, Michael—no harm will come to the girl if she's innocent."

"Susanna Collins can go to the devil for all I care!" Michael suddenly burst out.

"Has the girl done something to offend you? Has she broken your engagement? Do you not still wish to marry her?"

"We never were engaged, exactly. She never did promise herself to me."

"Well, the course of true love never did run smooth. She'll come around, and whatever the problem between you is, it will iron itself out, never you fear. Don't think Goody Burroughs and I didn't have our share of ups and downs at first. It's not easy, setting up a houshold and learning to live with another person. In a few years you'll look back on all this and laugh, after you've been married a while."

"Marry her? Not I! She's a liar and a cheat and a fornicator!" Then, in a flood, the story came out.

"This is serious," George Burroughs said gravely when Michael was through. "Have you been to Reverend Gilchrist?"

"No, I've been to no one."

"You should, you know, rather than let it eat away at you."

"Perhaps the things people are saying against her are true. She certainly witched me, with her graceful ways and modest talk. I thought her to be as straight as an arrow."

"You cannot carry this around inside you," Burroughs said earnestly. "It will eat away at you like a canker. Go and have a talk with Reverend Gilchrist, I tell you."

"Aye, I will," said Michael, turning his face back to the wall. Right now he wanted nothing but to be left alone.

When his master had left his misery was as great as it had been before, sweeping over him in a wave. Things had been going so well for him, and now this had happened, upsetting all his plans for the future.

Perhaps if he went and unburdened himself to Reverend Gilchrist he would feel better. If he talked to his minister Susanna would surely be punished for fornication. It was a serious offense, though, and while his anger against her was great, Michael was not sure that he truly wanted to see her punished. The problem was that one minute he wished to see Susanna Collins roasting in hell, and the next he wanted nothing so much as to have her back again.

Susanna was so busy during the days after her return that she had little time to worry about what her neighbors were saying. She began by preparing her beer for the next year. Malting—the process of sprouting and drying barley to increase its sugar content—was left to the village expert, but everything else Susanna did herself. After the barley had been malted she took the cracked malt and mashed it, steeping it slowly at just below the boiling point. Malting was a sensitive and smelly process, and was the most delicate stage of beer-making, which largely determined the success of the final beverage. If the liquid got too hot the final product would be sour. An experienced beer-maker could determine the taste whether or not the enzymes were working. Next the beer was brewed by boiling hops and herbs together with the smelly liquid. Finally, this liquor was cooled and mixed with yeast saved from other beer or bread. Within twenty-four hours of being mixed with yeast the brew was bubbling actively in Susanna's cellar.

In addition to putting up her beer and preserving food for the coming winter, Susanna had to replace her cloak, which she had left behind when she escaped from Metacom's men. Until she could weave a new cloak she was making do with an old one, shabby and much patched, which she had almost given to a beggar woman. Fortunately she had planned to make herself a new one anyway, although she had hoped to do it at leisure. Last spring she had traded a ham and flitch of bacon for some sheared wool, which had already been washed and had the burrs and tangled locks removed. She had carded the wool last summer, during the long summer evenings after her other work was done, combing the wool between cards that looked like brushes with stiff wire bristles until it was soft and fluffy. Then she had spun thread from the wool, standing at her tall spinning wheel and winding the wool a little at a time onto the end of the spindle while she pushed the big wheel with a stick held in her right hand. When the spindle began to whir, she pulled the wool out into a long, thin strip, which twisted quickly into thread. Before the thread was stored away to use in weaving, she had dyed it blue by dipping it in earthen jars of indigo.

Now, in the autumn, Susanna sat for many hours at her loom in the attic, weaving the blue thread into wool cloth. She tried to keep her mind off her troubles. She felt terribly sorry about hurting Micheal Hale, and she wondered if she and Raymond would ever be left in peace. She doubted that the Widow Harden would simply let him walk away. Although she dismissed it as foolishness at the time, she was also deeply distressed over Endurance Sheldon's hysterical outburst.

The Akins had given her more disturbing news. When she had gone to see them the day after her return they had embraced her with open arms, Hannah Akin's rheumy eyes filling with tears of joy over her miraculous escape and return. But Susanna was not the only person the Indians had captured, and the Akins told her that the others had not fared so well. Several inhabitants of Boston had been slain by marauding bands of Indians. One family, that of Nathaniel Bishop, had suffered a double misfortune. His son Reliance and daughter-in-law Chastity, a young couple who'd been married less than a year, had both been murdered by the Wamanoag. A town meeting had been called, and it had been voted that the militia should practice maneuvers every Saturday. "And they were out there, too, Saturday last," boomed Goodman Akin, "wheeling and turning on the town common, with flintlocks and pistols."

There was a mounting tension in the air that Susanna had never felt before. She spent most of her time at home, catching up on her work, but on the few occasions she ventured from her home she saw people looking at her and then exchanging grave glances, and there was whispering behind her back when she moved on. She imagined that people wondered at her escape from King Philip and his men, and surely there were some who resented the fact that her life had been spared when others had been killed.

On Saturday, Susanna was called to the home of Mercy Grant, who had a cough and was so congested that she could hardly breathe. Susanna took her some of her own cough syrup and some linseed oil to rub on her chest. On her way back she passed by the home of Nathaniel and

Waitstill Bishop, whose son and daughter-in-law's lives had been so tragically cut short.

Waitstill was outside, churning butter, as Susanna walked by. When she saw the girl Waitstill leaped up from her seat by the churn and dashed out into the road. "Away with you, you spawn of Satan," she cried, flapping her apron. "Don't darken our door with your shadow! Get off our land!"

"I am only walking home," Susanna said, alarmed. "I've been to take some medicine to Mercy Grant."

"Get off, and take your witch's potions with ye! How dare you show your face, when my Reliance and his Chastity lie in their graves, murdered by savages!"

"I was sorry to hear of their deaths, Goody Bishop. You have my deepest sympathy."

"I don't need your sympathy, you imp of Satan! A curse on you and your house! Why should you be alive and walking about when my firstborn lies dead!" Waitstill was following Susanna down the road, shouting at her. Several of her neighbors came to their doors to see what the fuss was about.

Susanna hurried on as fast as she could, and soon the woman's ravings faded in the distance.

That night after supper she took her Betty lamp, an iron dish full of oil from whose short spout hung a linen wick, upstairs to do a little weaving. She had just decided to quit when a knock at her door announced Raymond Galt. He had taken to walking to her house for a short visit each night after he got off work.

Tonight one look at his face told her that he was distraught. "What's troubling you?" she asked after they had kissed.

"Is it that obvious? I didn't want to alarm you unduly, but the truth is that ugly rumors are flying about."

"What kind of rumors?" she asked.

"I debated whether or not to tell you about this. I don't want you to worry, but I want you to be prepared. There's talk about town that you are to be charged with witchcraft."

Susanna turned pale, and sank slowly into her chair. "You can't be serious."

"As soon as I heard it I knew right away where it came from. Elizabeth Harden is furious at me, and at you for taking me away from her, and she's teamed up with that pompous fool Griggs, who dislikes you because you show him up for the incompetent he is. I went to see Elizabeth straight away, and said I'd break every bone in her body if she didn't stop her foolishness immediately."

"And what did she say?" Susanna breathed in a whisper.

"She said that the matter had been turned over to John Higgins and was entirely out of her hands. She said she couldn't stop it now if she wanted to." He didn't add that she had told him any number of people were ready to come forward and testify against Susanna.

"They've gone to John Higgins! The town magistrate! Raymond, what am I to do?"

"Don't worry, dearest. It's all a lot of nonsense."

"Then why are you frightened?"

That silenced him, at least temporarily. It was true that he feared for Susanna.

"These are hard times, Raymond. People are terrified of Indians, and resentful that I escaped from them when others were not so lucky." She told him of her encounter that afternoon with Waitstill Bishop. "And winter is coming, another long, snowbound winter that people are dreading. And there are the ususal hardships—illness and death, crop failures, reverses in business. They need a scapegoat and I'm an easy one. I'm all alone, with no family to protect me." She put her face in her hands, trying not to cry.

Raymond sat down beside her and removed her hands from her face. He took her chin in one hand and kissed her very gently. "No one's going to hurt you, Susanna, not while there's a breath in my body. And you're not alone. You have me. If worst comes to worst we'll run away together."

"Run away! Now you're talking nonsense. Boston is your home. Your future lies here. And where would we run?"

"To the Bahamas."

"The Bahamas! If I hear one more word about the Bahamas I'll go mad!" She jumped up and began pacing in her agitation. "When will you stop tormenting me with your tales of bare-breasted women, and islands that are warm in the winter, and birds that talk like people!"

"Stop pacing like a beast in a cage and come here." He caught her as she passed him, drew her down, and sat her on his knee. He did not appear to be at all put out by her outburst. "There's something I haven't told you—some good news, exciting news."

Susanna gave a short, abrupt laugh. "I could use some good news. I've certainly had enough of the other. What is it?"

"I've been talking to Samuel Coffin, and he's given me a ship."

"A ship? He has? Whatever for? He's usually one who keeps his pursestrings drawn tight enough."

"Yes, but he's always eager to earn more money, and I've convinced him that I'm the man who can do it for him. He's given me the command of a ship called the *Golden Plover*. Don't be misled by the name—it's not a fancy vessel—but with a little work she'll be seaworthy, and then as soon as I have a crew I'll be ready to sail. I've already given my notice at the shipyard."

"Ready to sail? Given notice at the shipyard?" Susanna stared at him dully. "Sail where?"

"To the Bahamas—where else?"

"The Bahamas! Surely you're not going off on a wild-goose chase looking for sunken treasure! I can't believe you're mad enough to entertain such a scheme!"

She jumped to her feet again, and recommenced her pacing. "Why can't you be content to be a carpenter? It's a good, steady living."

"I don't want a good, steady living. I want to be rich, and to make you rich as well."

She shook her head. "You're a lunatic, Raymond Galt! No sane man would talk such nonsense."

"Samuel Coffin is a sane man, is he not? And a sober one? And one, as you said, with tight pursestrings, who never invests his money foolishly? He's the one who's outfitting this ship, in return for a handsome share of the profits."

"That's true," she conceded reluctantly. "But why Samuel Coffin should put his good money into such a crackpot scheme is completely beyond me."

"Because I've let him in on my secret."

"Secret?" she said dully.

"You're repeating everything I say, like those talking birds from the tropics. Yes, love, a secret. My secret is that I've got a map. I'm not just sailing to the Bahamas on the off-chance that I might find a fleet of wrecked Spanish galleons. I've got proof that they're there, and I know where to look."

"Where did you get this map?" She looked at him skeptically.

"I bought it from a sailor."

She opened her mouth to protest. "I know what you're thinking," he interjected, "but it wasn't just any sailor.

This is a man from my home, from Montsweag. I've known him and his family all my life, and a more honest man was never born. His name was Ephraim Cramer. He sailed all over the world, and he wound up in Boston, right after I moved here."

"If this map is so valuable, why didn't he use it himself?"

"Because he was old and dying of a growth in his abdomen. He sold it for enough money to get home to Montsweag, so he could die among his family."

"And where did he get it?" she asked.

"He made it himself."

"He was there?"

"Yes. He swore he'd seen a sunken galleon with his own eyes, and that it was laden with chests of gold and jewels and pigs of silver. And I'm the only person alive who knows where it is and how to get there, and as soon as the *Golden Plover* is seaworthy and I've got a crew I'm going there. And you're going with me. And nothing is going to hurt you, not as long as I have anything to say about it."

"All right, Raymond." She was too tired to fight him. "I can see I'll not be able to talk you out of this. All I ever wanted was a quiet, decent life, with a steady, sober man whom people respected."

"If that's what you wanted then you should have married Michael Hale."

"Michael Hale! Did you have to mention him? Do you know what could happen to the two of us if he talks of what he saw? And why shouldn't he? I've betrayed him—at least that's the way he sees it. I do feel bad about hurting him. I'd rather it was anyone else who came bursting in upon us but Michael."

"You're tired, I can tell. There's no point in fretting over things you can't change. Young Michael will get over you and marry some other girl. He wasn't right for you anyway, Susanna, even if I hadn't come along. You'd not have been contented with him.''

She opened her mouth, but Raymond stopped her with a finger on her lips. "I'll be leaving you now. Get some sleep. I just wanted you to know what was happening. I don't want you to fret unneccessarily, but better to hear bad news from me than from someone who isn't a friend.''

"You're right. Thank you, Raymond, and I'll try not to worry. Although with so much going on, I don't know how I'll be able to help it. It seems to me that my life has suddenly gone careening out of control.''

She walked him to the door. When she opened it she saw Goody Akin on the other side, about to knock.

"Susanna! Quick! It's the Bishops' house—it's caught fire!''

Susanna and Raymond followed Goody Akin out and ran as fast as they could in the direction of the Bishops' house. They could see the fire long before they got there. Flames shot high into the air. It had been a dry autumn, and there was a brisk breeze blowing, fanning the flames. Showers of sparks flew about, and some of the outbuildings behind the house had already caught fire as well.

All of their neighbors stood in lines, passing buckets of water. Everyone was working frantically, but the house was past saving.

"We might as well give up on it," Nathaniel said as Susanna, Raymond, and Hannah Akin drew near and joined one of the lines of people passing buckets from hand to hand. Ebenezer Akin was already there, doing what he could. "Let's wet down the outbuildings and see what can be saved there," said Goodman Bishop.

All Susanna could think of was how this tragedy had followed so closely on the heels of losing their eldest son and his wife. When Waitstill Bishop saw Susanna she shouted, "Get away from my house, you witch! I won't have you here, bringing down more ruin upon us."

Susanna saw that others were looking at her in a strange way, muttering and dropping their eyes when she looked at them directly. "Go away, I said, and take your fancy man with you!" Goody Bishop screamed.

Susanna and Raymond looked at each other, wondering the same thing. Had Michael talked of catching them together? Obviously the link between them had been made in the mind of the public.

A great shower of sparks rose up into the air as the beams of the Bishop house collapsed.

"I'm not wanted here, Raymond. I think I'll go home," Susanna said.

"That might be best. Goody Akin can walk you home. She's too old to be out, doing this kind of work. I'll stay and see what can be done."

With a heavy heart Susanna turned away and went home.

On Sunday Susanna walked to church, as usual, in the company of Ebenezer and Goody Akin. She dreaded seeing Michael Hale, and did not know what she would say to him when she did.

As they drew nearer and nearer to the church the crowd thickened. People looked at Susanna as they had the night before—furtively, dropping their eyes when she nodded to them. She could feel the tension in the air.

As they approached the church Susanna saw that Reverend Gilchrist was standing by the door. He nodded to the other parishioners as they entered, but when Susanna drew near she was shocked to see him moving into the entranceway, blocking her path.

"You may not enter, Susanna Collins," he said in his sternest voice. "You have been accused of the sin of fornication, but a far graver charge has also been leveled against you."

Supply Proctor, the bailiff, stepped forth. "It is my duty to inform you that you have been charged with seventeen counts of witchcraft and sorcery," he said. "I am here to take you to jail, pending your hearing."

Susanna was stunned. Although Raymond had warned her, the idea of being charged with witchcraft had sounded so preposterous to her that she had thought, deep down inside, that nothing would come of it. And it had never occurred to her that she might be arrested in front of all her neighbors. The shame of it was too great to bear. Hannah Akin covered her face with her hands and began weeping silently.

"You must come with me." Supply Proctor nudged Susanna, as she had not moved. She had been standing stock-still before the door to the church. She nodded dully, and followed him without a word.

After she had been locked in the town jail, an unpretentious wooden building next to the town ordinary, she sank slowly onto the wooden bench running along one wall of the room reserved for women prisoners. Light streamed through the single barred window on the opposite wall, making a pattern of squares on her dress.

There was no other woman in the prisoners' room except Old Sally, a derelict who was routinely jailed for vagrancy. She was the beggar to whom Susanna had almost given the shabby old cloak she was still wearing.

"A witch they call you!" Old Sally said, shaking her wild gray hair and clacking her toothless gums. "Nay, I can tell them you're no witch. A kind, good girl you are, with always a bit of porridge for a poor old beggar woman. Kinder by far than many that has more."

"So you've heard, too. I suppose there's no one in Boston who doesn't know of my misfortune. Odd that I should learn of it so late."

Throughout the long day Susanna had to listen to the old woman's half-mad mutterings, but the truth was that she was glad for any company at all. And looking at Old Sally made her grateful for the blessings of her own life—health and youth, her own home, and a sound mind.

In the evening, after church was out, a crowd of women came surging into the prisoners' room, led by Waitstill Bishop. "Take off your clothes!" Goody Bishop demanded.

Susanna drew back instinctively, gathering her old cloak about her.

"Undress, I tell you!" Waitstill demanded.

"Whatever for?" Susanna stammered. There were so many of her neighbors in the crowd of women, so many people she had known all her life, but now they faced her as a hostile crowd, united against her, and she was frightened. There were people there whom she had healed, or whose husbands and children she had cured. She had never, to her knowledge, done any of them wrong, certainly not intentionally. Besides Goody Bishop, there were Goody Morris and Samuel Hubbard's wife. Patience Corwin was there and Silence Churchill, and so many more that she knew. Now they seemed like strangers to her, their eyes hard, their faces set against her.

"Take off your clothes now, I tell you, so we may examine you for witch's marks," Goody Bishop said.

"Nay, I'll not take off my clothes to have my body pawed at. What harm have I ever done any of you? It was your husband, Patience Corwin, I cured of the quinsy when he lay at death's door. And you, Silence Churchill, I cured of the throat distemper. And you, Mary Osborne, remember when all your children came down with the typhus? What would you have done without me then?''

The women dropped their eyes and milled about, muttering. "Perhaps we should send for someone else," said Silence Churchill.

"Nay, don't turn aside," Waitstill Bishop said to some of the women who had started drifting toward the door. "If she thinks she's too good to take off her clothes for us then we'll send for Supply Proctor, and John Higgins, and let them examine her."

The women stopped. "Would you like that better, Miss? They sent us for your own good. Someone has to examine you, and we thought to protect your modesty."

When Susanna saw that she had no alternative, she reluctantly removed her clothes. There was an indrawing of breath as two dozen eyes raked her unblemished and slender yet voluptuous body. Then the women surged forward. Running their hands up and down her nude form, they turned her this way and that, pinching and probing. They even took down her hair and felt her scalp.

"What are you looking for?" she cried when she could bear no more.

"The teat you use to suckle your familiar. If you're a witch you'll have one," said Goody Lawson.

"My familiar?" Susanna asked dully.

"The little imp you send about to do your bidding. Your little cat."

"My cat? My little tabby? Don't be ridiculous! She's just a little stray I found in the woods."

"Aye, but at night she turns into a bat or a mouse and flies about doing mischief. She can hide herself in the tiniest place, and put a hex on anyone who's crossed you," said Goody Lawson.

When a thorough examination of her body revealed no hidden witch's teat Susanna hoped that the women would leave. But she was not to be so fortunate. Goody Morris, who had left the group, now returned clutching a handful of pins. "We'll find her dead spot now," she cried, passing the pins about. To Susanna's horror the women came at her and began to prick her body here and there with the pins.

"Stop! You're hurting me!" she cried, trying to protect herself as best she could with her hands.

"Nay, lass, if you're a witch you'll have a place our pins can't hurt."

"I haven't got such a place—can't you see?" Susanna was on the brink of tears, tormented almost past endurance.

"Well, then, let her put on her clothes," Goody Bishop said. "If she can witch herself away from Indians she can conceal her witch's teat from us. And who's to say she's not only pretending we're hurting her with our pins?"

"Aye, we'll have to wait until she's in court to get her. Never you fear, she'll not hide her treachery from John Higgins. He'll wring the truth out of her, one way or the other," Goody Morris said, reluctantly collecting her pins.

The women turned and surged out of the prisoners' room, leaving Susanna to put her clothes back on. When she was dressed she sank into the straw on the floor, too stunned to think.

"Nay, don't worry, lass," said Old Sally. "You'll have your day in court. You'll prove to them all that you're no witch."

"How?" said Susanna. "They all seem to have their minds made up already."

7

S USANNA'S PRELIMINARY HEARING ON THE CHARGE OF witchcraft was held in the town ordinary on November 13, 1675, with the town magistrate, John Higgins, presiding. If Higgins thought there to be sufficient evidence against her she would be formally tried after seven judges and a clerk of court had been appointed by the governor. As many citizens as could crammed themselves into the community center to gape at the spectacle. The hearing was informal, and all who had evidence, either for or against the defendant, were urged to speak out.

Raymond Galt had been trying to see Susanna ever since her incarceration, but he was not a member of her immediate family and therefore could not get permission. The day before her hearing he bribed the jailer, a dim-witted old man named Makepeace Wyatt who got a meager pittance and his room and board in exchange for watching the jail, to let him have a few minutes alone with her. Raymond folded Susanna in his arms and kissed her, doing his best to reassure her.

"You're getting as thin as a rail," he said when his arms were around her. "Are they feeding you decently?"

"Yes, the food's not bad at all, but I have no appetite."

"You've got to eat, to keep up your strength. I wouldn't be overly worried, Susanna. It's so obvious to anyone with any common sense that it's Elizabeth Harden behind it all," he told her, rubbing her ice-cold hands and attempting to kiss the lines from her brow. "She's cooked up the whole scheme for revenge against you, with the connivance of that old sawbones, Dr. Griggs. It's just a preliminary hearing anyway, not a trial. Who's to speak against you, anyway?"

"Many folk have whispered about me and my mother, Raymond," she answered anxiously. "You haven't been here long, you don't know the tales they've spread. And then there's Michael Hale. He went to Reverend Gilchrist after the night that he surprised us together."

"I know, I know." He folded her in his arms. "No matter what anyone says, nothing can ever make me regret that night. All you have to do to recover your good name is to marry me instead of Michael. There was nothing formal between you, so there is no disgrace in severing the relationship. As for the two of us—fornication's a sin, 'tis true, but when it's done in anticipation of marriage it's more often than not winked at. I'll testify to anyone that I'm more than willing to make you my bride."

"What is the news about town? What are people saying about me?" she asked.

"There is one peuliar development," Raymond said. "Do you know a child named Endurance Sheldon?"

"Yes. She's a strange little thing, given to hysterical outbursts."

"She's been getting quite a bit of attention with them lately. She says that you're followed about by a Black Man that only she can see, and that the Black Man whispers in your ear, and tells you what to do. And she says you do his bidding, and that is how you cure people."

"I know. The child is clearly disturbed. She's been pointing at me and shrieking about the Black Man for years."

"Now other children are coming forward," said Raymond. "I think they're jealous of the attention Endurance has been receiving. They're concocting the wildest tales— that you've been presiding at witch's sabbaths, where the blood of babies is drunk and the Lord's Prayer recited backward—and more such nonsense."

The jailer came to the door. "Your time's up," he said, jerking his head. "You'd best get out. They'll be bringing her dinner, and I'll have to answer to John Higgins and Supply Proctor if you're found in here."

Raymond gave her a last kiss. "I've got to go now. You're not to worry"

"Not to worry? When my own neighbors invent such lies against me?"

"I wouldn't have troubled you with all this, but I didn't want you to be unprepared at your hearing. I thought it would be a worse shock to have it sprung on you."

With a last caution to her to keep eating and guard her health Raymond was gone.

To him, as to Susanna, it seemed incredible that anyone should listen to the tales of children, especially when the stories were more fanciful and elaborate with every telling. He could only think that when their accusations were examined in a court of law, and a woman's life was at stake, either the children would recant or their charges would be dismissed for the attention-getting devices they were.

Still, as Raymond stood in the midst of the crowd stretching and craning their necks to get a good look at Susanna as she was led into the ordinary by the bailiff for her hearing, Raymond wished he felt as optimistic as he had sounded when he'd talked to her. The truth was that the accusations were deadly serious ones, and that Susanna's life hung in the balance.

After the bailiff had conveyed Susanna to the front of the ordinary John Higgins called the meeting to order and read statements by Elizabeth Harden, Dr. Griggs, and Michael Hale, who had been persuaded to join their cause. "Are these the statements to which you swore earlier?" he asked each of Susanna's accusers when he had finished. Each rose in turn and swore that the statements were accurate.

"And what have you to say to these charges, Susanna Collins?" he asked when he was through.

"I am innocent of witchcraft," she replied, standing quietly but erectly in front of him. Her manner was modest but forthright. "It is true that I, and my mother before me, were skilled in the art of healing, but this gift came from God, not the devil. Would Dr. Griggs have been happier if those under our care had died? If they had died instead of living, would he have brought these charges against me? As to Mistress Harden's accusation that I used witchcraft to obtain the affections of Raymond Galt, I can only say that I have never resorted to sorcery to lure Goodman Galt or any other man." A low murmur went through the crowd at this, but Raymond could not tell if they were for Susanna or against her.

"And as for Michael Hale's statement, I can only say that I am sorry if he regards himself as being in the position of being wronged. I did not bewitch him into asking for my hand. It is true that he made me a proposal of marriage, a proposal which I told him I would consider. I had not accepted him, and there was no understanding, either formal or informal, between us. Raymond Galt has also made me a proposal of marriage.''

"Were you aware that he was already sworn to the Widow Harden?" John Higgins asked her.

"Yes, your honor, but no marriage agreement had been signed and the banns had not been read. He told me that he changed his mind after he met me, and it seemed to me that he had the right to do so.''

"And what of Michael Hale's other accusation, that he surprised you in a situation of intimacy with Raymond Galt?''

"Sir, I have been charged with witchcraft, not with fornication.'' Another murmur ran through the crowd, this one louder.

"You admit to it, then?''

"Sir, I repeat that I am not here to answer to such an offense. I do not believe it to be relevant.''

"I will be the judge of what is and is not relevant in this matter,'' John Higgins said sharply. He was clearly displeased by Susanna's reply, but he did not press the issue.

"Very well,'' he said, "you may be seated. This hearing, as you all know, is an informal one, and any who wish to give testimony for or against Susanna Collins may come forward. First, I will ask for the witnesses against her.''

Raymond was surprised at the number of hands that were raised. The magistrate recognized Samuel Hubbard.

"Aye, the woman uses witchcraft to tempt men, and it is not only Michael Hale and Raymond Galt who have fallen under her spell,'' Samuel Hubbard said when he gained the floor. "Everyone here knows me to be a hard worker, a loyal husband and decent family man. Wednesday before last as I lay down with my lawful bedfellow Susanna Collins did appear before me, naked and shameless in the moonlight, and she did beckon me, laughing and tempting me to break my marriage vows. 'Come, Samuel Hubbard, come with me, and you will taste such delights as Goodwife Hubbard never offered you,' she said in a low, mocking voice."

"And did you succumb to her blandishments?" Magistrate Higgins asked.

"Nay, I did resist, but so strong was her pull that I had to hold onto my bedpost to keep from being swept by her magic out of my door."

Susanna raised her hand in protest, and Higgins allowed her to speak. "Your honor, on Wednesday before last I was with the Akins until bedtime, and then I went home alone and went right to bed. You may ask them to verify this. Goddman Hubbard lives miles away from my house. It would take hours of walking to get there."

"That is not relevant, Mistress Collins," John Higgins said sternly. "It is well known that the shade of a witch can leave her body and travel about, and can even appear in two or more places at the same time." He motioned her to sit down and remain silent.

"But, sir," she persisted, "how then am I to defend myself, if you claim that I can be in three places at once? It is hardly my fault if men desire me. I have always carried myself modestly and behaved with propriety."

"Hold your tongue," Higgins barked. "It is my place to evaluate the evidence against you, not yours."

Susanna sat down.

"Do you have anything to add, Goodman Hubbard?"

"Aye, that I do. Wednesday before last was only one of many such occasions on which the shade of Susanna Collins appeared to me, tempting me. Sometimes she was

naked and would come right through the window into my
chamber, laughing and teasing me, mocking and holding
her breasts up to my face. Her hair was loose, tumbling
down her back, and she spoke lewdly to me, in such
language as a pure young maid never used, and she touched
forbidden parts of her body, and sang 'Come, Samuel
Hubbard, come sample my delights,' until she drove me
mad and frantic with desire. But always I closed my eyes
and ears, and refused to let her seduce me with her wicked
ways,'' he added self-righteously. ''Once she spit in my
face when I refused her, then turned into a bat and flew
out the window.''

Next rose his wife, an ill-favored woman who had a
mustache and warts on her chin. ''What my husband says
is true,'' Goody Hubbard said. ''For many a time I have
seen my husband with a vacant look on his face as he
made love to me. His thoughts were elsewhere. He was
being tempted by Susanna Collins's shade.''

After Samuel and Goody Hubbard sat down Deodat
Corwin arose and swore that Susanna's shade had appeared to him and tempted him, too. ''One night after the
goodwife was asleep I heard a scratching sound at my
window. I looked out, and there was Susanna Collins,
scrabbling to get in. I thought her to be in some kind of
trouble, and opened the window to her. She hopped down
from the sill and climbed into my bed, as bold and brazen
as you please.

''When I told her to be gone she pulled the sheet up to
her chin and cackled. I begged her to leave, asking her
what my wife would think if she woke up and found
Susanna in our bed. When that did not work, I threatened
her with a beating, and still she only laughed at me.
Finally I cried out 'Avoid, she-devil! In the name of the
Father, and the Son, and the Holy Ghost, avoid!' When

she heard that she shrieked and writhed as if in torment. And then she disappeared in a puff of smoke!

"And that was only the first of many times she disturbed my rest. Sometimes she came in her own form, and sometimes she appeared to me as a black pig, and once she appeared with the body of a monkey, the feet of a cock, and the face of a man."

"How could you tell it was Susanna Collins, when she assumed these other shapes?" Magistrate Higgins wanted to know.

"I could tell by her voice. Her form changed, but her voice was always the same. She sang lewd songs, and tried to lure me out of my house, and when I would not go she shook her fist at me, mocking and cursing me. She told me my children would die if I resisted her, and sure enough, our baby Preserved died. And it was all her fault, she that cursed the poor innocent."

Deodat Corwin was followed by Ezekiel Danforth, Jacob Churchill, and many more. Susanna sat rigid and silent, as man after man claimed that she had appeared before him in various stages of undress as he lay in bed at night and had tempted him. Nicholas Louder even claimed that she had climbed into his bed and fondled him lewdly and that he'd had to beat her off of his body.

After these men had testified, Abigail Woolcott, a young woman who had been disappointed in love, rose with a flounce. "Thomas Cheever walked me home from church on many occasions, and visited me in my home," she said in a injured voice. "He was going to ask me to marry him, and then with no warning he asked for the hand of Mary Osborne and married her instead. And how do you think this happened? I saw Mary Osborne hurrying away from Susanna Collins's house with something in her hand. It was a love philter, I tell you. And Mary Osborne put it in

Thomas Cheever's cider, and he fell in love with her. It was on account of the love philter she got from Susanna Collins that Mary Osborne was able to win Thomas Cheever away from me.''

Susanna asked to be recognized. "It was medicine Mary Osborne got from me. She complained of weakness and fatigue, and I gave her a tonic.''

"And what of me?" young Hannah Warren asked when she had been recognized. "I have had my eye on Michael Hale for a long time, and my father promised me a furnished house and twenty pounds for a dowry when I married, and then Michael Hale asked for her instead,'' she said with a sulky look in Susanna's direction. "She witched him away from me, I tell you. Else why would he turn down all I had to offer? What kind of dowry does she bring? And she is not even true to him. A fornicator, she is. And why should Raymond Galt want her, when he was already engaged to the Widow Harden? Susanna Collins witched him away, too.''

Elizabeth Glover rose next. "I scolded Susanna Collins once for examining the bodies of men and helping women in childbirth. I told her such conduct was unseemly in a woman unmarried.

" 'I will do as I wish, Goody Glover,' she said, as smart and fresh as you please, 'and a pox upon thy house for upbraiding me!' And sure enough, she put a curse on my house, and the next spring at planting time my husband's oxen died.''

Susanna had never spoken to Goody Glover in such a manner, but she remained silent. Next Goody Shattuck rose. "My goodman James be ill with the falling sickness. Last year he started wasting away, and this last week, after Susanna was brought to the jail before her hearing, I went to search her house and I found this!" People craned their necks this way and that to see the small doll Goody Glover held up. "It has my husband's face, and it be stuck full of pins!"

"I never saw that before, your honor!" Susanna cried out in astonishment. "Someone put it in my house!" She was so angered that she forgot to ask permission to speak.

"Order, order, I tell you, or I will have the bailiff clear this room," John Higgins shouted. "And if you speak out of turn again, Mistress Collins, I will have you removed from the room, and you will not be able to answer any of the charges against you!"

The next person to speak against Susanna was Nathaniel Bishop. "As you know, my son Reliance and his wife Chastity were killed by Indians at about the same time that Susanna Collins was abducted. How is it that she escaped, if she did not do it by witchcraft? How did she, a woman, frail, weak vessel that she is, escape from King Philip and his braves? No one else has ever done so before to my knowledge."

Many people in the crowd nodded their heads vigorously, and Susanna heard exclamations of "Aye, aye."

"There is more, your honor," Nathaniel said. "On the Saturday before her arrest Susanna Collins was walking past our house, and my wife ran out into the road, and cursed her in a fit of despair. Waitstill was wrong to do it, I freely admit it, and she is willing to accept whatever punishment is due her for it. She had lost our oldest son and his wife, and it seemed unreasonable to her that this girl's life should have been spared when she had lost those so close and dear to her. However wrong my wife may have been, it is a fact that the very night Waitstill cursed Susanna Collins our house caught on fire and burned to the ground. Many of those who helped me put out the blaze are here in this room today, and can testify that the house burned with an unearthly fierceness.''

"Are you suggesting that Susanna Collins used witchcraft to escape from King Philip and his men, and that she burned your house through witchcraft, because your wife cursed her?''

"Yes, sir, that is my contention.''

"Let it be so noted," John Higgins said solemnly to the scribe who was taking notes on the proceedings.

"And even if her account of her escape is true, she showed unseemly boldness in her murder of the savages that reflects poorly upon her," Nathaniel Bishop said before he sat down.

Susanna asked to be recognized. "I never claimed to have killed any of the Indians; I've told you all how I managed my escape. And would you rather I had behaved in a maidenly, modest manner, and been ill-used by King Philip and his men?" Susanna snapped, her eyes darting fire. She had sworn to herself that she would remain cool and in control of all her faculties, but her patience had been stretched to the breaking point.

"That would have been better," Nathaniel Bishop answered.

Susanna sat down, shaking her head. She decided that her best course of action was to remain silent. She seemed only to be hardening people's hearts against her by speaking out. At least this was only a preliminary hearing. She was sure she would be bound over for trial, but at her trial there would be seven judges, at least some of whom would be from outside the community. Surely they would be more impartial.

Next Goody Gray rose. "When my man was sick last year Susanna Collins came to visit him. And it was a foul day, cold and gray and raining, and she had to come quite a distance. But when she arrived at our house her shoes and skirt were clean and dry. And when I remarked on it she said, 'I scorn to have a drabbled tail.' ''

And then Goody Richards rose. "Last summer Susanna Collins came to me with bread she had baked and wanted to trade it for a thimble and some thread. But I did not need the bread and told her to be off. At that she flew into a temper and cursed the first thing her eye fell on, which was my best cow. And the cow's milk went sour, and then stopped altogether, and finally the cow wasted away and died.''

"Is there anyone else who wishes to testify against Susanna Collins?'' Magistrate Higgins asked when Goody Richards was through. "Very well, then,'' he said, "bring in the children.''

Supply Proctor left the room and returned with Endurance Sheldon and three other girls. They were all ten or eleven years old. Susanna recognized Hannah Cory and Martha Grey, and the fourth child she thought to be Peace Shattuck.

"Because of their tender years we have excluded these children from the rest of the hearing,'' John Higgins explained. "But now they must speak. Endurance Sheldon, step forward.''

Endurance, a thin, whey-faced girl, walked up to the front of the room. "Tell us about the Black Man,'' John Higgins prompted her.

Endurance turned around to face Susanna, pointing at a spot over her left shoulder. "He stands there.''

"Is he there now?'' Higgins asked.

"Yes.'' Suddenly the child went rigid. Then her chest began heaving, and she distorted her face into a grimace. Many in the room rose as the child started to scream. She fell to the ground, twisting and writhing.

"It's the Black Man!" she shouted. "He's tormenting me, so that I cannot speak against his handmaiden!"

The child wriggled and thrashed about the floor until her father came forward, protesting. "Let me take her away," he pleaded. "She can testify at the trial."

"Very well," John Higgins agreed. "Remove her from the court."

The other children had watched this astonishing performance with admiration and envy. "Now, Hannah Cory, come forward and tell your tale," the magistrate commanded.

"One night, as I lay in my bed, Susanna Collins came through the window and held out a piece of maple sugar and said she would give it to me if I came with her," Hannah said. "And she took me by the hand and we flew through the air to a clearing in the woods."

"Were you alone? Were there just the two of you?" Higgins asked.

"No sir, she had with her a little tabby cat—and two hogs."

"Go on. What happened in this clearing in the woods?"

"There were many folk there, standing in a big circle around a stone. And they were chanting."

"Did you know any of these other folk?"

"No sir. Many of them had their faces hidden in hoods. And some of them were Indians."

At this a loud murmur went up.

"This chant—did you recognize it? Could you understand the words?"

"No sir. They spoke very fast, and mumbled. It may not even have been English."

"Go on. What happened next?"

"After the chanting one of them came forth, and he held out a crucifix, but it was upside down. And then everyone recited the Lord's Prayer, only they said it backward."

"Go on," John Higgins prompted, when the child stopped.

"Next a man came forward with a large cup which he held up in the moonlight, chanting all the while. And he read from a great book with funny drawings in it."

"Can you describe the drawings?"

"No sir. They were odd, in very strange shapes."

"Please continue."

"And then the man who was chanting held up a knife and said something about the blood of a virgin. And then I feared that they meant to kill me, so I turned and ran back through the woods as fast as I could."

"Do you think you could recognize this clearing in the woods if you were taken there again?"

"Oh, yes sir. I would know the place," Hannah said.

"And you arrived home safely?"

"Yes sir."

"Do you have anything else to add?"

"No sir, except that after that I avoided Susanna Collins whenever I saw her."

"Thank you. You may sit down." He called the other two girls forward, one at a time, and each one told a similar story. Susanna was so stunned by these fabrications, and by the sheer inventiveness of the children, that she remained as still as a corpse. A dead quiet had fallen on the room, and it was clear that the crowd was impressed by what the children were saying.

After the children had testified Higgins had them removed from the room. "This concludes the testimony against Susanna Collins. Now I will ask to hear from those who wish to testify on her behalf."

Susanna could barely suppress her desire to count how many hands went up. She knew it would do her no good if Raymond Galt spoke for her, as his testimony would be suspect. Ebenezer and Goody Akin came forward, and stated that they had known Susanna all their lives. "There never was a sweeter girl, or a better neighbor," Ebenezer swore in a voice which quavered with age, strain, and emotion. "I don't know what we would have done without her help, now that we are getting old and slow."

There were others who testified to her modesty and good conduct, and many of her patients came forward annd spoke gratefully of her healing. Finally Reverend Gilchrist came forward. "I have always known Susanna Collins to be faithful in church attendance, and sober and responsible in her conduct," he said, "but I know that witches can deceive, giving the appearance of virtue to disarm their victims. I have prayed long and hard for a sign from God in this matter, but He has sent me none. Still, in the absence of any personal knowledge of witchery on her part, I can only speak in her favor." Susanna sighed. It was a lukewarm recommendation, but at least her minister had not spoken against her.

"Is there anyone else who wishes to speak on Susanna Collins's behalf?" John Higgins said. When no one came forward, he said, "It is clear to me that there is sufficient evidence against the defendant to have her bound over until such time as a court may be convened to try her on charges of witchcraft."

Susanna held her head high and tried to keep her face expressionless as she was led from the ordinary by Supply Proctor.

After her hearing Susanna was returned to jail. Old Sally had been released, so she now had no company at all. The nights had grown cold, and her patched cloak was poor protection against the chill. She tried to keep her spirits up, but there were times when she was hard put to ward off despair.

One evening as she was eating her supper she heard Raymond's voice outside, talking to the jailor. "Good evening to you, Makepeace," he said in his best hail-fellow-well-met voice.

"Well you might say it's a good evening," said Makepeace Wyatt, grumbling. "You'll be heading for your nice, cosy home. You don't have to sit here in the cold, and with but one prisoner to guard, too. If it weren't for that witch, I'd be on my way to a warm bed myself."

"I've got the next best thing for you, a nice hot sack posset."

"A posset?" the old man said eagerly.

"Aye—that will warm your bones. And all in exchange for a few words with Mistress Collins."

"Well—you may visit her for a minute. I see no harm in it," said the old man. "What's that you've got?"

"Only a cloak to keep her warm."

Inside the jail Raymond embraced Susanna swiftly. "I haven't much time," he said. "Here, I brought you this."

He held out a bundle. When Susanna unwrapped it she saw it was a green hooded cape of the softest wool. "Oh, Raymond, you shouldn't have. It must have cost a fortune. What's this?" Something fell out of the folds of the cape and fell to the floor with a metallic clang.

"It's a file. Now listen to me, and listen carefully. My ship will be ready to sail four days hence. I've been working night and day to get the *Golden Plover* seaworthy, and to put together a crew. The posset I gave Makepeace Wyatt has a sleeping potion in it. When he's asleep begin filing at the bars of your window. I'll come back tomorrow night with another drugged posset for Makepeace, and every night until we sail. You should have enough time to get through the bars by then."

125

"What if someone hears me?"

"Your window doesn't face the street, thank God. You'll just have to do your filing after curfew. It's a good thing you're the only prisoner, and that they didn't put you in leg irons. I could easily overpower old Makepeace, but we can't be seen together on the streets. It will be dangerous enough for you alone. Get to the waterfront as fast as you can four nights from now. The gangplank will be down, waiting for the crew to board the next morning."

"But when I'm discovered missing your ship is the first place they'll look for me."

"I've thought of that. I've fashioned you a hiding place until we're under sail."

"I don't know, Raymond," she said. "I'm afraid of facing my trial, but equally afraid of running away. My hearing was only a preliminary one, and some of the seven judges at my trial are bound to be impartial."

"Don't talk nonsense. You'll be convicted, because the powers that be want you convicted. Your execution will take people's minds off their troubles and off the inadequacies of those in high office, at least for a while. And your hanging will be quite a spectacle."

"No, I can't just run away. It will look like an admission of guilt. I must stand and refute my accusers."

"Refute them? How? Don't be ridiculous. Every man who ever lusted after you will say your shade appeared to him naked and enticed him, and there's no way you can disprove it. And every child who wants attention will invent fantastical stories of sorcery. At your trial they'll repeat what was said at your hearing, only there'll be more of it, and character witnesses will be reluctant to come forward for fear of reprisals or ostracism. You've already been convicted and hanged in the minds of everyone in Boston."

"If I run away I'll have to leave forever. I can never come home again."

"But if you don't you'll leave here forever anyway—in a pine box. Take it," he said, putting the file into her hands.

"What will I do later, after your voyage is over?" she asked.

"We have to take life one step at a time. Our immediate goal is to see to it you cheat the gallows. I've got to leave now—I haven't time to argue. Remember, the *Golden Plover,* four nights hence."

"All right," she said. "All right."

After he had gone, and she heard Makepeace snoring, she went to work as quietly as she could, filing away at the bars of her window. She could not believe that her life had come to this. Only a few short weeks ago she had been waiting for Michael Hale to propose to her, so she could be a respectable goodwife and raise a family. Now she'd almost been murdered by Indians, caught in fornication by Michael, stolen another woman's betrothed, stood accused of witchcraft, and was in peril of losing her life. It seemed to her that the fateful day on which Raymond Galt had appeared at her door, wounded and bleeding, had precipitated a chain of events that had snowballed recklessly out of control.

8

O<small>N THE NIGHT BEFORE</small> R<small>AYMOND'S SHIP WAS TO SAIL</small>
Susanna brushed her new cape, tidied her hair and dress as
best she could, and waited for Makepeace Wyatt to begin
nodding over his evening posset. However, as soon as the
old man began to grow drowsy he wandered into Susanna's room, something he had not done before. She could
not tell if he was suspicious or not.

"Tell me," he said, swaying slightly, "is it true what
people say about you—that you have lain with the devil?"

"Go on with your nonsense," she replied scornfully.

"Nay, I want to know. What was it like? Are his parts
the same as a natural man's?"

"Go on about your business, or I will lay a curse on
you."

"Nay," he said, retreating, "I'll be off."

Every night since Raymond had brought her the file she
had waited until Makepeace was asleep and then dragged

the bench in the women prisoners' room to the wall. Standing on the bench, she'd worked away at the iron bars over the single window until she could remove them and fit them back. It had taken her all night, every night, and during the day she would sleep, exhausted, after she had eaten her breakfast. She would wake at noon for her dinner, always the biggest meal of the day, and go back to sleep again. Halfway through the afternoon she would be awake and alert again, ready for the night's work.

Tonight she pulled her bench over to the window as soon as she heard Makepeace's snoring. Rolling her tattered old cloak, which she had decided to leave behind, into a bundle, she put it on the bench to give herself a little extra height. Quickly she eased the bars aside and punched the window out with her file. Dropping the file and her new cape outside, Susanna used all her strength and managed after a few minutes of fevered work to wriggle her way out and drop to the ground, thanking God that she was slender and her hips narrow. She wrenched her right shoulder in the fall, and struggled to her feet, rubbing her shoulder and shivering in the bitter November cold. Every morning since she had gone to work on the bars of her window there had been a hard frost on the ground, and tonight she could smell snow in the air. Quickly retrieving her cloak, she wrapped it about her, hoping to stop the chattering of her teeth. She picked up the file and slipped it down the front of her dress.

It was after curfew, and everyone was at home in bed except the town crier and folk such as doctors and midwives who might be called out on emergencies. Pulling the hood of her cloak well forward, she covered her face as well as she could and began slipping silently from the shadow of one house to another, taking small back streets and working her way toward the waterfront by a circuitous route.

"Eleven of the clock and all's well," she heard the crier call on his rounds. "A cold cloudy night with snow in the air." Twice she saw people scurrying along the streets on some late-night errand, but they did not bother her. There were clouds over the moon and it was not a bright night, which worked in her favor. She was about to think that she was home free when a voice behind her caused her to start in fright.

"Who goes there, and on what business?" she heard a deep male voice call behind her. She whirled around to see John Jacobs, a prosperous landowner and member of the town council.

Susanna had prepared a story for this contingency. She drew the two sides of her hood together so that most of her face was covered. "Rebecca Sewall," she said. "My father, Preserved Louder, has taken a turn for the worse."

"Is Preserved worse? I'm sorry to hear it. Why did your husband not come with you?"

"He has a bad headache."

"But it's not right to send you unescorted. Could not a servant have come with you?"

"Such was my distress when I received the message that I wanted to be off at once. I was still dressed, and I did not want to take the time for someone else to dress and accompany me."

"Well, then, Mistress Sewall, I must see you to your father's house myself."

This was what Susanne had feared. "Oh no, sir, thank you very much, but I wouldn't dream of putting you to the trouble."

"No trouble at all. Even with the curfew, there are always some unsavory characters from the waterfront hanging about. When you've a busy harbor in town it's impossible to keep everyone home. The streets are no place for a woman alone at night.''

''But surely you must be on some important business of your own.''

''It can wait. I can't leave a lady to make her own way on such a dark night.'' He held out his arm and Susanna was obliged to take it. She could be grateful for one thing—John Jacobs had very poor eyesight.

Her heart thudded so painfully she could feel it knocking on her ribs as they neared the home of Preserved Louder. What would she do when she reached the house?

''Thank you,'' she said when they were a few doors away. ''I can see myself the rest of the way.''

''Oh no, I insist on seeing you safely inside.''

When they stood before the house Susanna had no choice but to lift the brass knocker and let it fall. She had no idea what she would do when the door opened.

When no one came to the door at once, she said, ''The servants will be looking after Father. Someone will be here in a minute.''

''Very well, then, Mistress Sewall, I'll be about my own business. And give your father my best wishes.'' John Jacobs touched his hat to her.

''Thank you, sir, for your protection.''

As soon as he had turned the corner Susanna hurried as fast as she could in the opposite direction. She had only taken a few steps when the door of Preserved Louder's house opened, and a servant holding a Betty lamp looked out onto the street.

''You there,'' he called to Susanna, ''what do you want at this hour?''

''I'm sorry,'' she called. ''I knocked on the wrong door.''

She knew that undue haste would make her look suspicious, but she could bear the anxiety no longer. Picking up her skirts, she ran the rest of the way to Boston Harbor. As soon as she drew abreast of the water she pulled the file out of her dress and threw it in.

The moon was sufficiently bright for her to make out names on the sides of ships, and she had just spotted the *Golden Plover* when a pigtailed sailor, obviously drunk, came weaving toward her.

"Found no one to share your bed yet?" the man said, slurring his words and leering at her. "And you so young and fresh. I'll make the night worth your while." He fumbled in his pocket and drew out a coin.

"Leave me alone," she said, just as she saw, with enormous relief, the giant frame of Raymond Galt appear on the ship's deck.

"Is that you, Betsy?" he called.

"Aye, here I am. I'm sorry I'm late."

Susanna ran up the gangplank that Raymond let down for her and was in his arms in a minute.

"Quick, we've got to hide you at once," he said after they exchanged a hasty kiss. Inside the captain's cabin he removed three planks from the wall, revealing a small crawl space.

"It's crude and cramped but the best I can do. You'll have to stay here until we sail. I've put in a pillow and blankets. There's also some bread, cheese, and water. Did you have any trouble?"

"Not much," she said as she crawled in. There was barely enough room for her. After she was settled Raymond nailed the boards back. She lay for hours, shivering with fear, before she fell asleep.

She awoke when a violent motion threw her against one side of her tiny enclosure. Through cracks between the planks she could see daylight filtering in. At first she was frightened again, and then she realized that if the ship was moving they must be under sail. That meant that she was safe. Still, she would not begin to feel secure until Boston was far behind them.

She had not been awake long when she felt one of the boards covering her enclosure being wrenched open and a shaft of sunlight pierced the darkness. "Susanna." Raymond hastily unnailed the other boards and helped her out.

She winced, rubbing her neck.

"Are you all right?" he asked.

"Just stiff. What happened?"

"What I expected. The constable and a party arrived shortly after dawn and asked me if I had seen you. They weren't satisfied until they had searched the ship from top to bottom. I told them that you probably dematerialized or turned yourself into a bat and flew out the window. That, as a matter of fact, is very close to what that half-wit Makepeace Wyatt told them. He said when he went in to give you your breakfast you said, 'You'll not see me dance on a gibbet!' and vanished in a puff of smoke, leaving nothing behind you but your old cloak."

They both laughed. "I can see him telling that tale all over Boston, and being believed, too, if people give credence to half the nonsense that was said at my hearing."

"What did you do with the file I gave you?" he asked.

"Tossed it in the harbor."

"Good girl."

"When will it be safe for me to go outside?"

"Wait until we've been under way for a while. I'll have to explain your presence to my crew."

Susanna took as readily to sea life as if she had been born with gills and fins. Everything about Raymond's ship and the broad blue ocean fascinated her. She loved the intricate rigging and the sight of white sails bellying in the wind. She soon grew accustomed to the sight of bronzed, pigtailed sailors running up and down the rigging, wearing little besides breeches and a bright kerchief of scarlet, yellow, or blue tied about their heads. She loved the jargon of the sailors, and the stories they told each other of other voyages they had taken and of life in foreign, exotic places. She still thought that Raymond was on a fool's errand and wondered what would happen to her now that she had run away from her trial, but she learned to take life one day at a time and enjoy each moment for what it brought.

They had fair sailing, and as they sailed farther and farther south the weather gradually became warmer. At night she and Raymond leaned against the rail, breathing the fresh tangy air and bathing in the soft moonlight that sparkled on the deep blue sea like a trail of diamonds. Later they slept together in the captain's cabin.

It was an unbelievable luxury for the two of them to lie together in the same bed, naked and unafraid of the prying eyes and wagging, censorious tongues of neighbors. During the day Susanna grew accustomed to dressing lightly, sometimes even in sailors' trousers, and walking about with her hair blowing free or hanging down her back in a long braid. She brought the same freedom to their bed at night. Now that they could be alone together she and Raymond gave themselves to each other with a joyous abandon that Susanna had never even dreamed was possible.

On one such night she broached the subject that rose time and again to haunt her. "What's to happen to me, Raymond? I can't go back to Boston."

"Yes, you'll go back to Boston. You'll be my wife."

"But I couldn't do that to you. You'd be ruined, and I'd

be hanged. The fact that I ran away will be construed as an admission of guilt.''

He chuckled. "Love, when I go back to Boston I'll be so rich no one will dare lay a hand on my wife."

"You're mad, Raymond, you know that? Quite mad."

"That I am," he said. "Mad for you."

She opened her mouth to protest, but before she could speak he covered it with a deep, probing kiss that left her shuddering and eager for more.

"Wait until you taste papaya," he murmured.

"What?"

"Papaya," he said, his fingers making lazy circles on the tips of her breasts, rousing them to button hardness.

"What does that taste like?" she teased, knowing that his mind was on anything but conversation.

"Not as good as this," he muttered, lowering his head to nibble with erotic delicacy at one taut nipple. The gentle tugging at her nipple sent a tiny thrill of heat through her. "Good Lord, just looking at you sends me out of control," he said, his hand teasing her other breast. His lips and teeth pulled playfully at the hard tips, causing her to moan sharply as a jolt of desire rippled through her. When he had driven her to frantic impatience he moved slowly down her body with his lips, dropping a light trail of kisses along the way. His teeth bit teasingly at the softness of her belly, and she drew in her breath sharply. His hands were probing at the warm, wet center of her being, and she made a sound that was a half gasp at the incredible sensations he was producing. He looked up and gave a lazy smile of satisfaction. "I want you to sleep in my arms and glow with contentment."

She could no longer speak. Her breath was coming in hard little gasps, and his attentions were sending little shocks through every nerve in her body. "Susanna, it hurts," he moaned. "I want you so much it hurts." By the time he slid into her she had gone beyond impatience to a mad delirium of longing. He adjusted his rhythm to hers, sliding his hands underneath her and lifting her hips to fit him, and she instinctively drew up her knees and locked her legs around his back.

"You'll drive me crazy," he groaned. "Utterly crazy." By now Raymond knew Susanna's body as well as he knew his own. Throughout long weeks together he had grown expert in bringing her to the edge of mind-jolting release, then holding her back at the last instant. Now, only when her body moved as wildly and demandingly as his own did he take her with him in an erotic, star-studded explosion that left them perspiring and panting like two athletes at the end of a long race. They lay for a long time afterward, stroking and kissing each other, before Susanna drifted off to sleep.

Raymond stayed beside her, watching her breasts rise and fall in the even rhythm of sleep, and felt a wave of love for her so powerful he thought he would burst. Now that they were always together she pleased him in so many little ways he had never noticed before. He loved her poise and composure, the economy with which she worked and talked. When they sat together in the evenings, after they had eaten, she reminded him of a cat sitting contentedly beside a fire, its paws curled inward. She had the same kind of inner centeredness, a quiet, self-contained quality that was soothing and restful. It was not passivity. The first time he'd seen her, coming around the corner of her house and wiping her hands on her overskirt, he had known she was a resourceful and energetic woman. It was just that she never seemed to waste motion or words, but somehow knew the most direct and easiest way to do or say everything. Looking at her face softened by sleep and bathed in moonlight, her lips slightly parted, he knew he wanted her beside him always, every day of his life.

By the time they sailed into the azure waters of the Caribbean the air had grown warm and balmy. It had happened so gradually that Susanna did not stop to think that Boston would now be buried under drifts of snow until Raymond brought it to her attention. "It's January," he said, "and you told me that I was mad to say it would be warm in the winter."

"Winter," she said wonderingly, looking at the warm sand of an island basking in golden sun. "And I was dreading the winter." Less than three months ago she had wondered how she would survive this season, secluded and snowbound. She shook her head in awe.

They had reached the Great Bahama Bank, along the western side of the Bahamas. Here, in a vast expanse of shallow water, an occasional low key, or tiny island, lay like a lethargic alligator. Raymond had unrolled his precious map, and he consulted it constantly now, threading his ship through a maze of islets and keys. When he reached the spot marked with an "X" on his foolscap map he gave the order to drop anchor well clear of the sharp-edged, brightly colored coral reefs that lay beneath the surface of the water like the jagged teeth of a shark lying in wait for its prey.

They had anchored in the most spectacular place Susanna had ever seen. At the horizon a warm blue sky, studded with small puffs of cloud, met the clear blue-green of the Caribbean. Although they had stopped short of the reefs, Susanna had only to look down to see them clearly through the incredibly transparent water. "How deep is the water here?" she asked Raymond.

"Seven fathoms."

"Seven fathoms!" She knew that to be forty-two feet. It did not seem possible that the crystal-clear water could be that deep. She could easily see coral in every shade from white and pale pink to vivid purple, scarlet, and bronze. The coral swayed gently in the underwater current, bent into fantastic shapes—fans and feathers, clusters shaped like the antlers of deer, and long bony fingers reaching up toward her from the bottom, beckoning and waving. Schools of fish colored in every hue of the rainbow darted by.

"Can't we stop at one of these islands?" She longed to run barefoot on the sand.

"We'll stop soon enough," Raymond said. "We must take care of business first."

Raymond had gone ashore only once himself, to hire two native Caribbean divers, but he had forbidden his men to join him. Once ashore the temptations of bare-breasted maidens, cheap grog shops, and opium dens would prove too great.

"You'll all have shore leave after we've filled our pockets with gold," he promised his grumbling men. To the northeast the endless circle of the horizon was broken by a tropical island where clustered palms waved over its tangled undergrowth and broad beaches led down to gently-lapping waves. As Susanna gaped in wonder at the beauty of the island thousands of birds with gorgeous plumage of a deep scarlet rose squawking into the air.

"I never saw such birds!" she breathed. "This must be an enchanted place."

"They're called flamingos," Raymond said.

"Flamingos," she repeated slowly, mouthing the strange word.

"Enough of this," Raymond said, though he was relishing her enjoyment. "We've got work to do."

He gave his men the order to put the ship's longboat

over the side. "Let me go with you," Susanna pleaded. She could not bear the thought of missing even a moment of this adventure.

"Not now, not this time," Raymond said firmly. Susanna had to watch with wretched impatience while the longboat was lowered slowly and half-naked sailors ran down the rope ladder flung over the ship's side and stepped into the boat. Raymond was the last man to descend.

He sat in the stern of the longboat, taking their bearing with a quadrant. They had not rowed far—Susanna could still see the men clearly if she shaded her eyes against the sun—when Raymond gave the order to stop. " 'Vast pulling, bullies!" he shouted. "Way enough!"

In the boat's bow the leadsman threw his line. The heavy lead made a long curving sweep and hit the water with a plop. The leadsman measured their depth, and cried out, "By the mark, seven fathoms, Captain!"

His voice carried well over the water. Susanna smiled, proud that Raymond had been accurate in his guess of the water's depth.

The lineman's head, tied in a yellow bandanna, jerked up suddenly. "A wreck!" he yelled in a hoarse voice. "A wreck below!"

"I was right!" Raymond shouted, slapping his thigh. "Mark the spot with a buoy!" A weighted line attached to a buoy was lowered. Susanna saw the buoy bobbing on the surface of the blue-green water.

Everyone rushed to see the sunken galleon, so that the longboat was almost capsized. "To your stations!" Raymond roared. "To your oars or you'll have no rum tonight!" He nodded to the two native divers, and they slipped over the side of the boat and vanished into the ocean.

Looking down into the water Raymond could see the

wreck clearly. Its bow and elaborately carved stern were plainly outlined in the translucent water, and even the rows of gun ports for cannon along her side were visible. He watched as the two dark bodies neared the wreck and vanished.

They stayed under so long it seemed impossible to everyone that their lungs had not burst. Finally, after what seemed like an eternity, the divers emerged from the wreck and pushed off from the bottom, kicking swiftly to the surface. After they were pulled onto the longboat by eager hands they lay in the bottom, panting, while the sailors bombarded them with excited questions.

"There's a big chest in there, Captain," one of them managed to say between gasps. "And a hole in the side of the ship, big enough to pull it through."

Raymond began bellowing orders, and before Susanna had time to collect herself the divers had jumped in again, this time bearing drags attached to iron-clawed grapples. When they emerged again empty-handed after what seemed like an eternity, to collapse, winded once more, on the longboat's bottom, excited sailors began hauling in the lines. Slowly, against the pull of a ponderous weight, the lines were drawn in. A heavy, ancient chest, encrusted with coral and dripping seawater, was hoisted over the side.

The sailors crowded around it eagerly, but Galt insisted on returning to the ship before the chest was opened. Grumbling, the men went back to their oars, and, pulling with a steady rhythm, they soon had the boat alongside the *Golden Plover* again. Only after men, boat, and chest were safely aboard the ship did Galt give the order to break open the latter.

Numerous blows from a sledge were required to breach the oaken side of the chest, but the wait was well worth their while. A glittering stream of gold coins cascaded onto the deck of the ship, with a jingling noise that sounded like the sweetest music in the world to Raymond's ears. "Pieces of eight!" he shouted joyously to Susanna. Grabbing handfuls of the coins, he told her to hold out her skirt and showered them playfully into her lap like a golden rain.

Meanwhile he had sent the divers out again to search for more treasure. It was almost night by the time they returned, with the sad intelligence that there were no more chests in the hold.

"There must be more!" he cried. "There couldn't be only one. If not more chests, there must be gold bars, pigs of silver, something! Get down there and look again."

"The bottom of the ocean drops off sharply just beyond the wreck," said one of the divers, who spoke English reasonably well. "If the rest of the treasure was cast adrift and sank when she struck, we'll never get it back. It's too deep to go after it. Our lungs would burst from the pressure, even if we could hold our breath that long."

Raymond grunted, unconvinced. After further dives to the wreck the next day proved futile, however, he finally conceded. "The rest of it has either been cast adrift or was pulled up by others before us," he said. "Only one thing for it, men—keep looking for other wrecks."

For several days they stayed where they were, sending the longboat out on small expeditions to look for more sunken galleons. When they had covered the small area around them, Raymond gave the order to pull anchor and move farther west. At first their euphoria over having actually found sunken treasure kept his men going, but as days turned into weeks and their search for more plunder proved futile, grumbles of discontent grew into loud resentiment, and finally threats of mutiny were heard by the more impatient of the crew.

The skins of the sailors had become tanned almost to leather, and Susanna's hair was bleached quite blonde by the sun. "We've got to turn back," she pleaded against Raymond's obstinate insistence that they keep searching. "Look at your men. They're reaching the limit of their endurance." Salt spray had cracked and burned their lips, and their eyes, strained from searching the ocean and by the glare of the sun, were red-rimmed and had a hollow, vacant, almost haunted look.

Still Raymond pressed on. One day, when a brisk breeze relieved the heat and sent puffy white clouds scudding across the sky, a sailor who had climbed the mizzenmast to repair a sail cried out, "Ahoy, sir! Pirate ship to starboard!" Sure enough, coming toward them at a fast clip was a ship flying the Jolly Roger. It was only by putting up every bit of sail they could, and straining the ship's powers to its limits, that they were able to escape.

It was not the failure to find more treasure but the threat of capture by pirates that finally forced Raymond Galt to turn back. The farther they sailed the thicker the waters became with pirate ships, and the harder it was to evade them.

"Where do they all come from?" Susanna asked after they had changed course once again to avoid a ship that flew the skull and crossbones. It was night, and they were in their cabin.

Raymond grunted. "They sail out of their hideouts on Tortuga and Hispaniola."

"What would they do to us if they caught us?" she pressed. "Besides take our chest of gold, that is."

"Pray God you never find out," Raymond answered grimly. "If ever one caught us they'd come swarming over the side of this ship with grapples and boarding axes like a plague of locusts, throwing grenades and stinkpots filled with burning sulphur. They'd shoot most of us down with pistols and muskets, and finish the rest of us off with pikes and cutlasses. As for what they'd do to a beautiful creature like you . . ." He lifted a heavy strand of her hair, and let his voice trail off suggestively.

"To repel them we need a bigger ship with more cannon," he went on. "And we need more equipment. Even if we had found more treasure we couldn't have brought it up if it was really heavy. If we'd found big bars of gold and silver in that wreck we might have had to leave them for lack of proper hoisting gear. And we need diving tubs so the divers can stay down longer."

He pulled out a piece of paper and began sketching rapidly. "Now that I've actually been down here I know exactly what I need. I want two ships—one warship with plenty of cannon for protection against pirates, and another, a small light sloop we could anchor in close to the reefs."

"Will Samuel Coffin give you all of that?" she asked. "It sounds like an awful lot of money for such a tightfisted man to come up with."

"Nay, lass," Raymond said with a rueful laugh. "I'll never get what I need from Samuel Coffin. As a matter of fact, he told me not to show my face in Boston again unless I came back laden down with treasure. What he dreads as much as the damage to his purse is the laughter he and I would provoke in the town if I come back without a king's ransom after such wild boasting. Besides, there's you to think of. Nay, we can't go back to Boston yet."

"Then where are we to go? And where are you going to get the ships and equipment we need?"

"In England," said Raymond firmly, rolling up the

foolscap map that had made Samuel Coffin decide to back him. "We're going to go to England, and we'll get it from the king."

"The king?" Susanna said weakly. "You mean Charles II?"

"Of course I mean Charles II. What other king is there in England?"

"Do you have any connections with the king? How will you even gain an audience with him?"

Raymond pointed at his chest of treasure. "There is the only connection I need. Money. It's the universal language. I have proved there is treasure in these waters, and that I can get it. I can see now that I was hopelessly ill-equipped. If I got that with the resources I had, what could I not do with a king's backing?"

Susanna shook her head. "They'll send you to a madhouse," she said. "You must be a raving lunatic to think of seeking an audience with the king with no connections at court."

"You have to think big to get anywhere in this world," he said. "You're the one who scoffed at me for thinking I'd find anything down here, remember? And laughed at me for saying that it would be warm in the winter! I was right, wasn't I?"

"Yes, you were right," Susanna conceded. "Will we be going to London, then?"

"Not at first. We'll sail to Bristol first, sell this ship, and pay off the crew. Then we'll go to London to see the king."

"You can't sell the ship!" Susanna protested. "It belongs to Samuel Coffin!"

"Don't worry so much, Susanna. Just leave Samuel Coffin to me. I'll write him and explain that I'm selling the ship, and that I plan to invest it toward future profits for both of us."

"He won't like it. You should at least get his permission."

"I don't have the time, and besides, if I ask him he might say no. But don't worry, in the long run Samuel Coffin will approve of anything that gets him more money."

"But what if your scheme to get the king's backing fails? What will you tell Coffin then?"

"Well," he said equably, "if I fail to get the king's backing I suppose I'm damned all the way around. I won't waste months taking Coffins' ship back to him, and I don't dare entrust it to anyone else, so what choice do I have?"

Susanna just shook her head. "You're a madman, Raymond, a complete madman."

"Maybe so," he said, chuckling, "but you have to admit that life with me is never boring."

The next morning Raymond gave the order to set sail for England. His crew, little caring where they went as long as it was out of the shoals, reefs, and keys of the Bahama Bank, scurried up the rigging like monkeys and made sail. The white-winged vessel heeled before a spanking breeze and drew away to the eastward, her prow cutting a sparkling furrow in the bright blue sea.

Susanna, however, was deeply troubled. She did not know whether Raymond was not going back to Boston because he felt he could get no more money from Samuel Coffin, or because of her. It seemed to her that if a chest of gold would prove to the king of England that there was treasure in the Bahamas and that Raymond Galt could find it, then it would serve the same purpose with Samuel Coffin. She came to the conclusion that Raymond was only trying to protect her.

Night after night she lay asleep beside Raymond, tossing and turning. As long as she stayed with him she would be a liability. She knew that his ambitions all lay in New England. He might go to England seeking financial backing, but basically he was the kind of man—bold, aggressive, adventurous, and unimpressed by social rank—who belonged in the New World, not the old.

When he'd told her they would be sailing first to Bristol, a plan had begun to form in her mind. Bristol was not far from Chippenham, the town where Susanna's mother's cousins lived. When they reached Bristol she planned to run away to Chippenham, find her cousins, and begin a new life. The trip with Raymond had been a glorious interlude, an idyllic romantic adventure. But it couldn't continue—not forever.

At night, when they lay in each other's arms, he told her continually that when the time was ripe they would be married. But she knew that if Raymond married her he would never attain the heights to which he seemed destined by his abilities. As long as he was tied to her—an outcast, a woman accused of witchcraft who had sneaked off like a thief into the night to avoid prosecution—he would be hampered, unable to realize what she now believed to be his full potential. Although she loved him more than life itself, for his own good as soon as they reached England she planned to abandon Raymond Galt.

9

By the time Raymond and Susanna arrived in the port of Bristol on the west coast of England, spring had arrived, and the winter, so dreaded by Susanna only a few short months before, had passed her by entirely. Raymond put them up at an inn, paid off his crew, and entered into several days of negotiations to sell the ship.

On their first day in the port he hired a seamstress to make a dress for Susanna. "I want the prettiest dress in England, and damn the expense," he said bluntly.

"What do you want it made of?" the seamstress asked.

"What have you?"

"I can get anything you want—silk, taffeta, or the finest brocade."

"Brocade," he said slowly, savoring the word on his tongue. "I like the sound of it. It sounds rich."

"And what color?"

"What color goes well with green?" The only decent

garment Susanna had was the cloak of soft green wool he had given her. She had gone to sea with only the dress she had been wearing when she was taken to jail, and another one that Raymond had taken from her house before they sailed. Both were much the worse for wear, bleached by the hot sun and salt spray of the Bahamas.

The seamstress held up the cloak, stroking her chin and making small considering noises. "A rose brocade would provide a nice contrast to the cloak, and would set off Madame's beautiful hair and eyes and complexion to perfection."

"Very well, then, rose brocade it is."

"A very good choice, sir, if I may say so. I'll be back tomorrow for the first fitting." The woman took Susanna's measurements and departed.

When the seamstress returned the next day Susanna gasped when she saw the length of the gorgeous brocade that had already been cut to her measurements. "There must be some mistake," she said feebly. "I could never wear anything so magnificent."

"You'll grow accustomed to fine things soon enough," the seamstress mumbled, her mouth full of pins. "If I'm not very much mistaken your husband is bent on spoiling you. My advice is to enjoy it—there's any number that would be more than willing to trade places with you."

Susanna was about to tell the woman that Raymond was not her husband, then stopped. She was enjoying herself too much. She turned slowly as the seamstress pinned the lengths of fabric to her. There seemed to be enough material for three dresses. The sleeves were very full, ending just below the elbow, and the skirt billowed out like the sails of Raymond's ship. Susanna was sure she would never grow accustomed to such luxury.

On the day the dress was finished Raymond was out

negotiating with one of the men who had made an offer for the *Golden Plover*. The seamstress helped Susanna put on her new finery and volunteered to dress her hair.

"Let's fix you up proper before your husband gets back," she said. "He'll hardly recognize you when we're through." First she rubbed a little sweet-smelling pomade through the young woman's thick golden tresses. After most of Susanna's hair had been piled on top of her head the woman used repeated applications of a hot curling iron until tendrils curled about Susanna's face and neck in a most bewitching manner.

"Let me look in the mirror," Susanna said when her hair was finished.

"No—we haven't done your face yet." The woman opened a box she had brought with her, revealing an assortment of unguents and cosmetics.

"I couldn't paint my face," Susanna said disapprovingly.

"No one will know you've got a dab of paint on, I promise. Your husband will notice that you look prettier, but he won't know why."

Susanna let out a small yelp as her attendant began plucking her eyebrows. "How did you learn to do all this?"

"I used to be a lady's maid, before I married. Now hold still."

When her eyebrows had been plucked a fine dusting of powder was applied to her nose. A glistening ointment made Susanna's lips look as if they were begging to be kissed, and a little rouge made her cheeks glow until they almost matched the rose of her dress. A tiny drop of belladonna made her eyes look huge.

The seamstress held out three tiny vials. "Which of these scents do you like best?"

Susanna sniffed each one. "They're all lovely. What are they called?"

"This one is orange-water. The others are myrtle and millefleurs."

"Millefleurs—I like the sound." The woman dabbed a few drops of perfume behind Susanna's ears and at the pulse-points of her throat and wrists.

At last they were finished. "Now," the seamstress said triumphantly, leading Susanna to a full-length mirror, "look at yourself."

Susanna gasped at the beautiful woman who gazed back at her. She looked far too worldly to be a simple girl from Boston. "Where's the rest of it?" she asked.

"The rest of what?"

"The rest of the dress."

"The rest of it! You've been complaining for days at my extravagant waste of material!"

"Yes, but . . ." Susanna faltered, pointing toward her bosom. The dress was cut quite low, exposing the round creamy tops of Susanna's breasts.

"That's the fashion, Madame Galt."

"You mean even decent women dress this way?" Susanna said weakly.

"Decent! The more fashionable a woman is the more she shows! Rest assured that if Queen Catherine had your figure she'd give the court an eyeful! And both of the king's mistresses show a good bit more. They say you can see the tops of the Duchess of Portsmouth's nipples. And as for Nell Gwynne—she had her portrait painted completely bare-breasted!"

Susanna's head was spinning. She was surprised to hear it acknowledged so openly that the king kept mistresses, and she was still gaping at her reflection in the mirror. Her arms were bare from right below the elbow to her wrists.

The dress clung tightly to her midriff, then billowed out at the waist. Laced over its upper portion was a busk—a short, tight, little boned corset that forced her breasts high and squeezed at least two inches off her already slender waist. When she turned her skirt swayed, showing her ankles, and her shoulders and half her bosom were exposed. She'd known while the dress was being fitted that it was low-cut, but she assumed that something, a lace collar perhaps, would be inserted to fill the void.

"Just wait until your husband sees you, Madame," the seamstress said. "If you have any doubts about the way you look he'll set them to rest soon enough."

Sure enough, soon after the woman left, Raymond returned and he could hardly take his eyes off Susanna. He made her turn in a slow circle, raking her slowly up and down with a look that made her flush crimson.

"I'll give these to the maid who does our room," he said, picking up her two old dresses, "and when we get to London you'll have a dozen gowns as pretty as your new one and better!"

"Do you really like it?" she said doubtfully.

"Like it? I love it. You'll be the most beautiful woman at court. Now that I think of it, I'd better marry you as soon as we get to London, and keep you away from the king. It's well known that he has an eye for the ladies.

"I've got two men bidding on the *Golden Plover*," he continued. "We'll settle on a price tomorrow, and the day after that we'll be on our way to London! But first things first. Right now we're going to celebrate!"

Downstairs in the inn's tavern every head turned when Susanna entered. At first she was so embarrassed she refused to raise her eyes, but Raymond seemed to relish the way that people gaped at her, and after she drank several glasses of wine she relaxed.

She had never seen Raymond in a more ebullient mood. He insisted on buying drinks for everyone in the inn. When they had all been served he raised his glass. "To the king's health!"

Every tankard and glass went up. "To King Charles!"

The innkeeper saw to it that they feasted royally on a barrel of oysters, followed by roast beef, a roast duck stuffed with chestnuts, and a delicious cheesecake baked in a crust. Raymond talked with everyone, making no secret of his plans to go to London and seek an audience with the king.

The innkeeper claimed to have seen his sovereign once and was full of stories about him and the doings at court. "King Charles likes to dress as a commoner and go among his people without being recognized," he announced. "Once, while he was in a tavern, someone proposed a toast to the king, and he had no choice but to drink his own health!"

Later, in their room, Raymond insisted on removing Susanna's beautiful new dress himself. His fingers trembled as he undid her petticoats and tossed them into a crumpled heap on the floor. He unpinned her hair, letting it fall in a glorious tumble about her shoulders, and drew her to him, burying his face in her sweet-scented flesh. "When I'm a rich man I'll cover you in jewels," he murmured. "You'll have rubies and emeralds and sapphires, and diamonds on every finger."

"That would ruin me," she replied. "I was meant to be a simple goodman's wife. It's the only life I ever expected."

He silenced her with a kiss. The tender tips of her breasts were crushed against the coarse cloth of his shirt, sending shooting flames of excitement along her nerve endings. Raymond pulled off his shirt and pants and drew her down beside him on the bed, kissing her all the while. His hands were amorous and sure, knowing precisely where to touch her to inflame her desires. The mat of hair on his chest teased her breasts as he drew her close, making her mad with longing.

Susanna's eyes were half-closed, and there was a sound in her throat between laughter and moaning. Raymond bent his head, his gentle, probing mouth touching one of her breasts. His tongue caressed its rosy peak with a feathery touch, a light, elusive motion that started a delicious quivering in her stomach. She let her mind drift as he clothed her body in kisses, sending spirals of ecstasy through her. He ran his hand lightly up her thigh, over the jutting arch of a hip, along the line of her ribs, across her breast to her shoulder and down her arm. The touch of his hands, now more ardent and persuasive, sent a delicious anticipatory shudder running through her as one hairy thigh pried her legs apart and he lowered himself slowly onto her. Nothing he did was urgent. His mouth, his hands, his body pressing onto hers, were as unhurried as the lapping of sea waves by the Bristol harbor.

"Ah, Susanna." Now his kisses grew harsher, more insistent, searing a path down her neck and shoulders. When at last they were joined she felt that her body was made of light, glowing like a fire or a luminous mist at dawn that would disappear in sheer elation. The warm throb between her legs was a sweet singing that fired her very veins with delight. Her body became a vortex of fulfillment, and she was caught in the rapturous whirlpool that coiled and spun from one pulsating point of almost unendurable pleasure.

Raymond held himself back until they were both crazed with desire. Susanna dug her nails into his back, looking into his eyes with mute pleading. After release came like an explosion of shooting stars they collapsed onto each other, panting and moist and too weak to move.

Susanna lay back, her face flushed, mouth slack and open, every line of her body replete with gratification. She did not think that she could move even if the inn were to catch fire.

She lay awake for a long time, troubled, after Raymond had gone to sleep. If he planned to leave for London the day after tomorrow, now was the time to leave him. She had made inquiries, and found that the coach to London passed through Chippenham, where her relatives lived. She was convinced more than ever that the world into which Raymond was moving, was destined to live, was a world in which she did not belong, a world in which she would only be a liability to him. He could never return to Boston with her as his wife, and as for staying in England! The beautiful, worldly woman who had looked out at her from the mirror was an imposter. She did not look at all like quiet Susanna Collins from Boston. Susanna had no business with kings and courts. Let Raymond marry some sophisticated woman, some lady wise in the ways of the world and accustomed to court intrigue, someone who could help him further his ambitions.

The coach left at dawn, and she was afraid that if she went to sleep she would miss it. She lay throughout the night, holding Raymond in her arms and studying him in the moonlight, memorizing his face and body, to print them indelibly on her memory so that she would never forget them.

When the moon grew dim and the sky gray, she rose and dressed, leaving off the busk that accentuated her figure and fastening her green cape over the dress so that her bosom was covered. She would have felt more comfortable in one of her old dresses, but Raymond had given them both to the wench who cleaned their room and served as barmaid downstairs.

When she was dressed she leaned over and kissed Raymond very gently on the lips. He was still sleeping soundly, his lips parted, his face soft in repose. She smoothed his russet curls, steeling herself against their separation. Raymond stirred and mumbled in his sleep. For a moment her resolution faltered. Then she summoned her strength. If she was to leave him it must be this instant, before he wakened.

She did not have the heart to leave him with no word at all. Hastily seizing a piece of paper, she wrote, "Dearest Raymond—Marriage would never work for us. Please do not try to find me. Love always, Susanna."

Just as the rooster in the inn's yard crowed she slipped a handful of coins from Raymond's leather moneypurse, tied them in a handkerchief, and made her way silently down the stairs and into the courtyard. When the coach left for Bath and points east Susanna was on it.

As the coach traveled onward, bouncing over the rutted roads, Susanna looked out of her window, eager for her first sight of the English countryside. As soon as they were in the country proper the prospect was pleasing indeed. They went past fields newly planted with spring crops, and fields of green grass thickly sown with buttercups and daisies where sheep grazed. It was a cool, delicious day, with puffy white clouds scudding across a soft blue sky. The trees along the road, still clothed in new leaves of a tender spring green, shimmered in the breeze.

The only other passengers in the coach were a dozing parson clutching a Bible, whose spectacles were about to slip off his nose, and a stout woman who studied Susanna carefully and then ignored her. Susanna sat on the other seat, facing her two traveling companions. She tried to suppress her grief at leaving Raymond, and her apprehension over how she would be received by her relatives, by concentrating on the sights they passed.

The coach rattled over a plank bridge spanning a gurgling stream. A young boy fishing on the bank turned his head and watched them wistfully as they clattered by, no doubt wishing that he was going to a faraway place. The water where he fished was thick with reeds, and he sat on a bank awash with orange marigolds beneath a stand of willows whose hanging fronds swayed gracefully in the breeze. They traversed the bridge with such a great noise that the parson was roused from his nap, and then the road passed through a copse of aspen trees, their leaves shimmering like tiny jewels in the sun.

"It's a lovely sight, isn't it," the parson said, observing Susanna's enjoyment. "England in the spring."

"Yes, sir, that it is." Susanna could not help thinking of spring in Massachusetts. A wave of longing swept over her as she remembered the willows by the stream near her home. In the woods near her cottage fern fiddleheads and speckled jack-in-the-pulpit would have unfolded, and then blue violets and yellow cowslips would appear, dotting the meadows, suddenly ankle deep in new green grass. Delicate purple buds would swell on the lilac trees, and one day white blossoms would explode against the naked black limbs of cherry trees. In the morning she would be awakened by the song of bobolinks and redwing blackbirds, and that great imitator, the mockingbird, all pouring a flood of notes into the sweet morning air, like a liquid stream of gold.

"You're homesick, aren't you?" the parson asked, interrupting her reverie.

"Is it that obvious? Yes, I miss my home." He gave her a kindly smile, and within moments he was dozing again.

They drove through the city of Bath, rattling over the cobblestoned streets. It seemed a large city to Susanna, and she marveled at the number of fine redbrick houses. At the inn the stout woman got off the coach and an elderly man got on. Before they were out of the city he was as sound asleep as the parson, snoring gently in his corner.

They drove through more fields, where cows stopped wrenching lazily at the grass long enough to watch them pass. The cows turned their heads slowly, gazing with liquid brown eyes while the clumsy conveyance rumbled past, then bent their heads again. As the sun rose higher bushes along the side of the road were dotted here and there with washing spread out to dry by cottagers' wives.

At midday the coach stopped at the inn in Chippenham and Susanna got off. What she could see of the town pleased her. There were several tradesmen's shops on the main street—the blacksmith's cottage with his adjoining shop, and the homes and shops of the apothecary and the carpenter. Signs creaking in the breeze were painted with symbols, illustrating the nature of each business for those who could not read.

So this was where her mother had spent her childhood! She remembered the tales her mother had told her of growing up in Chippenham—of learning the healing art from her Aunt Elizabeth; of watching the blacksmith hammering horseshoes or stopping by the kitchen at the inn to beg a morsel of cake from the fat cook; of the day she and her cousin Mary had found a pregnant bitch and taken it home. They had been allowed to keep one of the litter of puppies and had given the others away.

Outside the inn, a building of mellow redbrick, a sign

painted with a golden boar swung over the street on a wrought iron arm. Inside the aged, silver-gray oaken timbers of the building's frame were visible, and there was a fair crowd gathered for the noonday meal. Susanna was hungry and thirsty, but too shy to eat by herself at the inn with strangers staring at her. She stopped only long enough to ask directions to the home of the Carvers.

"Carvers? Which Carvers be those?" asked the innkeeper, a stout man with a red face.

"I am looking for a woman named Mary Carver, who was first cousin to my mother. Her name was Cheever before she married."

"Mary Carver was your mother's cousin?" The man gave her a sharp but not unkindly look. "And who might you mother be?"

"Her maiden name was Abigail Norris. She lost both her parents when she was a child, and she came to live with her mother's sister, her aunt Elizabeth Cheever, here in Chippenham. Elizabeth and Samuel Cheever had a daughter named Mary and a son who was named Samuel also. Mary and my mother were the same age, and grew up as sisters. Mary's brother Samuel was younger. When Mary grew up she married a man named John Carver."

"Yes, I remember your mother now. She married a man named Nicholas Collins and they emigrated to New England. You're her daughter, say you?"

"Yes, sir. My name is Susanna Collins. My mother told me so many tales of growing up in Chippenham—I feel as if I know the town already. I don't suppose that things have changed much since she was a girl."

"No—we're slow to change our ways here. I suppose the rest of England changed a good bit under the Protectorate—people grew more sober, what with Cromwell banning the theater and confiscating the lands of the aristocracy. And then when King Charles came home, God bless his soul, everything returned to the way it had been. They say there was a great upheaval in parts of the kingdom. But here life has always been quiet, and we never had any aristocrats. We haven't even a manor or a squire's estate— just ordinary yeoman farmers, one and all. Have you been traveling?''

"Yes, sir."

"Then you'll be wanting a bite and a draught of ale. Come into the kitchen, and tell me of your family. I'm the proprietor of this establishment—my name's Philip Wheelwright.''

After she had eaten and refreshed herself with a pint of ale, Susanna felt much better. "There isn't much to tell," she said. "My father died when I was five years old, and now my mother is dead too. I came to England because my only relatives are here.'' She did not tell him that her mother had been dead nearly two years. Let him think that, she had come to England, seeking her only living relatives, because she had recently lost her mother. She certainly didn't want to have to account to anyone for the events of the past few months.

"You've had a long journey." He glanced at her rich dress, as if to say, if she could afford such costly apparel why couldn't she find a husband in America? No doubt the innkeeper was a major source of information for others in the small town, and a new arrival, especially a pretty young woman richly dressed, would naturally be an object of curiosity to everyone.

Susanna saw his desire for knowledge struggling with his reluctance to pry into her affairs. At last he said, "Is it true what they say of America, that it is full of painted savages with red skin?''

At first she answered his questions about America and

159

Boston willingly enough, but after a lengthy conversation that left him still eager for more Susanna began to grow impatient. "You'll be wanting to find your kin," he said at last, reluctantly. "I'm sorry to tell you that your cousin Mary Carver is dead of the smallpox these many years."

Susanna's face fell. "But her brother, Samuel Cheever, is alive," the innkeeper continued hastily. "And Mary Carver's husband John is still alive. He's taken a new wife. Samuel and Mary's parents, Elizabeth and Samuel Cheever, are both dead."

"I see." Susanna suddenly realized that she had put herself in a ridiculous position. She had relied on finding her cousin Mary, and felt confident of a welcome in her home. But Mary was dead, and her parents as well, and Susanna's only hopes were Mary's husband, who had remarried, and Mary's younger brother Samuel, whom her mother had rarely mentioned.

"I couldn't presume on John Carver now that Mary is dead," she said. "I don't even know that he ever met my mother, and he's got another wife. He's not even blood kin."

"I'm sure he'd be glad to see you," Philip Wheelwright said hastily.

"Where does Samuel Cheever live?"

"His place is at the far end of the town. He inherited his father's estate, so it will be the house your mother grew up in." He gave her instructions, and she set off down the uneven cobblestone street. At one end she could see a church, and from it half-timbered houses ran along either side of the street, each house with its own wooden gate. Thick hedges separated the houses from the road. Behind the hedges Susanna could see apple and plum and cherry trees in bloom, and a profusion of spring flowers—delphinium and hollyhocks and lilacs. Some of the houses had climbing roses clinging to arches over the gates. This is where I belong, Susanna thought—in a small, quiet town like this one. I could be happy here.

At the opposite end of the main street from the church was the village green. It was in this direction that Susanna had been directed by Philip Wheelwright, who told her that the last house before the green belonged to Samuel Cheever.

The two-storied house was of old brick covered with vines, and like most houses in the town had a thatched roof. There were several ivy-covered chimneys, and an arch entwined with honeysuckle framed the kitchen door. Against the walls of the brick-paved courtyard grew violets and hollyhocks and clumps of fragrant lavender. Blooming fruit trees added their sweet scent to the air.

Susanna sank onto a bench in the courtyard, in love with the house at first sight. This was where her mother had grown up. She could imagine Abigail and Mary playing here as young girls. It was here that her father had come to ask the elder Samuel Cheever for her mother's hand, and here that her mother had learned the skill of healing from Elizabeth Cheever. Behind the house would be an outbuilding the walls of which were lined with apothecary jars, like the small building Abigail Collins had had built for her medicines in Boston. Susanna was glad she had come, more than ever convinced that she could find a place here.

The kitchen door opened and a plump girl, perhaps a year younger than Susanna, ran out crying. She had her face in her hands and was too distraught to notice Susanna. She rushed by weeping noisily as Susanna rose to her feet, disturbed.

In a moment a woman who looked old and careworn followed, shaking her head. The woman showed signs of unhappiness and neglect. Her hair was pinned carelessly, half falling down, and her dress was none too clean. Beneath her skirt protruded a belly distended with pregnancy.

"What do you want, madame?" she said irritably when she saw Susanna.

"I am looking for Samuel Cheever," Susanna said, making a small curtsy.

The woman shot her a look of open hostility. "What do you want with him?" she said abruptly.

"He is my cousin. I have come from America to see him."

"America! All that way." The woman hesitated, considering, and while she did so her eyes raked Susanna up and down. "Very well, come in then," she said at last. "I'm Alice Cheever, Samuel's wife."

In the kitchen she offered Susanna a mug of ale. "Thank you, I ate at the tavern," Susanna replied. She looked about, trying not to let her face register her thoughts as she saw the mess about her. Two small tow-headed boys, obviously identical twins, came running out of the pantry, their faces smeared with jam.

"You two, out!" Alice Cheever said, flapping her apron at them. "If I catch you in the jam again I'll get your father to tan you to a fare-thee-well!"

The small boys scurried out the door. "I had to let my servant girl go just now," the woman said distractedly. "Bess was a slattern, but I could get no better, and had to put up with her as long as I could. I need any help I can get now, what with another baby on the way and me feeling so poorly much of the time." She rubbed her back at the base of her spine as she talked.

"You'd better sit down and take that weight off your feet," Susanna said.

"I wish I could! My feet are so swollen I can hardly get

them in my shoes. But I'm forgetting my manners. Come into the parlor."

Once in the best room in the house, which was furnished with old but comfortable furniture, Alice Cheever insisted that her guest take the best chair despite Susanna's protestations.

"So how is it you come to be Samuel's cousin?" the woman said when she had lowered her bulk onto a settle. "I never heard him mention any kin in America."

Susanna told Alice Cheever the same tale she had told the innkeeper. "Yes," Alice said, nodding her head thoughtfully, when Susanna was finished. "I remember hearing Samuel mention his cousin Abigail. She and Mary were five years older than Samuel and often had to watch him when he was growing up."

"I'm so sorry that Mary Carver is dead. My mother spoke of her so often, with such affection."

"She was a fine woman. She married a man much older than herself but he outlived her and has taken another wife. John Carver is a tough old soul—his mind comes and goes, and he's almost lost his sight—but he'll probably outlive all of us."

A young girl of about seven came running into the room, wailing loudly. "Hush, May, you're too old to be bawling like a baby," her mother said.

The girl's sobs subsided. "Alec popped me with his slingshot again," she said between sniffles. "Make him stop."

"Tell him his father will take care of him when he gets home. And you may have a scone. Now run along." The girl wandered off.

Alice Cheever gave a weary sigh. "You're more than welcome to stay with us if you'd like, although I certainly can't entertain you. You seem to be a lady of quality, and

I cannot provide you with many of the amenities, but I'll be grateful for the company.''

''I'd like that very much,'' Susanna said eagerly.

''We have nowhere to put you except the maid's old room in the attic,'' her hostess said apologetically.

''That will be fine with me. If you don't mind my saying so you seem to be in need of help, and I'm no stranger to work. I'd like to get out of this dress if you could lend me one of yours, something more practical.''

Just then a toddler lurched into the room, grabbed Susanna's skirt, and tried to put it in his mouth.

''Stop that!'' his mother said sharply. ''You'll ruin the lady's pretty dress!''

''How many children do you have?'' Susanna said, laughing as she gently disengaged the child's fingers.

''Six still living, three dead, and one on the way,'' Alice said. ''The trouble is that five of them are too young to be of much help. I don't know what I'd do without Sarah, my eldest. She helps me keep an eye on the others and handles much of the housework now. I've been so sick with this baby. I just can't cope.'' Helpless tears began rolling down her face. ''I'm sorry,'' she said feebly. ''I'm so sorry.''

''Nonsense,'' Susanna said briskly. ''You need some bed rest, and a good stiff tonic. Show me where I'm to stay and lend me a dress, and I'll get to work.''

''Bless you,'' Alice said as she led the way. She seemed to know instinctively that someone had come who would take charge. Alice gave Susanna a dress of plain brown cotton and pointed out the stairs to the attic.

The attic room had a steep, pointed roof, and Susanna had to duck as she entered to avoid hitting her head. But once she was in it she was pleased. It needed dusting, and it had little furniture except a bed and table and a few pegs for clothes, but it was cosy and had a leaded dormer window that looked out on the village green, where Susanna could see boys at play.

She changed her clothes hastily and was downstairs in a few minutes. She went to work cleaning the kitchen, and had just put some arrowroot broth to simmer on the stove when a man came through the back door.

"Hal-lo, love," he said coming up and grabbing her from behind. "What have we here? Another girl so soon, and this one a damn sight prettier than Bess!"

Susanna whirled around. "I'm your cousin Susanna from America," she said crisply, "and I've come to stay."

10

When Raymond awoke on the morning Susanna left him and realized she was gone he feared at first that she had been abducted again or had met with some other kind of foul play. At last he discovered her hastily scrawled note of farewell, but it made no sense to him. He puzzled over it for some time before folding it carefully and putting it away. Her new dress and a small amount of money were gone, and a few inquiries settled beyond any doubt that she had boarded the early morning eastbound coach, apparently of her own volition.

"Where does that coach go?" he asked.

"First to Bath, then through Chippenham, Newbury, Reading, Maidenhead, and finally London," the barmaid rattled off. She apparently assumed that Susanna's departure was prearranged between the two of them, but Raymond could not hide his distress, and the girl realized at last that Susanna had abandoned him.

"Easy come, easy go," she said with a shrug. "Here, sir, you'll be wanting your morning draught." She drew him a mug of ale.

"Nay, I'll have it later," he said distractedly. Upstairs in his room he sank onto the bed and stared out of the window with unseeing eyes, too stunned to comprehend what had happened. As the morning wore on it finally penetrated his mind that Susanna had deserted him, but for what reason he could not imagine. The girl downstairs had assured him that the only other passengers on the coach were a parson and a stout, middle-aged woman, so she had not run off with another man.

The longer he thought about it the only conclusion he could draw was that Susanna did not love him and did not want to marry him. He had told her they would travel to London on the following day and be wed there, so she must have waited until the last minute and bolted. So eager had he been to make his own protestations of love, so sure of their rightness for each other, that he'd never paid any particular attention to the fact that his pronouncements of devotion had not been returned. When he had thought about it he'd assumed her to be shy and reluctant to voice her emotions. It had never occurred to him that deep down inside Susanna did not return his love.

Raymond had always taken for granted that he could achieve whatever he went after, if he wanted it badly and pursued it doggedly enough. His father had scolded him for this trait when he was growing up. "You always assume that you can have anything you want," Geoffrey Galt had often said to his son. "Life isn't like that. I don't want to discourage your ambition, but things don't always work out the way you want them to." Susanna must have used him to escape the gallows in Boston, and then discarded him when she felt that she no longer needed him.

As he sat in his room on that dreadful morning, trying to come to grips with his feelings, he went back over his relationship with Susanna, searching for clues that would explain her desertion. She had always been quiet, but it was a quality he liked in her. She provided a foil for his own boisterousness, for his love of attention and streak of cocky exuberance. Two showy peacocks in the same family would have been one too many.

But now, as he thought back over it, he interpreted her silence differently. Perhaps she had never really cared deeply for him. He knew he had awakened her body, but he knew well that there was often a difference between lust and love. Perhaps Susanna had merely allowed herself to be swept along by the force of his stronger personality until she felt the time had come to do what she, instead of he, wanted.

Raymond knew he possessed such a strong will that sometimes it made life easier just to give in to him—his mother and sisters had told him this often. They would often take the easier path by letting him have his way, up to a point. When they felt he had pushed them too far they would rebel against his aggression and assert themselves. Perhaps he had been wrong to take her away from that dullard, Michael Hale. Perhaps she would have been happier and better off married to a man who would never be more than an artisan's assistant. Perhaps . . . Raymond's head began to ache from his speculations.

He considered pursuing her. He could inquire after Susanna in every town where the coach stopped between Bristol and London. A girl as pretty as she, dressed in the latest fashion, would surely be noticed. But what if she had gone all the way to London? It was a large, sprawling city, where she could easily get lost if she wished.

After considering the matter for some time Raymond

decided there was nothing for it but to bury his sorrow, to push Susanna resolutely from his mind. He had business to conclude. Today he would sell the *Golden Plover*, and on the morrow he would journey to London to seek an audience with the king.

He told himself that the world was full of women and he was not one to mope over a girl. Why, the barmaid downstairs was pretty enough and very attentive. She always jumped to serve him, even if it meant ignoring customers who had gotten there earlier, and her playful eyes and the husky insinuation in her voice indicated that she was more than willing to share his bed. That night he planned to take her up on the offer.

After Raymond had successfully negotiated the sale of the *Golden Plover* he returned to the inn and proceeded to get roaring drunk. The barmaid wound up putting him to bed, all right—alone, still dressed in his breeches and shirt. Or perhaps it would be more appropriate to say that she poured him into bed.

The next day he cursed himself as his aching head nearly split every time the coach to London jolted over a stone or a pothole in the road. At the first few stops he considered getting out and making inquiries about Susanna. But the day was bright, and the sunlight sent stabbing pains through his eyes into the back of his head. Devil take the girl—she could have her liberty if she desired it that badly. She was an accomplished temptress now, and would surely have no difficulty in finding another protector.

After a journey of two days Raymond arrived at last in London. London! The very name sounded like magic to his ears. It was a city he had always dreamed of seeing, and it did not disappoint him. He tried to drown his anger and raging sorrow over Susanna's departure, which were never far from his mind, with feverish activity. There was a great, sprawling city to be explored, and he had work to do.

After finding himself a room in a tavern he spent his first day in London simply walking about. The city was stinking and noisy, but beautiful and exciting, too, a pot-pourri of the old and the new. He commented on the many new brick buildings, and was told that a number of them were replacements for old half-timbered ones that had burned in the terrible fire of 1666.

The streets were narrow, some paved with cobblestones but most of them not. Along the sides or down the middle ran open sewage canals. Posts strung out at intervals attempted to separate the carriageways from the space left to pedestrians, but people flowed out into the streets, scattering only when a coach rumbled by. Across the streets houses leaned toward each other, each storey overhanging the one below it so that in narrow thoroughfares the sun was shut out almost completely.

The streets were filled with all sorts and conditions of people—merchants and beggars, peddlers and musicians, young men of fashion and ragged waifs, and elegantly-dressed ladies who hid their faces behind black masks. Raymond noticed that well-dressed men and women held scented handkerchiefs to their noses or carried small balls of perfume against the stench.

Even accustomed as he was to the raging of wind and weather at sea, the noise was enough to split Raymond's eardrums. Peddlers clanged bells and shouted their wares in an ancient singsong that was almost intended not to be understood. Coachmen shouted curses at each other over the noise of their vehicles' wheels while they struggled to maneuver their way through the jostling crowds. Apprentices lounging in shop doorways tried to lure shoppers inside by praising their masters' wares at the top of their lungs. Strolling musicians played and sang and street dancers performed for the amusement of the crowd, passing their hats for coins afterward. Porters staggered along with immense loads on their backs and cursed anyone who impeded their progress. Beggars displayed hideous deformities and ran after the well-dressed, shaking their outstretched hands for alms. "Make way, make way!" shouted the occasional liveried footman going ahead to clear a path for the sedan-chair of an aristocrat. Overhead signs painted with golden bulls or blue boars, red lions or King Charles's profile, creaked as they swung in the breeze. Above it all the bells of churches, the spires of which dominated the skyline, tolled sweetly the hours of the day.

After he had had his fill of sightseeing and gotten his bearings by familiarizing himself with the major landmarks of the city, Raymond asked to be directed to the best tailor in London. Accustomed to waiting upon noblemen and gentlemen of quality, the tailor looked disdainfully at the huge man in rough clothing who roared like a hurricane into his shop, throwing down a sack of gold coins and demanding the best suit in London.

After the measurements for his suit had been taken, Raymond sought out the city's best hatter and ordered a hat broader, higher, and more lavishly plumed than those worn by the most elegant dandies at court. At a wigmaker's he was measured for a black periwig curling to the shoulders. At the hosier's he purchased fine linen and ordered frilly lace bows, or canons, to adorn the tops of his knee-length stockings. His new square-toed shoes were decorated with silver buckles.

While he was waiting in his tavern for his wardrobe to be completed he asked the innkeeper, "Where does the king live?"

The question was greeted with general laughter. But when the innkeeper saw that Raymond was in earnest, he said, "Sometimes the king lives at Windsor Palace, but most of the time he's at Whitehall Palace. Why—do you have busines with His Majesty?"

"Yes I do," Raymond said, undeterred by the laughter. "King Charles and I are going to become business partners—he just doesn't know it yet!"

This provoked even more laughter. "I'm sure he's awaiting the opportunity with baited breath," said one man, holding out his mug for more ale.

Raymond smiled good-naturedly at the jest. "What's the best way to go about getting an audience with him?"

"Do you have any friends or connections at court?" the inkeeper asked.

"None whatsoever."

"Well, you're not alone. Many a man with no connections takes his petition directly to the king. You're not supposed to be able to gain admittance to the palace unless you've been presented at court, but security is lax and almost anyone can get through if he wants to badly enough. King Charles tries to make himself more accessible to the people than many of his predecessors. If the first Charles hadn't been so remote from his subjects he might not have lost his head, God rest his soul."

"What would be the best time of day to try my luck?"

The innkeeper scratched his chin. "Mid-morning, I'd say, while the king is taking his walk."

"And where does he do this walking?"

"I've never been to the palace myself, mind you, but I know the king has a great love of walking, and they say that after his morning council he usually takes a stroll through the Stone Gallery. Ask anyone at the palace where the Stone Gallery is—they'll know. That's where petitioners who want to get His Majesty's ear and have no connections at court try to reach him.''

After Raymond had gotten directions to Whitehall Palace he thanked the innkeeper and tipped him generously for the information. When his clothes were complete Raymond dressed carefully in his new wig and hat, a bright green coat, and a waistcoat so long-skirted that his breeches could hardly be seen. The silver buckles on his shiny new shoes twinkled and his new sword flashed in the morning sun as he walked. He thought he cut rather a fine figure as he set out to meet his sovereign.

The innkeeper had directed him to London Bridge and told him to take a wherry to the palace, which fronted directly onto the River Thames. At the bridge a host of watermen, most of them grizzled old ruffians with caustic tongues, fought over his business. After he had chosen one and negotiated the fare they set out, the wherryman poling them slowly down the Thames. They traveled toward the west, where the palace lay around a bend in the river.

Whitehall Palace was a sprawling, motley collection of buildings of all ages, sizes, and varieties of architecture. It had grown rather than been planned. The palace was honeycombed in a random fashion, with hallways and dozens of apartments opening into one another like a giant rabbit warren. In the outer parts lived the king's servants and a host of hangers-on. The central part was a mass of redbrick buildings dating mainly from the days of the Tudors and built so close to the river that the kitchens sometimes flooded at high tide. The largest structure, fronting the riverbank, housed the royal apartments and those lords and ladies who composed the King's court. Along the front of this building ran the Stone Gallery.

The gallery was a corridor almost four hundred feet long. Much of the magnificent art collection Charles I had gathered had been sold after he was beheaded, and Charles II, who was now trying to reassemble his father's collection, had lined the Stone Gallery with paintings by Raphael, Titian, and other masters. Only fifteen feet wide, the gallery was crowded with a throng of beautiful ladies in satin gowns, young men of fashion, soberly-dressed merchants, soldiers in uniform, and country squires and their wives.

Upon entering, Raymond could easily pick out the country folk, as their clothes were like those still worn by wealthy people in Boston. The squires were dressed in baggy, knee-gartered breeches instead of the short, wide-bottomed breeches now in fashion. They wore rough boots instead of stylish buckled shoes, and hats ornamented with silver buckles instead of waving plumes. Some of the country gentry newly come to town even wore ruffs, which Raymond now knew had not been worn by fashionable folk for years. In short, their clothes were hopelessly out of style. And not so long ago I dressed like them, too, Raymond thought, looking down at his elegant new clothes with satisfaction.

A man less aggressive than Raymond would have been daunted by the sheer size of the crowd. He plunged into the seething, elbowing mass of humanity until he came smack up against the broad back of a man in a blue velvet coat and could move no further.

The man turned around when he felt Raymond trying to get around him. "You'll get no closer today," he growled. "They're thicker than pickpockets at a hanging."

"Who are all these people, anyway?" Raymond asked.

The man shrugged. "Like us, they all want something from the king."

"How hard is it to get to see him?"

The man gave a short abrupt laugh. "Hard enough. I've

been here every day for a week, and gotten no closer than this. I'll just have to keep trying until I can catch his ear."

"Which direction will he come from?" Raymond was glad to have found someone willing to speak to him.

"He'll come from over there," his informant said, indicating a pair of velvet-shrouded doors. On either side of the doors stood guards in scarlet uniforms with gold lace running from shoulder to wrist, wearing plumed round hats with broad brims.

Struggling to hold his place in the sweating, surging crowd, Raymond suddenly heard a murmur sweep through the throng. "He's coming," the man in front of him said.

The guards stepped forward, pushing the crowd back, and then the velvet draperies were thrust aside and the doors opened. The crowd parted slightly to let the king pass.

Raymond strained forward, eager for his first glimpse of the monarch. Charles II, resplendent in crimson velvet, came down the corridor in long strides, a crowd of yapping spaniels at his feet. He was tall, almost as tall as Raymond, and had a marvelous physique, with well-shaped legs and a slender, lithe torso. He exuded robust good health and animal strength even though deep lines in his forehead indicated that he was no longer young. He had swarthy skin and glittering, black, heavy-lidded eyes, and Raymond would not have been surprised to learn that beneath his curled black periwig the king's own naturally luxuriant hair was turning gray. A narrow mustache crowned the upper lip of a full, sensuous mouth. Raymond could easily see why such a monarch would have no trouble establishing himself as a ladies' man.

For a moment after the king appeared a hush fell on the crowd, and then they moved toward him, each clamoring to make his voice heard over that of his neighbor. To one man who caught his ear King Charles said, "See me tomorrow night in my bedchamber." To another he gave a frown of annoyance, and an abrupt shake of the head. When the man followed him, persisting, King Charles stopped and focused on him a look so imperious, so scornful and withering, that it sent a shiver down Raymond's spine. The king stopped again to acknowledge a woman who sank to the floor in a deep curtsy. In the next moment he drew abreast of Raymond, and without so much as a glance in his direction, moved on.

After the king had gone and the hubbub had subsided, Raymond left the gallery, walked to the river, and was conveyed back to his tavern.

For a week Raymond went to the palace every day but never got any closer to the king than he had on the first day. If he had not been a man of unusual height he doubted that he would even have caught a glimpse of the monarch, so thick was the crowd seeking an audience. He noticed that many of the same people showed up, as he did, day after day.

He spent his afternoons roaming the city, until he knew half of its streets by heart, and frequented coffeehouses where he soaked up all the news and gossip he could, in the hope that some of it might be of use. He acquired a taste for coffee, an expensive beverage that was new to him, and took to smoking a long, thin pipe. He began to understand the character of the Londoner—boastful, convinced of his own superiority, hostile to foreigners, and contemptuous of colonials and English country folk. Raymond learned a great deal about London and the English, but he was still no closer to achieving his purpose.

Finally he realized that it would take some unusual strategy if he was ever to get a private audience with the king. One day he hired a porter and together the two of them managed to haul his massive treasure chest to London Bridge. The wherrymen, well accustomed to seeing Raymond every morning, did not question the presence of the battered old chest, its once polished fittings now green and tarnished by salt and seawater.

When Raymond and the porter arrived at Whitehall Palace they hauled the chest to the Stone Gallery. Cursing and swearing, they forced their way through the crowd, ignoring the hostile looks of those they pushed to the side.

At last the king appeared. As he drew near, Raymond and the porter opened the chest and tipped it over, sending a flood of golden coins spilling over the stone floor.

The king stopped. A dead hush fell on the crowd. "What is this?" the king said at last.

Raymond stepped forward and bowed deeply. "A tribute, Your Majesty."

"For us? This gold is for us?"

"Yes, Sire. A humble gift from a devoted subject."

The king looked Raymond over slowly from head to toe. "Where did you get it?"

"From the bottom of the sea. From a Spanish galleon laden with treasure that sunk on the reefs off the Bahama Bank in Your Majesty's waters many years ago."

The king rubbed his mustache, reflecting. "There is more where this came from?"

"Much more, for the man who knows where to find it."

"And you, we suppose, are that man?"

"I am. Allow me to present myself. I am Raymond Galt, from Massachusetts."

"Massachusetts! A colonial?" As he spoke the black, glittering eyes of the king raked Raymond up and down, taking his measure. Beneath the rich attire the king saw a strong, rugged man with a sun-bronzed face, hands that were no strangers to labor, and the love of adventure in a pair of extraordinary sapphire-blue eyes. He saw, also, that Raymond was a leader of men, someone born to command.

"Yes, Your Majesty. I have recently come from Massachusetts to London, with a business excursion to the Bahamas on the side that I hope might interest you."

"And what do you want from us?"

"Backing, Sire. Ships and equipment and a crew, in return for part of the treasure I find."

"You're sure there's more?"

"Oh, yes, Sire, quite sure."

"Hmm." The king looked again at the flood of gold coins. "Come to our bedchamber tomorrow morning at nine."

"Yes, Sire," Raymond said, bowing deeply to conceal his excitement.

Servants came forward to collect the gold and put it back in the chest, and many in the crowd turned around to look at Raymond with interest. In a moment the king was gone, continuing his promenade down the Stone Gallery.

The next morning Raymond was at the palace early. He was escorted by a servant to the king's bedchamber, a room hung with rich tapestries where Charles II, magnificent in a velvet suit of azure and silver, sat in an upholstered chair sipping his morning chocolate. Several of the small pop-eyed spaniels the king loved lolled at his feet.

For once Raymond's palms were sweating, but he managed to conceal his nervousness.

"Come in, Mr. Galt," the king said with a wave of his hand. "You may know," he continued when Raymond had entered, "that we have a great love of the sea."

"Yes, Sire, it is well known." Raymond had not, in fact, known this until he had heard it at a coffeehouse. He had been told by a man obviously acquainted with matters at court that whenever he could the king was off to Spithead, where his navy rode at anchor.

"There is no sight as lovely as a man-of-war with gleaming decks of cannon."

"I could not agree more, Sire. As a matter of fact, it is a man-of-war I need," Raymond said.

"For what? I thought you were going treasure hunting, not fighting."

"Yes, Sire, but I need protection from pirates." Briefly he told the king of his trip to the Bahamas. "I need a warship for an escort, and a smaller vessel equipped with the best diving gear to do the actual treasure hunting."

"Our navy, alas, is short of vessels. What kind of warship do you need?"

Raymond began outlining his requirements. The king raised his hand. "We classify our men-of-war according to six ratings, depending on size and number of guns. For example, our first rating includes our three-decker line of battle ships, mounting between ninety and a hundred guns. I assume that such a large vessel would be unsuitable for your purposes, even if I could spare one. It would be too large and clumsy to sail in and out of shallow waters."

"What would Your Majesty recommend?"

"I don't think you would need more than a ship of the fifth rate, a vessel of two hundred tons and twenty-two guns?"

"I'm sure that would be adequate." Raymond was beginning not only to relax but to enjoy himself, especially as the king was so knowledgeable about the sea.

"And the second ship?" the king continued. "What would its requirements be?"

"I need a light vessel of about fifty tons, with ten or so

cannon. I need diving tubs and other gear to hunt treasure—grapples, drag cables, tackles, and heavy blocks."

"You can get such equipment here?"

"If I cannot find it, I can tell coopers and shipwrights how to make it. And there is one more thing, Sire."

"Yes?"

"It occurred to me that it would be wise to carry a cargo so that pirates will think I have come to trade."

The king stared at the dark sediment in the bottom of his cup of chocolate. "An ingenious suggestion. You seem to have thought this scheme through carefully. What kind of cargo were you thinking of carrying?"

"Brandy, powder, scissors, clothing—anything that would look plausible."

"Hmm. I see. Very well. We will consider your proposal."

Raymond's heart sank. For a few wild moments he had thought the king was going to hand over everything he wanted with no argument.

"It is no secret that the royal treasury is seriously depleted," the king continued. "We don't need to tell you that we could put your sunken treasure to use, that is, if you can find it. On the other hand, if you return empty-handed we will have lost a considerable investment."

"I can find more treasure, Sire, of that I am confident," Raymond said.

"But we have other needs as well. You are obviously a man who knows the sea. Our navy needs reorganizing. We are not satisfied with the quality of work done by our admirals and administrators. You might be useful in that capacity."

Raymond chose his words carefully, trying to hide his disappointment. "With all due respect, Your Majesty, I do not think that I would be of much use to anyone if I was chained to a desk. I was not cut out to be that kind of man.''

"We will see, we will see. I take it then, that you would not be interested in a position at court either?'' He looked at Raymond intently as he spoke. Raymond had the distinct conviction that he was being tested.

He paused. He could flatter the king, or he could risk everything by telling the truth. "No, Sire, I would not.''

"How long have you been coming here seeking an audience? Perhaps you don't understand the kind of opportunity you are being offered.''

"I've been coming every day for a week, and I've seen enough to convince me that this is no place for me.''

"Why not? What observations have you made about life at court that gave you such a jaundiced view?''

"I've observed that every man here spends his life struggling to lift himself above his fellows. I've observed that men will kill for empty titles, or to climb one rung higher on a ladder that seems to be going nowhere. I can't spend my life plotting and scheming with knaves and rogues for empty preferments.''

He started to add that when the king's courtiers were not busy with intrigue they spent their time in endless rounds of whoring, or going to cockfights and the theater, but that was not so far from the life he himself had once led, and so he remained silent. He did not want to appear prudish. He also wisely refrained from saying that as far as he could see, acting as the king's pimp seemed to be regarded as the highest honor of all.

King Charles drew in his breath. "By the devil, a man who speaks his mind, even to his king. You are a rare creature indeed. We haven't encountered your like in a long while! And if you are not interested in empty preferments, what is it that you do want?''

Raymond opened his mouth, and then closed it again, confused. For indeed what he once thought he wanted and what he now desired seemed to be two different things. ''I thought I wanted to roam the world, to see everything in it, to eat and drink and wench and plunder to my heart's content.''

''And now?''

''After I've made my fortune I want to settle down and become a responsible citizen. I want a family. I want to make a contribution to my community.'' He was shocked to hear himself speaking these words—they seemed to be coming from the mouth of a stranger. No, not exactly a stranger—why, he sounded exactly like his father! He loved and respected his father, but he had always regarded him as a hopeless stick-in-the-mud!

''And by your community you mean this place in Massachusetts you come from, this, this . . .'' The king waved his hand.

''Boston.''

''Isn't it dreadfully uncivilized?''

''Not so uncivilized as you imagine. And there are opportunities there, limitless opportunities. The country is young and full of promise, waiting to be made by men with the courage to do it.''

''Well, any man who speaks to his sovereign the way you do is certainly not lacking in courage. We must say that your proposition intrigues us, but such an outlay requires serious consideration.''

''With all due respect, Sire, how long do you expect the decision to take?''

''I'm not one to rush into new ventures boldly, especially ones that are going to cost dearly. It could be several months.''

Raymond froze his face into an agreeable mask to conceal his dismay.

"But in the meantime a man of your talents and obvious knowledge of nautical matters could be very useful to me. Since Samuel Pepys left my navy has been administered most inefficiently, and your service will no doubt prove invaluable. You will be properly compensated for your services, of course. And we would like to hear more about Boston, and why it exerts such an appeal for a man like you. We must dine together soon."

"Thank you, Your Majesty." Raymond bowed his way out, beating a hasty retreat to cover his disappointment. He was flattered that the king wished to talk further with him, but he was an impatient man, and hanging about London with no useful employment forced home keenly his deep sense of loss over Susanna. He had hoped to have hard work to do, and soon. He itched to have another vessel at his command, to feel the sea breeze on his face once again, to keep moving, to do anything that would keep his mind off his loss. He had always found enforced idleness agonizing, and it could not have come at a worse time.

But at the same time it seemed to him that he was very close to attaining his goal. He had always known that if he could find someone with sufficient vision and capital to back him he could make a fortune, and the king was definitely interested in him. No, he must be patient, no matter what the cost. There was nothing for him to do but wait.

Back in his room at the inn he went over his conversation with the king in his mind. Something about it nagged at him, but it was some time before he put his finger on it. He had always presented himself to Susanna as a man seeking action and adventure, someone who would never have his fill of roaming the earth. He wanted to get married, but he had never stopped to think exactly how he would fit a wife and family into his life. He had seen women in Boston married to men who were always at sea, and he had always pitied them. They might as well have been widows.

When the king had forced him to articulate his ambitions, he'd realized that if he could make enough money he was ready to settle down. He could not blame Susanna for not wanting to marry a man with an incurable wanderlust, and she'd had no way of knowing that he had changed. How could she? He had not known it himself. Perhaps that was why she had left him.

11

Susanna spent her first afternoon in Chippenham cleaning and organizing her cousin's kitchen. When she had assembled enough food for a cold supper she left the house and went exploring. From her mother's descriptions she knew where to find each of the outbuildings, and it was strange to be in a place that was new to her and yet in a very real sense already familiar.

The door to the small building where Elizabeth Cheever had kept her simples and decoctions did not want to open. Susanna had to throw her whole weight against it, and once inside she was disappointed to see that it had not been in use for some time. The shelves, most of which had been stripped bare, were dusty, and there were cobwebs everywhere. It was clear that the building was used now only to store odds and ends—a stack of firewood stood in one corner, and those shelves that were not empty held a box of nails, some twine, and broken bits of farm equipment.

She was standing in the small room, looking about with an odd sense of loss, when a voice rang out sharply behind her. "What are you doing here?"

Susanna turned around to see a thin, blond girl of perhaps fourteen clutching a book to her chest. "That's my mother's dress," she said accusingly.

"You must be Sarah. I'm Susanna Collins. I'm your father's cousin. My mother grew up with him and his sister Mary."

As they walked back to the house together, Susanna gave an edited version of how she had gotten to England. Sarah listened with interest.

"That's odd," she said. "Of course I knew my aunt Mary before she died, but my father never mentioned growing up with a cousin named Abigail."

Inside, Sarah exclaimed at the immaculate kitchen. "I'm sorry it was such a mess," she said. "I don't know what you must think of us, but I can't do everything and Mother seems to be getting weaker and weaker. We can't afford more than one maid, and the last one wasn't much help."

"Why did you keep her so long?" Susanna asked.

"That was my father's decision," Sarah said, dropping her eyes. "Finally Mother put her foot down, and said either the girl went or she went."

"Several of your brothers were in and out of the kitchen as I was tidying up this afternoon," Susanna said. "I asked them their names, but I'm afraid I haven't gotten them all straight yet."

"After me, Mother and Father had a stillborn child and two who didn't survive infancy. The next surviving child was May, who's seven. Then there are the twins, Alec and Morley, who are five, and Evelyn, who's three, and then Christopher, who just turned two."

Together the two of them laid out the evening meal. "Where shall I sit?" Susanna asked as they set the table.

"Mother's not coming down," said Sarah. "You might as well take her place. Go ahead, she won't mind."

The children, all tow-headed blonds, straggled in one at a time, and Susanna noticed that they hadn't washed before eating. Their father was the last to arrive. He gave a quick glance at Susanna, sitting in his wife's place at the other end of the table.

"Is Alice in bed again?" he asked, drawing his brows together in annoyance. "You'll have to excuse my wife. Other women have babies without disrupting the whole household, but not Alice." Susanna said nothing, wondering that he criticized the children's mother in front of them.

Samuel Cheever was still a handsome man, although he was running to fat and his fair hair had thinned until there was little left on top. Throughout the meal he quizzed Susanna about her life in America. The children's manners were terrible, but he did nothing to correct them. Sarah had her hands full feeding both herself and the baby, and seemed to think it nothing out of the ordinary that the twins were shoving and pinching Evelyn.

"My mother told me so many stories about this house, I feel as if I already know it," Susanna said when she had satisfied Samuel's curiosity about New England. She tried to ignore the fact that the twins had quit tormenting little Evelyn and were now grabbing food off May's plate. "She talked more about Mary than you, of course, since they were of an age and such close friends. I'd be grateful for any memories of her you could share with me."

"I can't say that I remember her that well," Samuel said. "The girls were a good bit older, and, as you said, spent most of their time together. And then, of course, I was a boy, so we had different chores, and I guess as I got older the gap just grew wider and wider.''

After she and Sarah had washed up after supper Susanna carried a bowl of arrowroot broth and some port she had found in a sideboard up to Alice. "This will help build you up,'' she said, ''and tomorrow I'll brew you a good strong tonic.''

"Bless you,'' Alice said, sitting up on her pillows. "I don't know what I would have done if you hadn't come along. Sarah can't do all the housework, and she's not good at controlling the younger children. She's basically a good girl, but she loves books more than housekeeping. It's too bad she's not a gentleman's daughter.''

Alice sighed. "I feel terribly guilty about dumping all this on you. I'll start looking around for a new maid as soon as I can.''

"Don't worry about it,'' Susanna said. "I'm accustomed to hard work.''

During the succeeding days she had plenty of opportunity to prove her claim. With limited assistance from Sarah, who stole away whenever she could to bury her nose in a book, and from Alice, who insisted on getting up whenever she felt strong enough, Susanna soon had the house running smoothly, although there was a great deal to be done with so many little ones underfoot.

With the exception of Sarah the children were completely undisciplined. Their father ignored them unless they annoyed him, and Alice Cheever was temperamentally unsuited to motherhood. Her greatest fault was inconsistency. She alternately spoiled the children, lavishing them with affection and sweets, and then pushed them away from her with peevish irritation when she was feeling unwell or did not want to be bothered with them. There were rules that the children knew perfectly well they could break with impunity when their mother was in a good mood, but on other occasions they would be punished harshly for infractions of the very same rules.

Susanna tried to give her little cousins affection, but she also insisted on being strict and impartial, and, accustomed as they were to having their own way most of the time, they resented her at first and refused to obey her.

She found her cousin Samuel Cheever a difficult man to like. He was impatient with his wife and indifferent to her misery, reproaching her for "getting herself in the family way again" as if she had miraculously made herself pregnant. He was obviously pleased that the house was now running smoothly, but Susanna never heard a word of thanks. He seemed to think that good meals, a clean home, and well-brushed clothes were his due, although from the looks of things when Susanna arrived it had been a long time before her coming since he'd had them.

She tried a number of times to get Samuel to talk about her mother, eager as she was for any link with the past that would bind her to her new home, but he always put her off. He would repeat, with impatience, that Mary and Abigail had spent most of their time together and he could not remember Abigail well. He seemed to have some grievance against the two of them—that his parents had preferred the girls to him, or that Abigail and Mary had not looked after him well when he was young and their responsibility.

Before she had been in Chippenham a week Susanna knew she had made a mistake. The happiness she had hoped to find by going back to her mother's roots eluded her. The home in which her mother had grown up, a place she had always idealized, was no longer a happy place.

There was also an aching void in her heart left by Raymond's absence that was with her every minute of the day. Despite his boasting, wild schemes, and reckless bravado, all of which frightened her, she knew that she loved Raymond Galt with all her heart, and she missed him so dreadfully there were times when she wanted to die. Without his enthusiasm for living and explosive energy the world seemed dull and colorless. Then, too, there was the physical deprivation she felt. Night after night her body ached for him. She felt a pain that was truly physical in her limbs, in her heart, in her breasts.

She felt deep shame for the things that had happened to her during her last months in Boston. There were times when she could feel the eyes and hands of the women who had come to examine her body probing her naked flesh, and a wave of mortification swept over her, so keen that she felt as if she had been physically violated. Her imprisonment and witchcraft hearing were ordeals from which she sometimes thought she would never recover. The humiliation of having been caught with Raymond by Michael Hale, of having all Boston know she was sleeping with a man who was betrothed to another woman, when she herself was as good as engaged, had also left its mark.

Perhaps if she had talked about these things to Raymond she could have erased some of the pain, but after her escape she'd only tried to banish the terrible events of her last days in Boston from her mind, pushing thoughts of them away whenever they surfaced. She could see now that by ignoring them she had not made the hurt go away, but had only caused it to fester like an untended wound. And Raymond, who thought only of the future, had seemed to forget entirely that she had skulked away from Boston like a thief in the night. She could not talk to anyone here of her real reason for leaving Boston, for fear of being cast out again, so the pain lay, unexorcised, like a hard lump in the bottom of her heart.

She knew that Raymond loved her, and if he had been willing to assume whatever risks marriage to her might have entailed, who was she to argue with him? He was a resourceful man and could take care of himself. If they'd found it difficult or impossible to return to Boston, they could have gone to Virginia or Maryland or any of the other colonies.

The more she was tempted to indulge in these gloomy reflections, the gladder she was that she had plenty of work to keep her busy.

One afternoon when she had a bit of free time she decided to visit John Carver, her cousin Mary Cheever Carver's widower. His second wife directed her to a peaceful orchard of flowering fruit trees behind their house, where John Carver sat dozing in a chair, taking the afternoon sun with a blanket over his knees. He seemed very ancient, with a mass of wrinkles intersecting each other, and skin sagging in folds beneath his recessed chin. Wisps of gray hair clung to a shiny bald pate.

Reluctant to waken him, Susanna reached out tentatively and touched his gnarled, spotted hand. He opened his eyes at once. "I'm sorry to waken you," she said, "but your wife said it would be all right."

"Oh certainly, my dear," he said, smiling at the pretty young girl beside him. "Old people are like cats. We drop off to sleep and wake up at a moment's notice. What man wouldn't rather look at a beautiful woman than sleep, anyway?" he added gallantly. "I don't see too well, and perhaps my eyes deceive me, but I don't believe I recognize you."

"I'm Susanna Collins, daughter of Abigail and Nicholas Collins. My mother grew up with your first wife Mary. They were like sisters."

She had to repeat herself several times before the light

of comprehension finally dawned in the old man's eyes. "Abigail! Of course! Mary talks about you all the time. I'm so glad to meet you."

"No, I'm not Abigail, I'm her daughter Susanna."

"You married and moved to America before Mary and I started courting." He chuckled. "Many's the time I've heard Mary go on and on about you, I can tell you that. Your husband is named . . . ah, I forget."

"Collins. Nicholas Collins. But he was my father, not my husband."

"How is he now? In good health, I hope?"

"No, I'm sorry, but he's been dead for many years."

"So you've decided to come home. Sensible girl. Must be dreadful, living in the colonies. Must feel like you've been deported, or banished." He chuckled again. "I wish I could have seen the look on Mary's face when she opened the front door and saw you standing there!"

Susanna wanted to talk to the old man of her mother, and of what memories his wife Mary had had of her, but since he seemed to think that his first wife was still alive, and that Susanna herself was Abigail, it was difficult.

"What does Mary say of me?" she asked.

"Well, she told me that you were pretty, but she didn't say how pretty! I'm sure the Cheevers are delighted to have you back home. Do you have any children?"

"No, sir."

"Too bad. I'm sure Samuel and Elizabeth would love to have a grandson to dandle on their knees. Especially since young Sam seems to be turning out so wild and irresponsible. I don't know what will become of that boy."

He shook his head sadly. "Perhaps I shouldn't speak about it. Did they tell you about all the trouble he's gotten into while you were away?"

"No sir," she said.

"Well, then, it's not my place to speak of it. But I will say he's been a sore subject lately with Samuel and Elizabeth, and I'm sure they're still hoping he'll straighten out in the end. It's hard to turn your back on your only son. Perhaps I shouldn't say anything at all, but heaven knows if you've come home to stay you're bound to hear it sooner or later. He's your cousin and I know you and Mary helped raise him, but I declare I don't know if the lad will ever settle down. Perhaps marriage will sober him—it sometimes does."

"What's wrong with Sam?" Susanna asked.

"Do you mean why does he behave the way he does? I don't know. Who's to say? Samuel and Elizabeth certainly aren't to blame—they've given the lad as good an upbringing as anyone ever had. But sometimes children go astray despite the best efforts. The boy just seems to be selfish—grabs whatever he wants and devil take the hindmost. Takes for granted whatever his parents give him, and then reproaches them for not giving him more. He's borrowed money from Mary on the sly more than once, until I put a stop to it. Never paid her back, of course."

"Perhaps Sam was spoiled because he was the baby."

The old man shook his head. "Nay, Samuel did everything to make him straighten out except break the boy's head. But you should know—you were there."

He sighed. "He's been a sore trial to Mary, I can tell you that. The way young Sam carries on has made quite a change in her, quite a change, as I'm sure you saw. On top of losing the baby, it's aged her. But she's still young, and there will be other babies, God willing."

Susanna talked to the old man for a few more minutes, but his mind was hopelessly confused, and he clung to the belief that she was her mother. Finally she took her leave, saddened. At least John Carver had given her some clue to her cousin Samuel's character, however.

Back in the Cheever home she surprised Sarah, who was supposed to be weeding the vegetable garden, curled up in a corner of the kitchen with a book. The girl closed it with a guilty start and tried to hide it behind her when Susanna entered.

Susanna had become very fond of her shy, bookish cousin. At first she had been annoyed at her for not taking better care of the house and her younger brothers and sisters, but she'd come to see that in her own way Sarah was as undisposed temperamentally to deal with such matters as her mother. All things considered, the girl had done a fair job of coping with a difficult situation not of her own making.

When Susanna saw Sarah trying to conceal her book in the folds of her skirt she smiled at her. "You don't have to hide your books from me, Sarah. It's a fine thing to have a love of learning, and it's a shame you can't indulge it, although I myself have always preferred being out-of-doors or doing something active. What is it you find in those books that you love so much?"

"Oh, I don't know," Sarah answered. "It's hard to explain it to someone who doesn't feel the same way. It's just that the world of books is so much more beautiful than real life. Real life is full of crying babies and floors to be scrubbed and meals to be cooked. But books . . ." She sighed, and her eyes lit up with a dreamy, faraway expression.

"Books take me into an entirely different world. Sometimes I forget entirely that I'm just plain Sarah Cheever from Chippenham. I love to read about faraway places. I would love to go to Cathay—doesn't the name itself sound like absolute magic? The people there are yellow and have slanted eyes. Marco Polo went there, and had the grandest adventures! Oh, why can't I? I try to be satisfied with my lot, but it's so hard when I feel that I was destined to live in a different world—to travel, to learn, to explore. I wish I were a man, don't you?''

"Why no, what a notion!''

"I wish it weren't so hard to get books here in Chippenham. I have to read the same ones over and over. Then, of course, there's the problem of languages. If I only knew Latin there would be so many more books I could read.''

"I wish I could help you,'' Susanna said sincerely. "Sorry to change the subject, but how's your mother?''

The girl's face fell. "She's feeling very low today. She wants you to come up when you can.''

Upstairs in the Cheevers' bedroom Susanna thought for a minute that Alice was asleep. She lay back on her pillow, her skin a dreadful, waxy, pale color, and there were deep rings underneath her eyes.

When Susanna sat down beside her she opened her eyes. "Susanna,'' she said, reaching out to touch her cousin's hand. "How was your visit with the Carvers?''

"Disappointing, I'm afraid. The old man's mind is half gone. He thought that I was my mother, and that your aunt Mary was still alive.''

"Yes, his mind comes and goes. Sometimes he's sharp as a tack, and then there are days like today. Perhaps you should go back another time.''

"Sarah said you wanted to see me.''

"Yes, I did. I have a request, and I hope you won't think it a selfish one.'' She placed one thin hand on her distended belly. "I don't see how I can possibly live through another confinement.''

Susanna opened her mouth to protest, but Alice held up

a hand to silence her. "No, don't say anything. You've done everything you could, with your tonics and nourishing food, but I don't seem to be getting any stronger."

It was true. Susanna had been very worried about Alice's lack of response. She had tried every remedy she knew, but still the woman grew weaker and weaker.

"Somehow I don't think you'll be staying with us too much longer," she said. "It would ease my mind greatly if you would promise to stay with me until the baby comes. It should be any day now. I don't know what will happen to my poor children after that. I'm sure Samuel will remarry—I just hope it will be to someone who cares for them. I know I haven't been a good mother, but I do love my babies and I worry about them."

"Don't talk that way. I've delivered babies before, and together we'll get through your confinement. You'll just have to be careful not to get pregnant again."

Alice shook her head. "How am I to do that? The doctor told me not to have any more babies after Evelyn. I can't stop Samuel, and it's my duty as a wife to oblige him if he insists."

"There are methods of preventing conception." Heaven knows if there weren't I would probably be big-bellied with Raymond's child by now, Susanna thought.

"No, no." The woman looked at her in genuine horror. "I asked our minister about that once, and he says it's a dreadful sin. Bearing children is God's will—it's wrong to prevent it."

"Very well." Susanna did not wish to pursue the subject at the moment, since Alice was so agitated.

"I know you're not very happy here. Who could be? Samuel is a selfish man, and the children carry on like little heathens," Alice said with a sigh.

"No, it's not your family. It's my fault, really. I came

to Chippenham looking for something that isn't here any longer. I came to find the past, but the past is dead and gone. Life has to move on, I can see that now.''

"Are you sure there's nothing else?" Alice shot her a sharp look. "I've noticed that you don't seem to be happy. Has Samuel troubled you in any way?"

"Troubled me? How do you mean?"

"You know what I mean. You're a very pretty girl. Has he forced his attentions on you?"

"No, certainly not." Susanna was shocked. It was true that she had caught Samuel eyeing her speculatively from time to time, and he had a habit of brushing past her so that their bodies touched, or dropping a hand casually on her shoulder, but he had never done more than that.

"Good. That must mean he still has a woman in the village. Probably that slut at the Golden Boar."

"You mean he has other women, and you know about them?"

"Why certainly. The first time I accused him of carrying on with our maid was not much more than a year after we were married. He didn't even bother to deny it. I was pregnant at the time, and he said that as I was temporarily of no use to him it was perfectly natural that he should turn elsewhere. The very day you came I had to dismiss another girl for the same reason. She was carrying on with him right in front of the children.''

"You can't mean it." Consternation was written clearly on Susanna's face.

"Oh yes. You mustn't be too hard on Samuel. I know he's a thoroughly selfish man, but I still love him anyway. I could have married someone else, and my parents strongly opposed the match, but I would have Samuel Cheever or no one, and the truth is that if I had to do it over again I'd still marry him.''

Her eyes grew misty, looking into the past. "Fifteen years ago he was the handsomest man you ever saw in your life, and he could be such fun! I suppose he was partly after my dowry, but I think he really cared for me in the beginning. I was pretty then, believe it or not."

"I believe it." Even now, Susanna could see the remains of a fine-boned, delicate beauty in the woman's careworn, ravaged face. It was the kind of beauty that faded quickly unless it was nurtured and protected.

"What is worrying you, Susanna, if it's not Samuel? I know something is preying on your mind."

"I's just that I came to England wih a man, someone I love very much. I thought we would both be better off if I left him, but I was wrong. I miss him dreadfully."

"I see. Are you pregnant?" Alice asked.

"Good heavens no! Whatever put that idea in your mind?"

"Thank God for that at least. But you are lovers."

"Well . . . yès."

"Lord, child, you needn't be shy with me. I was five months gone by the time I dragged Samuel to the altar. If I hadn't been my parents would never have allowed me to marry him. If you love this man you must find him. Do you know where he is now?"

"In London. At least, that's where he was going."

"Would you know where to look for him?"

"No, that's the problem. And since I ran away I don't know if he'd be glad to see me. He was going to try to get financial backing from the king, so if I could get to court somehow I'm sure someone there would know of him."

"The king! He certainly isn't lacking in ambition. Have you any money?"

"Just a little—hardly more than the fare to London," Susanna admitted.

"You must go there and do everything in your power to find him. He'll forgive you, I know he will. But if you can't locate him I hope you'll think that you always have a home here."

She lay back, deathly pale, and took a few deep breaths before she went on. "Look in the wardrobe over there. You'll find a carved wooden box. Bring it to me."

Susanna fetched the box. Alice unlocked it with a tiny key she kept on a chain around her neck, and took out a small leather sack of coins.

She held it out to Susanna. "It's not a fortune, but it will help."

"No, I couldn't!"

"Nonsense. You've done enough for me. It's the least I can do."

Susanna still hesitated.

"Go on, girl, take it."

Susanna held out her hand reluctantly and took the small bag. "Thank you," she said. "I'll repay you when I can."

"Well, I'm glad it will be put to good use. And it will ease my mind, knowing you'll be here until the baby comes. If only I knew that someone capable would be with my children afterward, I wouldn't mind dying." Alice lay back on her pillows and closed her eyes.

A week later, in the evening, Alice felt her first pains. The next morning, after hours of labor, the baby seemed no nearer to being born, and Alice was too tired to push when Susanna told her to. Susanna, who had sent Samuel away and sat with Alice throughout the night, examined her as soon as the light was good enough. She had hardly dilated at all.

There was nothing that Susanna could do except to give

her medicine to ease the pain. Throughout the day Alice's agonizing labor continued, and toward sunset she was delivered at last of a stillborn son.

The woman lay hardly conscious as Susanna washed the pitiful, inert little corpse. She approached the bed, wondering how to tell Alice that the child had not lived, but she could see, from the tears trickling down the woman's face, that no explanation was necessary.

"There's no sound," Alice said weakly. "No crying. He's dead, isn't he?"

"I'm afraid so," Susanna said. "It's dreadful, I know, but you have so many healthy children to be grateful for."

The woman acted as if she had not heard. "I'll not be far behind him."

"Don't talk that way," Susanna began, but Alice stopped her with a feeble wave of her hand. "There's no point in pretending. I know I'm dying. I'd like to see my family now."

Susanna waited outside while the children went in, one by one. Sarah came out sobbing, and even the younger children were sobered. Alice asked to see her husband last. They spent some time together, and when Samuel came out his face wore a look of heavy sorrow. He gave Susanna a look full of self-pity. "Who's to take care of us now?" he asked.

After the family had gone back downstairs Susanna returned to Alice's room. The woman, exhausted by the labor and her emotional interviews with her family, lay flat on her back. Her eyes were surrounded by black circles and sunk deep in her face. Her skin was as yellow as wax, and her breathing so shallow that for a moment Susanna thought she was dead.

When she became aware of Susanna's presence beside her, she opened her eyes slowly. "I'm dying," she said in a weak voice, "but it's curious. Except for worrying about what will happen to my children I don't mind. I'm so tired. I just want to drift off . . ."

She closed her eyes. Susanna nursed her throughout the day, until finally she sank into unconsciousness. Late that night, with only the light of a few candles illuminating her thin face, Alice breathed a heavy sigh and stopped breathing.

Susanna tidied the bed and arranged the body, folding Alice's hands neatly on her breast. Then she woke up Samuel, who was sleeping on a makeshift bed in the parlor, gave him the sad news, and climbed slowly to her own room in the attic. She was so tired from her lengthy vigil that spots danced before her eyes.

Taking off her dress and not bothering to remove her petticoats, Susanna lay down and dropped off immediately. She did not know how long she had been asleep when something woke her. She was still dazed and exhausted, and it took her a minute to realize that someone else was on her bed.

"Who is it?"

"It's me—Samuel," a muffled voice said. The man had his hands on her and his mouth was buried in her neck.

"What in the world are you doing?"

"Come on, love, give us a kiss." His mouth, wet and tasting of ale, came down on her lips.

The shock brought Susanna fully awake. She struggled to push him away from her. "You're an animal," she hissed. "Your wife lies dead downstairs, her body not yet cold, and you . . ."

"Precisely," he said, pinning her down with the full weight of his body. "She's no longer of any use to me. I've heard that there are those who relish it, but I've no desire to roger a corpse."

Susanna lashed out at him, kicking and clawing. The

nails of one of her hands raked across his face. He drew back, cursing, and held his cheek. "What's wrong with you, girl? You want me, I know you do. I've seen the way you look at me. Come on, give us a kiss."

"You're disgusting." Susanna struggled with all her might to free herself.

"I'll marry you, I promise I will." He was still trying to kiss her, even though she was swinging her head from side to side so that he couldn't find her mouth in the dark.

"You filthy abomination, I wouldn't marry you if you were the last man on earth."

The loathing in her voice brought him up sharply. He drew in his breath with a hiss and sat up, freeing her. "You're just like your mother, aren't you, and that bitch sister of mine, Mary. Always looking down on me, always disapproving. Punishing me whenever they got the chance, and putting on fine airs, as if they were a pair of ladies.

"And you—who the hell do you think you are, to play high and mighty with me? You've been wearing my wife's clothes, that I bought her, and eating my food, since the day you arrived here. You're living off my charity. God only knows what kind of trouble you got yourself into in the colonies to get kicked out. You must have nowhere else to go or you wouldn't have come here in the first place."

"Get out," Susanna said with a steely coldness in her voice that surprised even her. "Get out or I'll kill you."

Samuel Cheever stood up slowly, holding his bleeding cheek, and backed out of the room. "I want you out of here by morning," he said. "And good riddance to bad rubbish, I say."

"You needn't have bothered to order me to leave. I wouldn't spend another night under this roof for a king's ransom."

Susanna got up and dressed in her gown of rose brocade and green cloak. She was leaving Chippenham exactly as she had arrived in it. She felt sorry for the Cheever children, especially Sarah, whom she had come to care for, and felt bad about leaving them with no explanation, but she could not spend another minute under Samuel Cheever's roof. She would have to write Sarah a letter later with some explanation.

She walked in the dead of night down the main street of Chippenham, which she knew well now, until she reached the inn. She knocked on the door for some time. Finally Philip Wheelwright answered it, yawning in the light of his candle, with a dressing gown thrown hastily over his nightshirt.

"I need shelter for the night," Susanna said. "Tomorrow I'm taking the coach to London."

12

SUSANNA WAS DISMAYED BY THE CITY'S CROWDS AND NOISE, but at the same time excited by its life and beauty. She had no idea how to go about finding Raymond in a place as large as London. Indeed, she had never even dreamed that a city so huge existed. As the coach from Chippenham rumbled in she knew only that somehow or other she would have to contrive to get to court and make inquiries. She had no doubt that Raymond would have succeeded in seeing the king, and someone at court would surely remember him. Raymond Galt was not the kind of man one forgot, even at a king's court.

The inn where the coach stopped refused to give her a room. When she made the request of the innkeeper's wife in a faltering voice, the woman raked her with hard eyes and said, ''Get on with you! I'm not running a bawdy house. Ply your trade elsewhere.''

Susanna was shocked to be taken for a prostitute, but

she knew that it was highly unusual for a woman to be traveling alone, without masculine protection or even the company of a servant. She had no choice but to set out in the street by herself, shaking with humiliation.

She was turned down at several other inns. As she walked along one street after another, seeking a room, she could not help being fascinated by all that she saw, despite her fear. She watched a man perform on a tightrope for a gape-mouthed crowd. At an open-air market she saw two women fish vendors in a screaming fight, whacking each other with large flat flounders until they were pulled apart. A grimy urchin pulled a silk handkerchief from the back pocket of a stout gentleman who stood talking to a well-dressed lady, and neither man nor woman noticed a thing. Susanna witnessed a brawl between porters and a band of apprentices. And on street corners everywhere women vendors beckoned to customers, singing the praises of their great baskets of oranges, onions, spring mushrooms, and sweet potatoes.

She noticed that apparently respectable women traveled about the city on their own, but with their faces covered by black masks. When she saw some in a store window she ducked in and bought one for herself.

When she left the store, wearing her mask, her attention was drawn to a small group of expensively dressed young men coming out of an inn across the street. Their faces were flushed, and they were shoving and cursing each other in an affectionate manner.

A small coach stopped in front of the inn, and the most beautiful woman Susanna had ever seen leaned out and tapped the side of the coach with her fan. She had red-gold hair, violet eyes, and a white complexion. "Jerry!" she cried, trying to attract the attention of one of the men in the group.

They were making too much noise to hear her. "I say, you there, Lord Marston!" she called out.

At last the young man looked up. "Marry come up, it's Lady Everdeen!" He made a deep bow with exaggerated courtesy.

"I never saw such a fuss! And all drunk, the lot of you, in the middle of the day," the woman said, looking at them with mock exasperation. "I'll have you arrested for creating a public nuisance if you don't pipe down!"

"By the devil, Barbara, would you treat us so? We throw ourselves on your mercy!"

"Mercy be damned! You'll have no mercy from me! I'm angry at the lot of you! I've invited you to see me twice, Jerry, and you haven't come! And where have the rest of you been? You, Lord Amesbury, and you there, Skiffington! You're all avoiding me!"

"Why should we come see you?" the one she'd called Jerry said. "By the devil, you've turned into a dull creature! Married three months, and still faithful to your husband! I vow and swear, you'll give the court a bad name! The Black Boy himself will banish you to the country if you don't mend your ways!"

The others broke into raucous laughter, and the four of them walked out into the street and crowded round the window of her coach. Traffic was beginning to back up behind them, but they ignored the curses and shouts of coachmen and porters.

"Now what are you scurvy rascals fighting over?" Lady Everdeen asked.

"It's Lord Amesbury here," Jerry said. "He won't share his whore with me. Curse my stripes, it's a selfish man who won't share his whore with a friend—don't you agree?"

"Indeed I do!" Lady Everdeen said. Their voices were

being drowned out by the angry curses from the stalled coaches behind them, so Susanna could not hear the rest of their exchange. At last the coach moved on and the four young men made their noisy way down the street.

Susanna continued walking, learning from everything she saw. At the next inn she came to, which had a swinging sign ornamented with what she already recognized as the king's coat of arms, she asked to see the innkeeper, thinking that she might have more success with a man than a woman. When the proprieter came out, she introduced herself as Mrs. Collins, and told him that her husband was at sea. "He will be home shortly, and I'm to meet him here."

The man scrutinized her carefully. The woman was young, very pretty and well-dressed, but she had no luggage and no servant. Nor had she been brought to the inn by her own coach, which surely would have been the case if she'd been a woman of means from out of town. He did not believe her story for a minute, but somehow she did not impress him as being a prostitute either. His guess was that she was pregnant, and looking for a place to hide until she had her baby. It was as easy, perhaps easier, to get lost in a large city as in the country.

"All right," he said. "I'll give you a room." He named an exorbitant price. Susanna gasped at the amount. She knew that he was taking advantage of her, but she felt that she had little choice. She had been walking all afternoon and dusk was approaching. She was tired, and all she could think of was having a place to lay her head. The thought of still being out on the street at nightfall filled her with panic.

She tried to bargain with him, but he refused to come down on the price. "All right," she said reluctantly. "I'll take it, if you'll have my meals sent up to me."

The innkeeper agreed, and led Susanna up to her room. It needed dusting and the sheets were none too clean, but there were no bedbugs as far as she could see. She undressed, and was in her petticoats when a girl brought up a meal of roast beef and browned spring potatoes with parsley, with a piece of cheesecake for dessert. At least the food was excellent.

Susanna spent the next few days roaming the streets, talking to shopkeepers and any other folk who seemed harmless. She learned that the king lived in Whitehall Palace and that the best way to get there was by boat, but she still had no idea how to seek an audience with someone at court.

She tried to think of places that Raymond might frequent. She could not go to the coffeehouses, as women were not allowed there. She was afraid to go by herself to the New Exchange, a fashionable lounge and meeting place for gallants and their ladies, for fear of being taken for a prostitute. She looked in the expensive shops around Covent Garden, and spent a good bit of time walking about in Hyde Park, where fashionable ladies and gentlemen went riding.

Her money was disappearing at an alarming rate. The inkeeper refused to extend her credit, and she had to pay for each day's lodging in advance. Without the money that Alice had given her she had no doubt that she would have been tossed out on the street by now.

On the day she gave the innkeeper her last coins for that night's lodging she went to Hyde Park and sat on a bench, at a loss for what to do next. She did not even know that Raymond was still in London. For all she knew he could be on a ship by now, halfway to the Bahamas. She was sitting by herself, trying to plan and not to panic, when she was approached by the four young men she had seen outside the inn on her first day in London.

"Marry come up, Skiffington, where has this ravishing creature been keeping herself? Have you seen her before?"

"I'd remember her if I had, I vow and swear! Allow me to introduce myself," he said with a deep bow. "Algernon Skiffington, at your service, madam."

"How do you do," she said. "I am Mrs. Collins." She did not like this boisterous crew with their rough language, but they were lords and no doubt familiar with the court. Maybe one of them could help her find Raymond. Besides, she had observed that even the most elegant folk thought little of cursing. Perhaps these fellows meant no harm by their coarse talk.

"A great pleasure, I'm sure, Mrs. Collins. I blush to admit that these disreputable fellows are my friends. Allow me to present them—Lord Amesbury, Lord Marston, and Lord Richfield."

Each of the gentlemen bowed in turn. "You must have just come to town," Skiffington said.

"I haven't been here long," she conceded. "I'm waiting for my husband to return from the sea."

"Her husband out of town! Ho, here's a merry state of affairs!" said Lord Marston.

His attention was distracted by a coach rattling by. "Curse my tripes! There goes Allen Garvey with his fancy-boy! He kept his fondness for beautiful boys well concealed when he was single, but now that he's wed he leaves his poor wife at home and never goes anywhere without the lovely lad!"

"His wife doesn't miss him," said Skiffington. "She hadn't been married a week when she was caught in bed with her page!"

"And there goes Lady Grove with that ugly daughter of hers," said Lord Richfield. "She's looking everywhere for a husband for the girl, but 'tis said when she finds one she plans to bed the man herself."

Susanna dropped her eyes in confusion. "We're being dreadfully rude," Lord Marston said. "Here we are with a beautiful woman, and we can do nothing but look about to see who's riding by, while we ignore this little treasure. I say, Mrs. Collins, if you'd give me a pretty ribbon from your dress I'd put it to good use, I vow and swear I would!"

"A ribbon? What would you do with it?"

"I'd tie it in the prettiest bow you ever saw, about a part of me that I've now got well hidden. But I'd be more than delighted to show it to you, let me perish if I wouldn't!"

The other three men roared with laughter at this sally, and Susanna felt herself flushing crimson.

"Why, the lady's blushing!" said Skiffington when he could control his laughter. "Can it be possible? Have we found a woman in London who is both beautiful and modest?"

Susanna was growing genuinely distressed, but the young men took no notice.

"What shall we do with her?" Lord Amesbury said.

"I saw her first," said Skiffington, "so I have the first claim."

"Surely you'll share her?" said Lord Richfield.

"I'll think on it," Skiffington replied.

Susanna buried her face in her hands, appalled by their rough talk but trying not to cry. "Go away, the lot of you!" she said in a muffled voice.

"Come now, Mrs. Collins, we didn't mean to upset you," one of them said, bending over her.

"Get away from her, you louts." A voice lashed out, deep and authoritative, as sharp and hard as the crack of a whip. "You, Skiffington, I'll have your father tan your hide. And you, Jerry—you should know better."

Susanna looked up. A handsome old man, immaculately

and richly dressed, stood before her. "I am Lord Lansdown, madame," he said gently, bending over her. "May I offer you my protection?"

"Oh, thank you, sir. I'm in the most dreadful fix."

"Come and tell me all about it. My carriage is over here," he said, taking her elbow. The young men stepped back and let them pass.

She was afraid of jumping from one precarious situation to another, but she had little choice but to accept his offer of protection. The young bloods were proving too much for her.

He led her to his carriage and helped her in. "Now, there, dear, what's the matter?" he said after he had lent her a fine handkerchief. "Bye-the-by, what is your name?"

"Thank you, sir. My name is Collins, Mrs. Susanna Collins. My husband's at sea, and I'm supposed to meet him here in London, but the money he gave me has run out, and I'm about to be tossed out into the street, and I don't know what to do next. Perhaps he's dead. I could be a widow by now for all I know."

"There, there," he said, patting her arm reassuringly. "I'm sure everything will be all right. You can come home with me, and later we'll leave word at your inn so your husband will know where to find you when he gets in. I'm sure he's all right."

He tapped the top of the coach with his walking stick. "Take us home, James."

As they rode Susanna was able to examine her benefactor at leisure. He was tall and slender and carried himself well. He had a long, kindly face, eyes of a clear, deep blue, and a gentle, bemused expression, as if he were well-acquainted with the world and forgave it for its folly. His hands, which were folded over his walking stick, were wrinkled, but he had long, beautiful fingers. Altogether she thought him remarkably well-preserved for his age, which she calculated to be at least seventy.

"We'll get you settled, and then we'll send to the inn for your things."

"I have no things. Everything I own in the world is on my back."

"Well, then, my dear, we'll have to remedy that. My daughter Lucinda has recently been widowed and has returned home to live with me. We'll turn you over to her. There's nothing she loves more than planning a wardrobe and fussing over clothes."

Susanna knew that some of the most fashionable houses in London were in St. James Field, and it was in front of one of these homes, a handsome red brick townhouse, that they stopped. Lord Lansdown helped her down and into the house.

It was by far the most elegant place Susanna had ever seen. She looked wide-eyed about the drawing-room, which was hung with heavy draperies of gold-green and had the most beautiful silver chandeliers and wall sconces. The marble fireplace had a plaster overmantel reaching to the ceiling, lavishly decorated with carved figures of flowers and animals. The furniture was all either gilded or inlaid with ivory and mother-of-pearl.

Lord Lansdown watched her eyes move from one object to another and smiled, obviously, relishing her enjoyment. He summoned a maid and directed her to prepare a room for the lady. "Would you like a cup of tea while your room is being aired?" he asked. "I'm afraid I don't have much company, and things do get musty."

"Tea, sir?" she said. "I don't believe I've ever tasted it."

"It's not much drunk in England, but the queen loves it, and it has become fashionable at court."

"Well then, I'll try it."

Lord Lansdown summoned a servant and ordered tea, and requested that his daughter join them. In a few moments the doors to the drawing room opened, and a pretty young woman Susanna reckoned to be in her early twenties, came running in. She was soberly dressed in a dress of dark green silk. "Papa!" she cried in a light musical voice, bending over to kiss him.

"Lucinda, this is Mrs. Susanna Collins, who is going to be staying with us. This is my daughter, Lady Lucinda Mott."

After the two women exchanged greetings Lucinda sat down and immediately broke into an excited chatter, but Susanna could tell that she was being examined out of the corner of Lucinda's eye. The young woman was fresh and dainty, with her father's clear blue eyes, sandy blond hair that was drawn up in back and dressed in curls about her face, and a little nose that tipped up at the end.

"Oh, Papa, it's so dreadful to have to wear mourning! I saw the most gorgeous material this morning in a little shop on the Strand! It was a chartreuse velvet, and I could just see myself in it, with a cloak to match!"

"Since you cannot have it perhaps it would look good on Mrs. Collins. She's blond, too."

Lucinda shot a sulky look in Susanna's direction. "Are we dressing her, too?"

"Mind your manners, Lucinda. While you're under my roof you'll be polite to my guests."

Just then a maid came in with a silver tea service. "Will you pour, Lucinda?" Lord Lansdown asked. "Mrs. Collins is about to have her first cup of tea."

"Her first cup! Are you from the country, then? Everyone at court has started drinking it."

"I'm originally from Boston."

"Oh." Lucinda sniffed disdainfully. "A colonial."

The tea was served with little frosted cakes. "It's very good, and it smells wonderful," Susanna said after taking a sip. "Did you say that the queen drinks it? I should love to go to court."

"Ambitious, are we?" Lucinda's voice was sweet as honey, but her eyes had narrowed to slits.

Her father ignored Lucinda's cattiness. "Well, my dear, perhaps that can be arranged. Now, Mrs. Collins, I'm sure you'd like to rest and freshen up before dinner. Agnes will show you to your room."

A maid took Susanna upstairs to a beautiful bedroom. The bedstead was covered with cloth-of-silver and the hangings were of green taffeta. Wardrobes were built into the wall, and there was the most adorable little daybed with a fringed canopy and tight-rolled bolster. Two chairs were also covered with cloth-of-silver. It quite took Susanna's breath away.

After she was left alone she examined the walls of the room carefully, to see if there was a door connecting it to another chamber or any kind of secret passageway. She had heard that fashionable folk had such arrangements to facilitate liasions with guests, and she had no illusions about Lord Lansdown's motives in picking her up. Although he seemed very old to her it was apparent that he was aware of her as a woman.

Soon she had satisfied herself that there was no way to enter the room except through the door to the hall. She could hardly see Lord Lansdown playing the impetuous lover, climbing a trellis to slip through one of his lady-love's windows, so her privacy was at least assured. She removed her cloak and dress, lay down in her petticoats, and was asleep almost at once. She had no idea what her future held, but temporarily at least she felt comfortable and secure, confident that she had found someone who would take care of her.

For days Lord Lansdown did little except show Susanna around London, taking great relish in her pleasure at everything she saw. He took her to the finest shops, and before long Susanna knew the best places to purchase anything, from ribbons to the costliest jewels. They went riding in Hyde Park, past the houses of the gentry in St. James Field and Pall Mall, and through the fashionable suburbs that lay between Temple Bar and Charing Cross.

If Susanna saw the best of London, she also saw the worst. She saw prostitutes being beaten in Bridewell, and the bodies of criminals hanging on Tyburn Hill.

"What have they done?" she asked, nodding toward the corpses swaying back and forth in the wind.

"It could have been anything, from robbing coaches to stealing a loaf of bread," said Lord Lansdown.

"You hang people for stealing bread when they're hungry?"

"Don't worry about it, my dear," he said, patting her hand. "It doesn't concern you."

One day she asked to go to Bedlam, the infamous insane asylum, where poor wretches lay chained to the walls in their own filth and howled at those who came to jeer at them. She also insisted on being driven through a slum, where filthy, starving children with sunken eyes and pinched faces swarmed through the streets like rats.

Meanwhile, dressmakers were busy fashioning a new wardrobe for her. No expense was spared. She did have a dress made from the chartreuse velvet Lucinda had admired, and a cloak of topaz velvet to wear with it, which matched her golden-brown eyes almost exactly. There were other dresses, all of the richest satins and velvets—plum purple and garnet red, primrose yellow and flame red. Her favorite was of black and honey-colored satin, with an overskirt of exquisite lace. They were all cut low, to expose her round, high bosom, and had full sleeves, trimmed in ribbons and lace, that ended just below the elbow.

The shock of seeing herself transformed into an elegant lady, which she had experienced first in Bristol, had worn off, and now she loved dressing up and looking pretty, although she still could not bring herself to use rouge on her cheeks or carmine on her lips, or to place tiny little beauty patches on her cheeks and beside her mouth as other ladies did. Her hands were bleached with lemons and softened with creams, and she brushed her teeth until they gleamed white and flawless. Pumice-stone removed every trace of hair on her arms and legs and rubbed smooth the rough patches on her elbows and ankles. She bathed in milk and rubbed her entire body with her favorite jasmine perfume. Every morning her hair was done in the latest style by Lucinda's maid.

As soon as she was settled she wrote a long letter to Sarah Cheever. She could not think of a convincing excuse to explain her sudden flight in the middle of the night, so she simply told the girl the truth. Susanna knew that Sarah was well aware of her father's misconduct anyway.

Susanna had no idea why Lord Lansdown was doing so much for her. He usually went to bed after the rest of the household, and for a while she held her breath every night when she heard him climbing the stairs, waiting fearfully for a knock on her door. But he never attempted to force his attentions on her—indeed, he never even touched her except to give her a fatherly pat on the hand. She never lost sight of her ultimate goal—to get to court and find Raymond, but for the moment she was content simply to enjoy herself.

She did notice one flaw in her benefactor. Lord Lansdown was unquestionably a vain man. He watched his diet very carefully and was most particular about every article of clothing he wore. He was also particular about his carriage, the furnishings of his house, and indeed all of his possessions. His carriage had to be spotless, his horses groomed to perfection, his table the best in London, and his liveried servants perfectly trained. Beneath his worldly, urbane kindliness lay a man who cared very deeply what other people thought of him. Susanna had a vague feeling that she was nothing more than another beautiful acquisition, another ornament for his home.

As time passed Lord Lansdown became aware that she was unversed in the arts pursued by fashionable ladies of leisure. When Susanna was not riding about with him, Lucinda, at her father's insistence, undertook their guest's education. Accomplished London society ladies, she learned, spent their time painting, doing fancy needlework, riding, playing cards, and sometimes reading—that is, when they were not dancing and flirting. Susanna took painting lessons with Lucinda's teacher, although she was sure she would never be any good at it, and Lord Lansdown hired a dancing master for her. She was a ready pupil there, and soon she had mastered the intricate steps of the coranto, a dance performed by one couple at a time, and the allemande, in which several couples participated.

An impoverished gentlewoman was hired to teach her proper etiquette and deportment. Fortunately she had a naturally erect, graceful carriage, and sat and moved well. She was taught how to sink to the floor in a deep curtsy, how to address various levels of the aristocracy, and the correct way to behave at court. She learned to her surprise that it was proper etiquette for ladies to ask the king to dance and not vice versa.

One day after Lord Lansdown had bought her a beautiful garnet necklace during one of their afternoon drives about the city, she asked him why he was being so kind to her. "Must I have a motive?" he asked, with his genial, indulgent laugh. "It's such a treat to have someone fresh and unspoiled to show all of this to. It's like seeing London myself again for the very first time. Now what else would you like to do?"

"I don't know," she said. "We must have seen and done just about everything!"

"Nonsense!" he said. "We've hardly started."

"Well," she said hesitantly. "I should like very much to go to court."

"You surprise me. You seem lacking in social ambition, but you've mention several times that you'd like to go to court. I'm not sure I want to take you. The Black Boy himself might steal you away from me."

"Who's the Black Boy?" She remembered that the young nobleman who had been baiting her on the day that Lord Lansdown had rescued her had referred to the Black Boy.

"That's the king's nickname, because he's so dark."

"Well, I think there's little likelihood that the king would be interested in me. I'd just like to see the court, that's all."

"All right, my dear, I promise to have you presented. But we can't do that this afternoon. How would you like to go to the theater?"

"The theater!" Folks in Boston heartily disapproved of the theater, and she had been taught to regard it as a dreadfully wicked place, but she was curious about it.

"Would you like to go this afternoon? You look so beautiful wearing your new necklace, it's a shame to keep you all to myself."

"Oh yes! What are we going to see?"

Lord Lansdown smiled. "Who knows? It doesn't much matter. Most of the people at the theater are more interested in looking at each other than at watching what's happening on the stage."

She found what he said to be true. The theater was crowded, and the play already under way when they arrived. As they made their way slowly to one of the front boxes every head turned to scrutinize Susanna, and a murmur ran through the crowd. "Lord Lansdown . . ." "Who's the woman?" "Smashing beauty . . ." she heard as they passed.

The play was a tragedy by Beaumont and Fletcher, full of battles and deaths, frightening ghosts who rattled chains and prophesied doom, and gruesome torture scenes. Susanna could not follow the plot, but she enjoyed the experience immensely. Through it all the audience kept up a lively chatter, so that the actors had to shout to be heard.

The entire bottom floor of the house was called the pit, and there, on long benches, sat foppishly dressed young dandies who talked loudly with each other, and a few flamboyant, painted women. "Who are they?" Susanna asked in a whisper, inclining her head toward the women.

"Prostitutes," Lord Lansdown answered.

Shocked, she scrutinized them closely, but they seemed to her to be ordinary women, although they were highly painted. Walking about in the pit were six young girls with baskets over their arms, selling fruit and sweetmeats.

A low balcony divided into boxes reached close to the stage, which jutted out into the pit, and here, around Susanna and her protector, sat gentlemen and fashionable ladies, dressed in satin and velvet and dripping with jewels. The fashionable folk were still discussing Susanna. "Lansdown has a woman," she heard someone say.

Above the boxes was another gallery with the cheapest seats. Here sat poorly dressed women and young men wearing the rough clothes of apprentices. They stamped their feet to signify approval, or let out loud jeers and catcalls when they were displeased with the performance.

When the play was over, and the hero had died, covered with blood from a punctured pig's bladder fastened inside his shirt, a number of ladies and gentlemen surged forward to Lord Lansdown's box. He introduced them all to Susanna, who lowered her gaze and blushed as their sly, worldly eyes sized her up.

One of the first to arrive was the beautiful red-haired woman she had seen on her first day in London. Again, Susanna thought that with her white skin and mass of red-gold hair she was the most beautiful creature she had ever laid eyes on.

"Marry come up, Roderick, you're a fine one, keeping this lovely girl all to yourself!" the woman said when she entered, rapping him playfully with her fan. "How long have you been hiding her?"

"Lady Everdeen! What a pleasure to see you!" Lord Lansdown beamed. "How are you enjoying married life!"

"It's dull as dishwater, I vow and swear! I had ever so much more fun when I was single! And now I suppose I shall have to produce an heir, and go into seclusion, and lose my figure!" She pouted prettily, running one hand from her voluptuous bosom, which was all but popping out of her gown of green satin, down to her slender waist.

"I doubt that. But allow me to present Mrs. Susanna Collins. Mrs. Collins, Lady Everdeen."

Susanna nodded her head, and the other woman subjected her to a frank and rather embarrassing scrutiny. "Aren't you full of surprises, you old rogue!" she said, her eyes narrowing as she examined Susanna's new necklace, no doubt trying to estimate its worth. "Keeping a woman at your age! But you know what they say—just because there's snow on the roof doesn't mean there's no fire in the chimney!"

Lord Lansdown chuckled. "Barbara, you're incorrigible. Mrs. Collins is only staying with Lucinda and me for a while."

"And I'm supposed to assume that you're 'only friends,' as they say? Nonsense, Roderick. I can spot an infatuation when I see one. And you're about as innocent as a fox in a henhouse."

Lady Everdeen was only the first of a stream of people to visit them, all curious to meet Susanna. Lord Lansdown seemed very happy and expansive, gallantly stooping to pick up Susanna's fan and the little fur muff he had bought her, and solicitously fastening her cloak about her shoulders. He was being very considerate, but something about his manner bothered her. All of the people he introduced her to clearly thought the two of them were lovers, and his halfhearted disclaimers only reinforced rather than dispelled the notion.

At last she realized why he was lavishing her with so many gifts and so much attention, taking her everywhere and introducing her to people of quality. Her benefactor didn't want a mistress—he just wanted everyone to think he had one.

13

LORD LANSDOWN WAS AS GOOD AS HIS WORD, AND NOT long after they went to the theater he arranged to have Susanna presented at court. When the night arrived she dressed with special care. She knew she looked beautiful in a long-trained gown of cloth-of-gold covered with gold lace. Her neck was encircled with a topaz necklace Lord Lansdown had given her especially for the occasion.

For once Lucinda was nice to her, helping her dress and keeping up a steady stream of chatter. "You must tell me about everyone you meet," she said, "and what the ladies are wearing, and what the king says to you when you're presented," and a great deal more in the same vein.

She insisted on making up Susanna herself. For the first time Susanna was invited into Lucinda's bedroom, which, Susanna thought, was overcrowded with cabinets, screens, trunks, silver plate, a hanging shelf lined with the latest romances, repeating clocks, and a tea table. Her dressing table was even more cluttered. In addition to several mirrors, it held a glue pot, a pot for pomatum, washes, unguents, and a wide assortment of cosmetics and perfumes.

"You must rouge your cheeks," Lucinda insisted. "Everyone is doing it."

"Very well. Just a little," Susanna conceded.

"And a touch of carmine for your lips."

Lucinda dabbed Susanna's face with scented powder, and got her maid to insert combs in her hair which made it stand out and seem even thicker.

"You're a vision!" Lucinda exclaimed, clapping her hands together when she was finished. "Now, all we need are a few little beauty patches—one to accentuate your high forehead, one at the corner of your eye, and one beside that voluptuous mouth!"

"Oh, no, Lucinda, I couldn't." Susanna had to draw the line somewhere.

Lucinda tried to persuade her but gave up when she saw that her entreaties were in vain. "Very well," she said, "we'll wait until next time." Susanna, in her opinion, was still resisting being totally made over into a lady of fashion.

Lucinda could not be present at official court functions because she was still in mourning. She was furious that she would miss seeing Susanna's presentation. "It's not fair to be a widow so young," she said, pouting. "What good did Frederick ever do me! Died of smallpox at four-and-twenty, and didn't even leave me a son to inherit his title! You'll have to tell me all about it when you get in."

"We may be late," Susanna told her.

"Don't worry—I'll be waiting up for you."

As their coach drew up to the palace she made no attempt to disguise her nervousness.

"Never mind, my dear, you'll do beautifully," Lord

Lansdown said. He had no way of knowing that Susanna was more anxious about getting news of Raymond Galt than she was at the prospect of being presented to the king and queen.

As it turned out, the queen was indisposed, so the king sat alone in the Presence Chamber, on a raised dais canopied with crimson velvet swagged with gold and silver fringe. At one end of the room musicians tuned their instruments in preparation for the dancing to come. The king was surrounded with his own attendants and the queen's ladies, all dressed in gorgeous satins and velvets. The richly-draped room was ablaze with thousands of candles, in chandeliers and wall sconces, and Yeomen of the Guard held smoking flambeaux. Spectators thronged the gallery. As those being presented to him drew near, the king held out his hand to be kissed.

"Earl Hargreave! Countess Hargreave!"

"Baron Dexter! Lady Dexter!"

"As each couple was called, they came forward slowly, sank into a deep bow and curtsy, kissed the king's outstretched hand, and then moved to the side to make room for the next couple. On either side, courtiers and ladies gossiped, keeping up a running commentary on the new arrivals. The king, bored almost to tears, stifled a discreet yawn or two behind the hand that was not being kissed.

Susanna held her head high and kept her eyes straight ahead, outwardly calm and serene but quaking inwardly. Was Raymond here tonight? Would she find him at all? Had he met another woman?

Finally their turn came.

"Earl Lansdown! Mrs. Susanna Collins!"

Ladies and courtiers drew in their breath as the pair walked slowly down the red carpet. Every eye was on Susanna. "Her train isn't very long," one woman sniffed.

"Her hair's too thick, and I don't like the way it's dressed," another said loudly.

"Her cheekbones are too high. If her eyes were any bigger there wouldn't be any room on her face for her nose!"

"Her lower lip looks as if it's begging to be kissed."

"I'll wager it has been—and many times, too!"

Susanna was not disturbed by the commentary. She knew the ladies were jealous or they would be criticizing her worst features instead of her best ones.

When she approached the dais she sank into a deep curtsy and kissed the king's outstretched hand. "What have we here?" Charles II slipped his hand under her chin and raised her. "Another jewel to ornament our court." When he spoke to her a dead hush fell, and people leaned forwardly eagerly to catch his words.

The king saw before him a rather tall young woman with a slender but voluptuous figure, who had about her an air of tranquil poise and self-containment. She had a modest shyness that seemed to him as incredible as it was genuine, and the roué in him at once sensed a challenge. He was determined to seduce her.

He suspected that making Susanna his next mistress would not be easy, even though he was a king. He sensed that Susanna had an inner core of integrity. She might adopt the latest fashions in dress, but here was no will-o'-the-wisp to be cast hither and thither by the latest fads in speech and behavior.

With a knowledge born of much experience, he knew, too, that beneath her cool exterior lay a passionate woman. Her full lower lip, almond-shaped eyes, and firm, full bosom produced in him emotions that had lain dormant for a long while. He could not remember the last time he had been so excited by a woman. He could not help wondering, as he looked into her eyes, which regarded him frankly and coolly, if the passion he sensed in her had ever been awakened. Not by Lord Lansdown, he'd wager.

Susanna found herself looking back into a pair of glittering, black, heavy-lidded eyes. The king had a long, lean face, a long nose, and heavy black brows, the threatening appearance of which was offset somewhat by a sensual mouth. He had a swarthy complexion, and a thin mustache curled over his upper lip.

The king looked very tall and magnificent, and quite handsome, too, although he was much older than she had expected, as he had a deeply lined forehead and even deeper lines running from his nostrils to his mouth. He studied her quite openly, but she remained calm beneath his gaze. When he was apparently satisfied, he nodded. They moved on, making way for the next couple.

"Why did everyone grow so quiet?" she asked Lord Lansdown in a whisper.

"Because the king showed you special favor, and because you're a fresh face at court. You wouldn't believe how bored most of the people here are. Court society is terribly inbred. They see the same faces, and repeat the same gossip, endlessly."

"Bored? How could anyone be bored with all this?" She looked around at the richly hung room, the beautiful assembly of lords and ladies glittering with jewels, and the musicians, who were dressed in taffeta suits and wore garlands on their heads, and wondered how anyone could ever tire of it all. She had never dreamed that she, plain Susanna Collins from Boston, would ever be dressed in satins and jewels and be presented to the king. She felt like pinching herself to be sure that she was not dreaming.

As the presentations continued she glanced about her everywhere. She was pretending to be taking in the others present, but in fact she was looking for Raymond. He wasn't there, or at least she couldn't see him anywhere.

At last the presentations were over. At a signal from the king the musicians began to play. A page came over and bowed to Susanna.

"Mrs. Collins, the king would like you to ask him to dance."

"Me?" For all her newfound composure Susanna was rattled.

"I told you the Black Boy would steal you from me," Lord Lansdown said with a smile. "Go ahead, my dear."

Again silence fell on the court, and every eye was on Susanna as she made her way to the king's dais.

She sank into another deep curtsy before him. "May I have the honor of dancing with Your Majesty?"

"It would be my pleasure," the king said.

The first dance was a coranto. As they moved through the slow, intricate steps Susanna prayed that she would not make a mistake.

The king was a superb dancer. He had the shapeliest legs she had ever seen, and a very fine figure, for all of his age. Every eye was upon them. Once, when Susanna turned, she saw a woman glaring at her with a look of such undiluted venom it made her shudder. She was a handsome woman, but no longer young, with chestnut hair that Susanna suspected was dyed piled high atop her head. She made a mental note to ask Lord Lansdown who the woman was.

The dance seemed to go on forever. When it ended at last everyone applauded as the king escorted her to the place against the wall where Lord Lansdown awaited.

Susanna expected the king to leave, but he stood there, looking down at her, scrutinizing her from under those bright, heavy-lidded eyes. "What a beautiful ornament you have brought to our court, Roderick," the king said at last.

"I thought you would appreciate her, Sire," Lord Lansdown said with a touch of asperity.

The king turned to her, apparently waiting for her to speak. "I am very sorry the queen could not be here tonight," she said at last in a faltering voice.

"Why, my dear?" the king said. "She is only a queen, but you are a goddess."

Susanna only smiled politely in return. Just as the king thought, her head was not easily turned by flattery.

His remark was overheard, and spread through the crowd like wildfire. The woman Susanna had noticed glaring daggers at her while she danced with the king stood not far away from them, and Susanna could see her out of the corner of her eye. When someone whispered to her the exchange between Susanna and the king, the woman turned angrily aside and flounced away, drawing a long satin train behind her.

The king ignored the disturbance. "Surely you have not been in London long, Mrs. Collins?"

"No, Your Majesty. This is all very new to me."

"But you like our city?"

"Very much. Oh yes, I love it." For it was true. Now that she had been presented at court, and the king himself had singled her out for favor, she felt that she owned the whole world. If only she had Raymond to share it with her!

"You do us great honor. Perhaps you would care to dine here one day soon? With Lord Lansdown and Lady Mott, of course." Lord Lansdown had told Susanna that his daughter Lucinda could go to private parties, but could attend no official court functions until she was out of mourning.

"Yes, Sire, I would love to."

"Good. Is next Tuesday satisfactory?" He turned to Lord Lansdown.

"That will do very well, Your Majesty."

"Then it's settled."

The king left and returned to his seat on the dais.

"Well, my dear, I told you it would happen. You've made quite a conquest on your first night at court, not to mention quite an impression on everyone else here."

"Who was that woman who was glaring at me while I danced with the king? She got very angry when he came over to speak to us."

"Oh, that's Louise, the Duchess of Portsmouth," Lord Lansdown said in an offhanded manner. "She's one of the king's mistresses, but she's rapidly falling out of favor. She's taking the wrong tack with him—throwing tantrums and displaying temperament when he shows favor to other women. It's only driving him farther away from her."

"How many mistresses does he have?" Susanna started to say that he was awfully old to be carrying on so, but checked herself in time. Age was a sore subject with Lord Lansdown.

"The king only has two mistresses at the moment. There's Louise, and the other is Nell Gwynne."

"Is Nell Gwynne here tonight?"

"No, she doesn't attend official court functions. Nell's from a very humble background—used to be an actress, and even worse, they say. She makes no attempt to deny it. Once she was coming to see the king, and some people mistook her carriage for that of the Duchess of Portsmouth. Louise isn't very popular, because she's a Roman Catholic. Some boys started pelting Nell Gwynne's carriage with stones, and one of them said, 'It's the king's Catholic mistress.'

"Nell Gwynne stuck her head out of the coach. 'No,' she cried. 'It's the Protestant whore!' " Lord Lansdown laughed heartily.

"She called herself that?" Susanna was shocked.

"She says that's what all the king's mistresses are, but she's the only one honest enough to admit it. Her honesty does her no good, I'm afraid. She's the only one of the king's mistresses he hasn't made a duchess. If she herself didn't emphasize her humble origins the king might forget about them."

For the rest of the evening Susanna was deluged with partners. She did not deceive herself into thinking that everyone was overwhelmed by her charms. Rather, she suspected that what Lord Lansdown had said was true— everyone at court was heartily bored. Life at court was so monotonous and inbred that an attractive newcomer was showered with attention from the gentlemen and became the target of spiteful comments from the ladies.

Susanna knew she would have to take advantage of her novelty to establish herself; in a very little while people would be accustomed to seeing her and she would settle into whatever position she had been able to win when she was a fresh face.

On the evening they had been invited to dine at the palace Susanna and Lucinda spent the afternoon deciding what to wear. Lucinda was delighted to have a special invitation from the king, as the rituals of mourning weighed heavily on a young woman so full of vitality. She knew that it was Susanna who was responsible for the invitation, and again Lucinda seemed to be pleased with her at least temporarily.

"The king isn't overly fond of Papa," she said as Susanna went through her dresses, deciding which one she thought Lucinda should wear. "I think it's because they're two of a kind—both proud as peacocks!"

Susanna had decided to wear her gown of chartreuse velvet and her hooded cloak of topaz velvet, with the beautiful topaz necklace that matched her eyes. Lucinda eventually settled on a dress of deep blue satin, with a velvet cloak to match. "I feel like wearing my coral satin!" she said fretfully, stamping her foot. "It's so dreadful to wear these dark old colors."

When they finally finished dressing they found Lord Lansdown waiting for them patiently at the bottom of the stairs. "I'm escorting the two prettiest women in London tonight!" he said gallantly as he handed them into his coach.

The servants at the palace were expecting them. The small party was escorted to a room richly hung with velvet and priceless tapestries and lit with chandeliers of solid gold.

There were about a dozen people in the room, sipping wine and talking while they waited for the king. Susanna greeted the ones she knew and was introduced to the others. Once more, she seemed to be creating quite a stir, and again she suspected that any pretty young face just arrived at court would be the object of similar curiosity and excitement until her novelty wore off.

The invited guests were exchanging pleasantries about the weather and other harmless topics when two yeomen pulled back the velvet draperies over the doors with great fanfare and in walked the king—with Raymond Galt beside him!

Susanna had to look twice to convince herself that it was indeed Raymond, so elegantly dressed was he. He was wearing a gold-and-silver brocade coat over fashionable short-puffed breeches of pale green satin. The finest linen hose covered his long, muscular legs, and his russet hair was concealed beneath a black, elaborately curled periwig. Altogether, he looked like a different person entirely from the carpenter in leather breeches who had been carried to her door last October. Only the sapphire-blue eyes and stunning physique belonged to the Raymond she knew.

Although Susanna had been looking forward to this moment ever since her flight from Chippenham, she was so shocked that she wished for a moment that the floor would open up and swallow her. For one stunning instant their eyes locked. She could see that Raymond was no less startled, although he recovered more quickly.

"Mrs. Collins, may I present one of my advisers on naval affairs, Mr. Raymond Galt. Mr. Galt, Mrs. Susanna Collins." The king himself performed the introduction.

Raymond bowed low over Susanna's hand. "Your Majesty's court continues to be full of surprises," he murmured.

"Isn't she lovely?" the king said. "And Lord Lansdown has been keeping her all to himself for the longest time."

After the king exchanged polite greetings with his guests he indicated that he was ready to eat. With a great flourish the doors to a dining room were opened by a pair of servants. Inside the dining room candles blazed everywhere, and the table was laid with more gold and silver plate than Susanna had ever seen in one place. Great bowls of fresh flowers were placed everywhere.

The king seated himself at the head of the table. He had placed Susanna at his right, and to her utter dismay she saw that Raymond was to sit directly across the table from her, on the king's left. Lord Lansdown and Lucinda were far away at the other end of the table.

"Mr. Galt wants to go treasure hunting in the Bahamas, Mrs. Collins, but I want to keep him here to advise me," the king said. "Why do you think a man would want to embark on such a risky venture, when he has gained his sovereign's favor and has a secure place at court?''

"Well, Sire, there are some people who are excited by a challenge," Susanna said.

"On the other hand, there are others who like to play it safe," Raymond said, boring into her with eyes that were as hard and unforgiving as steel. "Why throw in your lot with one who has yet to make his fortune, when you can ensnare one who can give you wealth and a title overnight?" He looked down the table at Lord Lansdown, in case Susanna had missed his point.

Susanna wanted to die then and there, so great was her misery. Raymond thought she had used him to escape Boston and get to England, then had thrown him over because he was not rich in favor of someone who already was. He probably thought she had met Lord Lansdown in Bristol, and had been carrying on a secret intrigue behind his back while he was out negotiating the sale of the *Golden Plover*.

"Do you think I should let him have the ships and financial backing he wants?" the king continued, apparently oblivious to the strange current flowing between them. "He assures me that he can bring both ships back laden with gold, and heaven knows the royal coffers could use filling."

"That depends. Does his scheme sound like a reasonable one to you, Your Majesty?" Susanna asked.

"Well, offhand it is a little implausible, but young Galt here impresses me as a sane, levelheaded man. I'd hate to miss an opportunity because I lacked the vision to invest in an ambitious young man."

"It sounds like you do stand to gain a great deal," Susanna said. "On the other hand, there are many people who jump to hasty conclusions on the basis of scanty evidence and come to regret it later.''

"Then you advise caution," the king said.

"When dealing with Mr. Galt I imagine a great deal of caution is in order.'' As she spoke she looked into Raymond's hard eyes, with a steady, unwavering gaze.

Later Susanna could not remember the rest of the conversation, nor could she for the life of her recollect what she had eaten, as she was only able to choke down a few bites.

After a flaming dessert had been served with a great flourish the small party retired to the receiving chamber for an evening of dancing. Raymond sauntered over to Susanna, bowed, and said, "Please introduce me to your friends, Mrs. Collins.''

"Lady Mott and Lord Lansdown, allow me to present Mr. Raymond Galt, of Boston, Massachusetts.''

"A pleasure, I'm sure.''

As she sank into a deep curtsy Lucinda looked up at Raymond through her long lashes and gave him her most bewitching smile, the one that brought out the dimples in her cheeks.

"Do all the men in the colonies grow to your height, Mr. Galt?" Lucinda asked coquettishly. "I vow and swear, you tower over the king."

"There are about as many men of my height in the colonies as there are women with your beauty in England, Lady Mott. Would you care to dance?''

Susanna was deluged with partners, but Raymond was not among them. After the first dance was over he brought Lucinda back and launched into a flirtatious conversation, rather pointedly turning his back on Susanna. Raymond and Lucinda were speaking in low, intimate tones, and she had to strain to catch fragments of their conversation.

"The king seems to hang on your every word. . . ."

"A pity that you must wear those dark clothes. I can picture you in lavender velvet, or a lovely blue to match your eyes. . . ."

"You must tell me about your adventures at sea. . . ."

"I would rather talk about you. . . ."

Raymond danced with Lucinda several times, causing jealousy to wash over Susanna in painful waves.

Toward the end of the evening Raymond at last asked her to dance. There was nothing personal in the way he touched her as they moved through the graceful steps of the allemande.

"Well, madame, you seem to have done extraordinarily well for yourself in such a short time, with a doddering old man doting over you and the king practically in your pocket! Which do you plan to do first—become the king's next mistress, or marry Lansdown in the hopes of becoming a rich and titled widow in a few years? You've turned out to be quite the little opportunist."

"It takes an adventurer to suspect it so readily of another," she snapped. "You have the gall to accuse me of using the king, when you crossed the ocean for exactly the same purpose. I haven't noticed you avoiding anyone who could help you."

She wanted desperately to tell Raymond how she came to be there, but she was angered that he had leaped to conclusions without giving her a chance to explain herself. "And speaking of titled widows—you certainly seem to be dancing attendance on Lady Mott. It wouldn't hurt you to marry a titled lady and acquire her fortune. Then you wouldn't need the king's backing."

"I just might do that. It's not a bad idea at all." They glared daggers at each other and went through the remaining steps of the dance as stiff as a pair of mannequins.

As soon as the piece ended Susanna walked directly to the king, curtsied, and asked him to dance, without another word to Raymond. While they were dancing the king leaned over to her and whispered, "Will you come and have supper with me? Alone, I mean."

Susanna's heart was thudding. How could she refuse? "When do you want me?" As soon as she spoke she regretted her choice of words.

"I want you now, but unfortunately I will have to wait until next Wednesday."

"I don't know if I can get away." She would have to put him off as long as she could.

"I'll be waiting for you anyway. If you can't give Lansdown the slip I suppose I'll just have to restrain my impatience. There will be a special sentry posted to admit you at the Holbein Gate—on this side. Do you understand?" He smiled at her with a look of complicity.

"Perfectly, Sire."

When the evening was over Lucinda was excited and talkative on the ride home. "It was so wonderful to be out again! I do so hate being in mourning! What did you think of that Raymond Galt, Papa?"

"He's an impressive young man. Knows a great deal about the sea."

"The sea! Pooh!"

"He has a sharp head on his shoulders," Lord Lansdown added.

"I'm more interested in what he has between his legs than in his head," Lucinda said bluntly. "Let's face it, Papa, I just wasn't intended for celibacy. And from the way Raymond Galt looked at me, I'll wager he's no monk either. He's terribly handsome and I quite fancy him, even if he is a colonial. Can we invite him to dinner?"

"If you wish."

"Soon?" she pressed.

"Whenever you like, dear," Lord Lansdown said indulgently.

"How about next week?"

"All right, if you wish."

Susanna was ready to die from jealousy and longing. Why hadn't she told Raymond while they were dancing that she came to court only to find him? She had considered it, but he had been so cold to her, so distant and aloof. Perhaps he no longer cared for her. Perhaps he had decided to set his sights higher—on Lucinda or some other elegant lady at King Charles's court.

It was torture to hear Lucinda rattle on about the evening—what she had said to Raymond and what he had said to her. When she had exhausted that subject she repeated the other conversations she had engaged in or overheard, and discussed the gowns and coiffures of the women who had been present, usually to their detriment.

As Wednesday neared Susanna went through a dozen schemes in her mind to avoid the king's invitation to dine with him privately. She had little doubt as to his intentions. And what would Lord Lansdown think if she went?

On Monday her benefactor took her for a ride in Hyde Park. The day was gray and rainy, with a fitful wind blowing gusts of rain against the side of the coach. The unpredictable English weather had turned suddenly cold, and both of them wore fur-lined cloaks and a fur-lined robe lay across their laps. Each of them had their feet on a little brazier full of burning coals, so it was warm and moist inside the coach.

Susanna had suggested that they delay their ride until the morrow, as she had noticed that Lord Lansdown had been coughing at breakfast, but he insisted on going anyway. "A little inclement weather never kept a Londoner indoors," he said. "Otherwise most of us would never go anywhere!"

After they were settled, and the swaying coach had taken off, he reached over and took her hand. "I can't help noticing that you are unusually subdued, my dear," he said. "Is something troubling you?"

She decided that the best thing to do was to tell the truth. "Yes, Lord Lansdown."

"Please, my dear, I do wish you'd call me Roderick."

'Very well . . . Roderick. I'm troubled because the king has asked me to dine with him on Wednesday, and I couldn't think of an excuse to say no."

"Do you need an excuse?"

"I couldn't just turn the king down bluntly!"

"No, my dear—I mean, don't you want to go?" Lord Lansdown asked.

"But he wants to dine alone—just the two of us."

"I understand."

"But his intentions are anything but honorable."

"My dear, the king's intentions are always honorable."

"You mean, you wouldn't be upset if he seduced me?" she asked.

"Certainly not! It would be a great honor, as a matter of fact. It would enhance my position at court. Most of his mistresses are married women. Surely you don't think their husbands stand in the way, do you?"

Susanna shook her head. Just when she thought she understood these people, they did something else to surprise her.

"I certainly won't stop you, if you want to go, that is." A fit of coughing seized him. "Or is the problem that you don't want to?" he said as soon as he could speak.

"No, sir, I do not!"

"Are you sure? The king's mistress has a higher standing that anyone in the land, except the king himself."

"Even higher than the queen?"

"Oh, yes. Not officially, of course. But unofficially, she has much more power than the queen, because she has the king's ear, and can get him to dispense favors to those to whom she is favorably disposed. Besides, if you have any staying power at all, he will probably make you a duchess. As I told you, he's done so with all his mistresses, except Nell Gwynne."

"I still don't want to."

"Do you mind telling me why?" Lord Lansdown asked.

"I'd rather not."

"Very well, then don't go."

"I told him I didn't know if I could get away. He said he'd post a special guard, just in case."

"At the Holbein Gate?"

"Why yes. How did you know?"

He chuckled. "That's the way his mistresses always enter the palace. It's known as Cuckold Gate." Another fit of coughing convulsed his frame.

"You're getting ill, sir—I mean, Roderick. That cough's turning nasty. I think we should go home."

"Perhaps you're right." He tapped his cane. "Home, James."

By the time they reached Lord Lansdown's townhouse a rattling, persistent cough had settled in his chest. As he stepped down from the carriage a sudden spasm of pain wrenched his face.

"Where is the pain?" Susanna asked.

"Here—in my chest," he replied. "Don't worry—I'm sure it will pass."

"James!" Susanna called. "Help him in."

"I'm all right," the old man said, shooing James away.

He got into the house alone, but inside another spasm hit him, and he had to admit that he needed help up the stairs. He refused to be carried, but leaned heavily on James as he moved slowly and ponderously, making his way one step at a time.

In his bedroom Susanna pulled the cord that summoned the maid. "Build up the fire and tell the cook to start heating lots of water," she ordered. "Bring me all the hot water bottles you have and plenty of blankets. I'm going to make out a list for you. I want you to go to the apothecary's and get everything on it."

Lucinda came running in to find out the reason for all the commotion. One look at her father told her that he was ill. He had gone deadly pale and was too weak to stand. "Papa! What's wrong with him, Susanna?"

"He's got a bad cold, which could be turning into either pleurisy or pneumonia."

Lucinda motioned her outside so they could talk without being overheard. "How serious do you think it is?"

"If it's nipped in the bud, not too bad. But if complications develop it could be fatal for a man his age."

Lucinda paled. "Should I send for the doctor?"

"I think not, not right away. I know as much about these things as any doctor. Rest assured, I'll do everything I can to save him."

14

AFTER JAMES HAD GOTTEN LORD LANSDOWN INTO HIS nightshirt Susanna covered him with blankets and surrounded him with hot water bottles. As soon as the maid returned with the medicines Susanna had ordered she began dosing him regularly, and sat up with him through the night, catching little catnaps when she could. On Wednesday she sent a note to Whitehall Palace by a footman explaining to King Charles why she could not honor his request to dine.

After several days of constant nursing the crisis in Lord Lansdown's illness came. His fever broke without turning into pneumonia, and from then on it was only a matter of quiet bed rest and a nourishing diet until he was well again. Susanna continued to nurse him, and noticed that as soon as he was out of danger he seemed to enjoy being ill and all the attention he got as a result. She even suspected

him of exaggerating his discomfort in an attempt to pro-
long her presence at his bedside.

One day as she was watching her patient sleep Susanna
thought that one good thing at least had come from his
illness—she had had a legitimate reason for avoiding an
intimate tête-à-tête with the king. As she watched him
Lord Lansdown's eyelids flickered and slowly opened.

"Are you still here?" he said slowly. He smiled, and
reached out to touch her cheek. "You've taken such good
care of me. I'd probably be dead by now if it weren't for
you. I should like to wake up and always find your pretty
face beside me. Will you marry me, Susanna?"

"Oh, sir—I mean, Roderick—that's the illness talking.
You go back to sleep now."

If Lord Lansdown was fond of Susanna before his illness, he positively doted on her afterward. The first thing
he did when he was completely well and had his strength
back was to buy a coach for her. It was a beautiful little
gilt affair, with padded scarlet upholstery trimmed in swags
of gold rope and tassels, and six matched grays to pull it.

Susanna imagined he would forget that he had proposed
to her in a moment of weakness, but when they went out
together for the first time in her new coach he asked her to
marry him again.

"I'm sorry, Roderick" she said, lowering her eyes,
"but I can't marry you."

"I know I'm an old man, and in some ways it wouldn't
be much of a life for you. But I can lay the world at your
feet. There would certainly be compensations."

"It's not that, sir. I'm very fond of you."

"Is there someone else?"

"Yes, since you ask. I told you on the day we met that I
already have a husband."

"I hope you'll forgive me for saying that I believed that to be a polite fiction."

She tried to look astonished. "Why ever would I invent a tale like that?"

"I don't know. At first I thought that perhaps you were going to have a baby. After that, I couldn't guess. I sent word to the inn where you were staying that you could be found here, and no one has called for you. It's been some time now, and you don't seem to be greatly bothered by your husband's absence. I don't mean to alarm you, but perhaps he's been lost at sea."

"No," she said. "He's very much alive."

"Very well, I won't press you. But if you ever change your mind, or if you ever need any kind of help, you're to come to me. Agreed?"

"Agreed." Impulsively she reached over and kissed him on the cheek.

As soon as his strength returned Lucinda began plaguing Lord Lansdown to honor his promise and invite Raymond Galt to supper. When he did, and when Raymond accepted, Lucinda went into paroxysms of joy. "An actual virile, red-blooded male, and he's coming to see *me*!" she exclaimed, flying into Susanna's room and waving Raymond's note of acceptance under her nose. "Whatever shall I wear! Oh, I won't dress in somber mourning clothes! They make me look like a withered old hag! It's so dreadful—I can hardly remember what Frederick looked like, and I have to mope about as if I'm stricken with grief!"

"Didn't you love him?" Susanna asked.

"No, not exactly. I liked Freddy well enough, but the marriage was arranged between our parents. And we were only married a couple of years."

"Perhaps since it is a private occasion your father will

let you wear something pretty,'' Susanna said. "No one will be the wiser.''

"He'll do it if you ask him. You can get him to do anything! Will you?''

"Of course.'' Susanna smiled. Now that Lucinda was being nicer to her she could not help liking the young woman. "I'll see what I can do.''

"I know you'll bring him around. Raymond Galt said he wanted to see me in lavender, but I haven't a lavender dress, at least not one that's in fashion. I'd love to wear red, but I don't think I dare!''

"That would be going a bit too far,'' Susanna agreed. But red would go well with Lucinda's sandy blond hair and blue eyes.

"Susanna, is it true that you really don't mean to marry Papa?''

"Whatever put the notion into your head?'' Susanna had said nothing of Lord Lansdown's proposals, or of her rejections. She thought it would hurt his vanity if it got about that she had turned him down.

"Don't be coy with me. The whole household knows that he proposed to you twice—once when he was sick, and again the first day he took you riding in your new carriage.''

"Is nothing sacred? Is it impossible to have a bit of privacy here?'' She knew the servants gossiped, but how they knew virtually everything that went on in the house was beyond her.

"Oh, you silly thing—you can't keep secrets here! The first time the upstairs maid heard, and of course in the carriage James hears every word.''

"Well, yes, then, it's true. He did ask me, and I did say no.''

"Then I apologize for being so nasty to you. It's just

that from the very beginning I was sure you intended to marry Papa and steal my inheritance. He's so completely infatuated with you, you could get him to do anything you wanted."

"Lucinda! The thought never crossed my mind! I love Lord Lansdown like a father, and I'll be indebted to him for the rest of my life, but I could never marry him!"

"What a relief! When he asked you the first time I thought perhaps you were just being coy when you said no, but when word got about that you'd turned him down a second time I was pretty sure you meant it! I know I've been dreadful to you, and I'm ever so sorry. I really do like you."

"And I you." The two women embraced, and when Susanna caught Lord Lansdown in a good mood she brought up the subject of Lucinda's attire, and he gave his permission for her to wear a pretty dress when Raymond came to dine. "As long as it's not too bright," he said. "Red or yellow won't do."

Lucinda flew into ecstasies when she received the news, and immediately began going through every garment in her wardrobe. She settled at last on a light spring green satin, which looked ravishing with the necklace of priceless emeralds she had inherited from her mother.

She insisted that the whole house be cleaned from top to bottom in honor of the occasion, and supervised the food preparations herself. "We're going to start with crawfish bisque," she told Susanna on the day of the great event, "and then we'll have lamb stuffed with oysters, and a flaky meat pie, and our cook's best pudding for dessert."

"It sounds wonderful."

"You don't sound very excited. It's the first time I've had someone here who even remotely resembles a suitor. Of course, I couldn't marry Galt, a mere colonial, even if he were rich. Unless he decides to stay at court and the king gives him a title.''

"Do you think that's likely?'' Susanna and Lucinda were up in Lucinda's bedroom, helping each other dress. Susanna was wearing her most brilliant red velvet, having defiantly decided to look her best. Raymond Galt could go to the devil for all she cared.

"It's certainly not beyond the realm of possibility,'' said Lucinda, who was pasting a beauty patch high on one cheekbone. "They say the king has taken a great fancy to him, and keeps him by his side night and day.''

At last they were ready. In the drawing room, where they sipped wine before going in to dinner, Lord Lansdown joined them with their guest. Raymond was once again splendidly attired in a coat of gold and purple brocade and breeches of pale green satin.

"Good evening, Lady Mott,'' he said, bowing over Lucinda's hand. "And to you too, Mrs. . . . . Collins, was it?''

"Susanna Collins,'' Lucinda said. "She's the cleverest woman, Mr. Galt. You wouldn't believe it. She's just nursed my father through the most dreadful illness. I'm sure we all would have given him up for dead if it hadn't been for Susanna. She knows all about medicine, and is the best nurse.''

"I'm sure Mrs. Collins will receive her reward,'' Raymond said wryly.

"I hope you won't mind that we're dining *en famille*,'' Lucinda said. "I thought of inviting some more people, but to tell the truth, I hated to share you with anyone. I found your conversation at the palace so fascinating I wanted to have you all to myself. I hope you'll be satisfied with whatever the cook sees fit to put before us.''

Raymond murmured something appropriately reassuring, while Susanna smiled, thinking of the days of preparation Lucinda had gone through to make the evening as perfect as she could.

Once they had settled themselves at the table Lucinda turned the conversation around to Raymond. "You've made quite an impression at court, from all reports." After meeting Raymond she had sent out all her spies to learn everything about him they could. "They say the king dotes on you, and wants you with him morning and night."

"Unfortunately in this case court gossip is accurate for once," Raymond replied. "At first I thought it would be to my advantage to win my sovereign's favor, but I'm afraid I've overdone it. I thought if he liked me he would give me what I want, but instead he only draws me closer to him."

"You're not enjoying life at court?" To Lucinda this seemed impossible.

"Frankly, it grows rather tiresome after a while. Why, look at the king—even he is bored to death half the time. No, Lady Mott, I'm afraid King Charles's fondness for me has done little more than make me feel like a monkey at the end of a rather short chain."

"And what is it you want, then?" Lucinda knew perfectly well what Raymond was after, but she thought to ingratiate herself with him by getting him to tell her himself, and by hanging on each of his words as he did so.

"I came to court seeking the king's financial backing. I want to go treasure hunting in the Bahamas. There are wrecked Spanish galleons there, full of plunder, ripe for the plucking."

At Lucinda's insistence he described his plans in greater detail.

"Two ships," she exclaimed. "And a lot of equipment. It sounds dreadfully expensive."

"Unfortunately it is, or I should not have had to cross the ocean to find a patron." While Raymond talked Lucinda flirted with him shamelessly, one minute drawing her fan across her face until only her saucy blue eyes showed, the next minute favoring him with her most bewitching smile, while Susanna looked on, writhing inwardly.

"Does His Majesty seem favorably inclined to your scheme?" Lucinda asked.

"One day he does, the next day he doesn't. He keeps me dangling. Just as soon as I'm sure I'm making headway, he says that he needs me beside him and can't let go."

"And that doesn't please you?"

"I don't delude myself into thinking my sovereign finds my services indispensable. I think I'm little more than a court jester—someone who amuses him and distracts him from his cares."

"But I'm sure that's not true," Lucinda insisted. "He told me at dinner that you have a great knowledge of the sea, and that you've given him invaluable help in reorganizing the royal navy."

"Perhaps I have been of some small use along those lines."

"And if the king does give you the backing you seek? After you find this fortune—what then?"

"I don't know. My plans are not firm at the moment," Raymond said.

"Surely you don't plan to return to that provincial little town you live in, do you?"

"I may."

"But how could anyone go back to the colonies after having tasted life in London! You've had such a success here, too—do you know how many men would give any-

LOVESPELL

thing to have gained King Charles's favor the way you have?"

"Let them have it then. I don't fancy spending the next thirty years playing games with court politicians. There are already any number of them that would love to have my head on a platter."

"Oh, pooh! You can take care of yourself! Court intrigue can't be any more dangerous than life in the colonies, with all those ferocious red savages ready to massacre decent folk at a moment's notice! I heard only recently that there's been great trouble in that quaint place you're from," Lucinda said.

"Massachusetts."

"There is Indian trouble right now, isn't there?"

"Yes, according to the latest reports, which are several months old. They're calling it King Philip's War, after the Indian leader who's at the heart of the trouble. Frankly, Lady Mott, I'd rather face King Philip and all his tribe than navigate the treacherous shoals of life at your court."

"Well, then, we shall have to do everything in our power to alter your opinion of us, shan't we, Papa?"

Susanna ate mechanically, in mute agony. Raymond paid her not the slightest attention. Lord Lansdown, on the other hand, lavished attention on her, selecting choice bits of meat to put on her plate, pouring her wine himself, and beaming fatuously. What must Raymond think? Lord Lansdown did everything to give the world the impression that they were lovers.

The excruciating evening finally limped to a close. "Lord Lansdown, may I have permission to take your daughter riding in Hyde Park tomorrow, if the weather is fine?" Raymond asked as he was about to leave.

"Why yes, I don't see why not," Roderick answered, chuckling affably. "As long as you keep the windows

249

covered," he added hastily. "Remember, dear, you're still in mourning."

"Covered windows will suit my purpose exactly," Raymond murmured, bending over Lucinda's hand.

For weeks, as Raymond continued to dance attendance upon Lucinda—taking her for walks and rides, dining with her, bringing her a pop-eyed little spaniel from the king's own kennels—Susanna's misery grew. Raymond always greeted her politely when he came to call on Lucinda, and then proceeded to ignore her completely. He acted as if she did not exist.

Susanna's spirits were not lifted by a letter she received from Sarah in Chippenham:

Dearest Cousin Susanna,

Thank you so much for taking the time to write and explain your sudden flight from our home. You needn't feel bad or guilty—I knew from the start that it would be only a matter of time before my father forced his attentions upon you. He had his eyes on you from the moment you set foot in our house. The only thing that prevented him from approaching you earlier was his attachment to a barmaid at the Golden Boar.

He is still seeing this girl. Her name is Ellen. She is not much older than I am and a thoroughly bad lot. I live in fear that he will marry her. She cares nothing at all for the children and if he weds her I will still have to do everything. I have been reduced to a household slavey and have had no time at all for my books.

I am sorry to write you such a depressing letter, but I would do anything to escape my circumstances here. If you are ever in a position to give me some kind of employment please send for me. I hate to leave my brothers and sisters, but if I do Papa will have to marry someone responsible, or at least hire some decent help. If I don't get away soon I'm sure I will never get married. It will be forever until all the children are grown and by then I will be an old maid.

Love always,

Your Cousin Sarah

Susanna contemplated sending for the girl at once, but did not know how to introduce her into Lord Lansdown's household. She kept the letter, and decided that if her own situation were ever to stabilize she would send for the girl.

The king, meanwhile, apparently decided that he had acted too hastily in asking Susanna to dine with him alone. She received several more invitations from Whitehall Palace, but Lord Lansdown and Lady Mott were always included.

At a number of these occasions Raymond was present. After one evening of dancing, at which Raymond had icily ignored Susanna, she could not stand the tension any longer. Back home in her room she broke into frantic weeping.

She heard a knock at the door. "Susanna? It's Lucinda!"

"Go away!" she called, trying to muffle her sobs.

"No I won't! You must let me in!"

When Lucinda refused to leave, Susanna at last, reluctantly, opened her door. "Whatever is the matter?" Lucinda asked as soon as she was inside.

"Oh Lucinda—I've made the most dreadful mess of my life! I wish I were dead! I have nothing to live for!"

"Now, now—what's this! You're the one who's always so calm! Whatever would make you carry on so, Susanna?

Here's a handkerchief. Dry your eyes, and tell me all about it.''

Susanna did as she was bidden. "Before I confide in you, I must know one thing."

"Of course," Lucinda said, genuinely distressed over Susanna's unhappiness.

"Do you love Raymond Galt?"

"Love him? Heavens, no! He's the first attractive man to pay any attention to me since my husband died, that's all!"

"Oh, I'm so relieved! I thought you wanted to marry him!"

"Marry a colonial? You must be mad! Especially as he seems to have every intention of returning to that uncivilized place! But what has Raymond Galt to do with you?"

Slowly, hesitantly, Susanna told the tale of how she had run away from Boston with Raymond, omitting only her imprisonment and hearing on the charge of witchcraft. Lucinda's round blue eyes grew larger and larger as Susanna recounted the tale of their adventure in the Bahamas, the discovery of the treasure chest, and their journey to Bristol.

"So you left him because you couldn't see yourself as a lady, and thought he should have one for a wife?"

"Because of that, and in the belief that I would find family and friends willing to receive me in Chippenham."

She gave a brief account of her adventures there, and how she had come to London. "But I still love him, Lucinda. I love him most dreadfully. And I know now that I'm as good as most of the fine ladies at court! They have nothing but a set of manners anyone can learn, and a few foolish occupations which anyone can cultivate, and a great many pretty gowns and jewels!"

"You're a good deal better than most of them, if the

truth be told," said Lucinda. "Then why is Raymond so cold toward you?"

"Because he thinks I've abandoned him for someone who's already rich, who is already established."

"My father."

"Yes."

"I can hardly blame him. I thought the same thing myself for a long time. You could easily have married Papa, and he can't live forever. You'd have been young, wealthy, and titled, with the whole world at your feet!"

"I don't want the whole world. I only want Raymond!"

"Ooh!" Lucinda said when Susanna was through. "Do you suppose Raymond has been dancing attendance on me all this time just to torment you? The devious wretch!"

"I don't think so. I'm sure he finds you quite attractive, but of course I can't help hoping that he still loves me."

"The knave! And all this time I thought he was smitten with my charms! Men—you can't trust a single one of them! I wouldn't give a farthing for the whole lot of them!"

She blustered on in this fashion for some time, until finally Susanna started laughing. "You don't really want him, but it infuriates you that he might not really want you either!"

Lucinda started laughing too, her innate good humor overcoming her bruised vanity at last. "Well," she said. "This is a fine kettle of fish! We've got to get your Raymond back for you. What's to be done now?"

"Nothing!" said Susanna. "There's nothing you, or anyone, can do for me!"

"Nonsense," Lucinda said firmly. "I'm not without influence at court. It will come out all right, you'll see."

Susanna knew that it was only a matter of time until the king would attempt to see her alone again, and she was not surprised when she received a note from him, asking her to join him for supper.

"What do you plan to do?" Lucinda asked her when Susanna showed her the invitation.

"I'm going, of course. I haven't any excuse for putting him off this time."

"You don't sound very pleased."

Susanna shrugged. "What difference does it make what happens to me? I've lost Raymond. I might as well become the king's next mistress."

"You can't be serious!"

"Why not? At least he doesn't discard them like old rags when he's through. I wonder what he'll make me the duchess of?"

Susanna's maid helped her into her dress of black and honey-colored satin, and adjusted the overskirt of black lace. She tightened a busk around her midriff, defiantly pushing her breasts up until they were ready to pop out of her bodice.

After she was dressed Lucinda helped her make up her face. At last, under Lucinda's urging, she consented to have a small beauty patch placed beside the corner of her mouth, and another one on her temple.

"You're a vision!" Lucinda said when her toilette was complete. "I'll have your maid wait up for you," she said as Susanna put on her gloves. She giggled. "We won't be expecting you early."

Susanna felt nothing but an icy calm as her small gilt coach rattled over London's uneven streets. At the Holbein Gate the guards were expecting her. Her carriage drove up to a secluded side entrance to the palace, and she was helped down by two liveried servants. The same men saw her through a maze of corridors until they stopped at last in front of a door draped with velvet hangings.

One of the servants gave a soft, discreet knock, and the door was opened. "Mrs. Collins?" another liveried servant asked.

"Yes."

"Right this way, please."

Inside a small fire was burning against the night chill. The room was elegantly appointed, and before the fire a table had been set for two.

After Susanna removed her gloves the servant poured her a glass of wine. She had not been nervous at first, but as time passed and she continued to sit alone, she began to feel a small but insistent tug of apprehension. She had a plan, but she did not know if it would work.

At last an inner door opened with a flourish and the king walked in. Susanna rose and sank into a deep curtsy.

The king took her hand, kissed it, and gave it a small squeeze before he released it. "I am honored that you accepted my invitation," he said as they seated themselves.

"The honor is mine."

A few musicians were seated on a dais, hidden behind a tapestry, and as the king sipped a glass of wine they began to play. At a nod from him servants began to enter bearing food.

Susanna nibbled at her meal. The king was very smooth and relaxed, as indeed he should be, Susanna thought. He's done this often enough before! Seated as she was only inches away from him he seemed even older, every line and wrinkle magnified.

Between the wine and the king's easy manner, Susanna soon relaxed herself. When they had finished dining, and the last dishes had been cleared, the musicians stopped playing and silently withdrew, leaving them entirely alone.

The king poured Susanna another glass of wine. As she sipped it he took her hand in his and lifted it to his lips, kissing it softly. "I have looked forward to this moment, when the two of us would be entirely alone, so often," he said, piercing her with his glittering black eyes. "The first time I saw you, you aroused feelings in me that I had begun to think were long dead."

He rubbed the inside of her palm slowly with one thumb. "If those who envy me could walk in my shoes for a few days they would doubtless be content to live out their lives in quiet obscurity," he continued. "It isn't easy being a king. I have always needed someone to help me forget my burdens at the end of the day." He moved an inch closer. "Are you willing to become that someone, Susanna?"

It seemed to Susanna that she was watching a play being acted out in which she had no part. "I will give myself to you gladly, Your Majesty, if you will do me a favor in return."

"You may have anything you ask," he said. "Titles, land, jewels. Of course I will not expect you to continue living with Lord Lansdown. I will be more than happy to set you up in your own establishment."

"What I ask is not for myself, but for someone else at your court."

He raised his eyebrows, a startled expression on his face. "Someone else?"

"Yes, Sire. I will become your mistress if you will give Raymond Galt what he wants of you."

"Raymond Galt?" The king dropped her hand. "What is Raymond Galt to you?"

"I once loved him," she said in a low voice, dropping her eyes. "That is over. But I hate to see him hanging about from one day to the next, hoping for royal favor."

"But he has my favor already. So much so that I don't wish to let him go."

"I know, Sire. That is the problem. He came to court hoping to ingratiate himself with you, and unfortunately he succeeded all too well."

"Do you know what Galt wants of me?"

"Yes, Sire. He wants two ships, financial backing, and equipment to go treasure hunting in the Bahamas."

"How are you so well acquainted with his plans?"

"I came to England with him. I, too, am from Boston. I was on his ship when he found the treasure chest he presented to you when he first came to court."

"I see." The king snapped his fingers, and a servant materialized out of nowhere. "Show in Raymond Galt."

Susanna gasped. "He is here?"

Before the king could reply the door opened and in walked Raymond. He bowed deeply before Charles II, and then inclined his head slightly to Susanna. If he was surprised to see her dining privately with the king he did not show it.

"Mrs. Collins informs me that the two of you are acquainted. Is that true?"

"We were close to each other at one time."

"Do you love her?"

"Certainly not, Your Majesty."

"I do not think you are telling the truth for once, Raymond."

"You are certainly entitled to your opinion."

"Raymond, if there is one thing I have had considerable experience in, it is matters of the heart. You yourself know that I am no stranger to amorous intrigues. That is why I spotted at once that there was something between the two of you."

"At once, Sire? I don't understand." Raymond was icily polite.

"The first time Mrs. Collins dined with us here at the

palace the two of you were seated across from each other. I could hardly fail to observe the tension between you. I would have had to be blind not to notice it."

The king rose and began pacing rather restlessly around the room. "I noticed the same tension every time you were brought together after that, so I made some inquiries and discovered that you had come to England together."

"It seems that nothing escapes Your Majesty," Raymond said drily.

"You landed in Bristol and sold a ship called the *Golden Plover*. The day before the two of you were to come to London together Susanna left you and went to Chippenham."

"Chippenham?" For the first time since she had been presented at court Raymond looked at Susanna as if she was a human being instead of a reptile. "Why in the world Chippenham?"

"She has relatives in Chippenham, with whom she hoped to make a home," the king continued. "Unfortunately the conditions there were not favorable, and she came to London hoping to find you. Instead she found refuge with Lord Lansdown and his daughter."

"Refuge? Is that what they are calling it now?"

"Yes, refuge. I am sure it was nothing more. I am correct, Susanna?"

"Yes, Sire."

"She's a scheming little opportunist," Raymond said, biting off his words. "She used me, and then she used Lansdown, and if you let her she'll use you too."

"I think not. Lord Lansdown has made her an honorable proposal of marriage, which she turned down."

"Turned down?" Raymond turned to Susanna, searching her face. "But why?"

"Because, you dolt, she still loves you," the king said. "If I hadn't figured it out for myself, I received a letter from Lady Mott explaining it all. You've been pretending to court her for some time now, but you were really only seeking an excuse to see Susanna, weren't you?''

Raymond ignored the question. ''Forgive me, Sire, but if she loves me, what is she doing here?''

''She has just offered to give herself to me, if I will give you the financial backing you came to court seeking.''

Raymond swallowed an expletive. ''You did this?'' he said to Susanna.

''Yes.''

''I am about to make you a counter offer,'' said the King. ''I will give you the backing you desire, but you must take Susanna with you.''

''Let me be sure I understand you,'' Raymond said. ''You will give me the ships and equipment and money I need, but I must take Susanna Collins with me to the Bahamas?''

''Those are my terms,'' said the king.

''May I ask why you are doing this, Sire?''

''I don't know. Perhaps I'm just getting old and sentimental. I've certainly broken up enough romances. Instead of tearing a couple asunder perhaps I rather like the idea of bringing one back together for a change, that's all.''

''Very well, Your Majesty,'' Raymond said with a bow. ''If those are your terms, I accept them.''

''And you, Susanna?''

Susanna's heart was pounding so hard she could hardly speak. She had come prepared to sacrifice herself to the king in order to advance Raymond's ambitions, sure that she had lost him. And now! Could it be true that they would be together again? But it was only by the king's command. Raymond's eyes were as cold as steel. He was only taking her because it was a condition of the king's backing. But still—they would be together. She had a chance. Surely she would find a way to mend their misunderstanding.

"I accept your conditions, too, Sire. And I thank you with all my heart."

"Good," the king said. "Susanna, give me your hand. And you, too, Raymond."

He put Raymond's hand on top of Susanna's. "Whatever foolish misunderstandings have torn you apart, do you promise to resolve them?"

"I do, Your Majesty," Susanna said. Raymond gave a murmur of assent.

"Very well, then. I'll send for your carriage now, Susanna. You've got a lot to do—you'll be needing your rest."

15

WHEN SUSANNA RETURNED HOME LUCINDA WAS WAITING up for her. "Well?" she demanded, pouncing on Susanna's bed. "What happened? How was he? Is it true what the say about the king's sexual prowess?"

"Slow down," Susanna said, laughing. She told her briefly what had transpired.

"Then it worked!" Lucinda said. "I wrote to the king about you and Raymond. I told him everything—I hope you don't mind. But I never got an answer or any kind of acknowledgment. I thought he was dead set on having you for himself at all costs, and had chosen to ignore it. But Susanna, this is wonderful—does it mean that you and Raymond are reconciled?"

"I don't know," she said. "He was no more than polite to me."

"But now he has to take you with him."

"Yes, there's that at least."

The next evening Raymond called. After greeting him Lucinda withdrew and left him alone with Susanna. "I'll make provisions for you on one of my ships," he said stiffly. "But I want you to understand that the only reason I'm taking you with me is that the king commanded me."

"I think he intended for us to be more than shipmates," Susanna said. "His intent was that we should be friends again."

"A king, even one like King Charles, doesn't have absolute control over his subjects' emotions. There are some things that can't be legislated," Raymond replied.

"You mean you'll take me with you, but you'll not promise to care for me again."

"I'm glad we understand each other." He rose. "If you'll make my apologies, I'll be leaving. I'm swamped with work and I've had a long day."

"That was his stiff male pride talking," Lucinda said when they were alone together later in Susanna's bedroom. "He'll come around. Just give him time. I've explained everything to Papa and he won't do anything to stand in your way."

"He's not angry at me? I mean, for deceiving him? I did tell him rather a pack of lies when we met. I thought if he knew the truth he wouldn't befriend me."

"No—you're not to worry about it. He knew something was peculiar about your story from the beginning. He says he realized he probably couldn't hold onto you for long, all things considered."

Susanna spent the next few days in a flurry of preparations for her departure. Her parting gift from Lord Lansdown was a handsome set of trunks to put all her new gowns in. One night she tapped on Lucinda's door and presented her with a jewelry chest. "I shouldn't keep these," Susanna said, holding out the jewels that Lord Lansdown had given her. "They really should belong to you."

"Nonsense," Lucinda said, pushing the chest back. "They're yours. You've given my father a great deal of pleasure. It's not every old codger who gets to gad about London with a beautiful young woman on his arm. And you were a good friend to me, too—that is, when I allowed you to be."

Raymond, meanwhile, had his hands more than full. He searched the teeming London docks looking for just the vessels he wanted. Ships with gilded hulls gleaming, their tall masts bare skeletons shorn of sails, lay on the quiet water in great numbers, but his specifications were exacting, and few that he saw pleased him.

After Raymond had finally found several ships that appeared to be likely candidates to serve as his armed escort he badgered Admiralty officials for days at Wallingford House with requests to give him the vessels he wanted. He was mired in a sea of bureaucractic red tape that drove him half-mad with frustration. He was eager to be off, but officialdom was not to be hurried.

At last he was given an adequate man-of-war, one of two hundred tons burden, mounting twenty-two guns. The vessel had optimistically been named the *Success*. He got no crew, as the navy was short of men.

"I can't sail across the ocean with no men," he said, his temper at the breaking point. "The king said my vessels were to be properly provisioned and manned."

"Then let the king find your men," he was told. Afraid of pressing his luck, Raymond let the matter ride. At least he was making headway.

After scouring the docks again he found a ship that

would do for treasure hunting. For this second vessel he chose a fleet sailing sloop called the *Star*. He had decided to put all of his cannon on the *Success*, so as to lighten the second ship further for navigating shallow waters. While he wrangled with the navy he was also assembling diving tubs and other treasure hunting gear—grapples, purchases, drag cables, heavy blocks, and tackles.

The money the king had granted him had seemed like a great sum, but it dwindled at an alarming rate. In addition to the two ships and diving equipment, Raymond outfitted his ships with a legitimate cargo—brandy, powder, knives and scissors, clothing, and other English goods that the islanders imported.

By the time all this was done he had exhausted his financial resources, and he still had no crew. Raymond was forced to haunt the lowest dives and cheapest sea-men's boarding houses along the waterfronts of Limehouse and East London, assembling a motley crew that was willing to sign on with him for a portion of whatever booty they might find.

"And a scurvy lot they are, too," he said one evening when he had been invited to dine at Lord Lansdown's house. "You've never seen a more villainous assembly in your life! Here an eyepatch covers an empty eyesocket, there a livid welt on a man's cheek shows that a cutlass has left its mark. Many of them have backs that show they've been flogged half to death at one time or another. They look nothing so much as a pig-tailed, kerchiefed, earringed, tarry-smelling lot of pirates!"

"Do you feel safe setting sail with such a crew?" Lucinda asked apprehensively.

"Oh, I've no fear that I can control them," Raymond answered with his usual self-confidence.

When Susanna was packed Raymond conveyed her trunks to the harbor and saw them safely stowed aboard. "This will be your cabin," he said, in the new, curt, businesslike manner that hurt her so. "I'll be next door—not out of any particular choice. I just took the best cabin for myself and decided that as you are a lady you should have the next best. My officers are men accustomed to a certain amount of discomfort.

"You are free to take your meals with me and the other officers on board. Otherwise I intend to be left alone. I can't be bothered with a woman's foolishness while we're at sea. You will have to amuse yourself." His eyes were hard and unforgiving.

On the day they were finally ready to set sail Lord Lansdown and Lucinda saw Raymond and Susanna down to the docks with baskets laden with wine, cheese, and nonperishable delicacies for the trip. "Don't forget to write when you have the chance!" Lucinda said, embracing Susanna with tears in her eyes.

"Don't worry. We'll be back," Susanna said.

"We've got to be," Raymond said. "Don't forget I owe an enormous debt to the king."

"You'll succeed, Raymond, I know you will," said Lucinda, standing on tiptoe to receive a brotherly kiss on the cheek.

"I have no choice," he said grimly. His mind was already at sea. Susanna could tell that he was planning and scheming, impatient to be off. "If I fail I'm done for. Not only am I in debt to the king, but I've still got to pay off Samuel Coffin."

"Samuel Coffin!" Susanna gasped. "I'd forgotten all about him! That was his ship you sold in Bristol, and you pocketed the money! And half of the treasure in the chest you gave the king was rightfully his!"

"I'll pay him back for his ship," Raymond growled. "It's a good thing I had this money—what do you think I've been living on all this time, after I gave every bloody doubloon we found on our first voyage to His Majesty? Come on, girl," he said impatiently to Susanna. "Be quick with your good-byes. We've a fresh, spanking breeze and I'm anxious to be off while the tides are with us."

"Thank you, Lord Lansdown, for everything you did for me!" said Susanna, embracing the old man warmly. "I'm eternally in your debt!"

"It was my pleasure," he said gallantly.

Susanna could hardly believe that she was to be at sea once more with Raymond until the ship's great sails were unfurled, and the *Success* and *Star* moved slowly out of the harbor.

When they were on the open sea she stood on deck, watching as England receded. Finally it was nothing more than a speck on the horizon, and she was surrounded by the vast blue ocean.

Susanna was not afraid of the voyage before them. She was a good sailor, and was soon reaccustomed to the rolling and pitching motion of the ship. She loved life at sea, loved the motion of the ship and the smell of salt air and the beautiful sight of white sails billowing in a stiff breeze. She was deeply troubled, however, that Raymond treated her with such icy courtesy, as if she were a stranger. Every night she dressed with care in one of her beautiful gowns and joined him and his officers for dinner, and every night Raymond spoke to her in the same chilly manner he had shown toward her since King Charles had made their reconciliation one of the conditions of his patronage.

The more Susanna watched Raymond's crew the more

apprehensive about them she became. There were a few she thought decent, trustworthy men, but most of them looked like they would slit their mothers' throats for a piece of gold. There was one in particular that she disliked—a huge, hulking brute of a man named Ramon Garcia. He had swarthy skin pitted with smallpox scars, black, greasy hair, broken teeth, and a perpetual scowl. He rarely spoke, but she could see him sizing up Raymond when the captain was not looking. He seemed to her to be taking Raymond's measure, wondering, if it came to a contest between them, which one would emerge the victor.

When they reached the Bahamas she could not help remembering with nostalgia her first trip there with Raymond, when the two of them had been so happy together. The tropical islands with their broad, white beaches, exotic vegetation, and gorgeous birds evoked a thousand memories of happier times. The warm, balmy air and unbelievably clear blue-green water, through which one could see darting schools of fish and brilliantly colored coral swaying in its sparkling depths, produced in her a thousand pleasant sensations. Night after night she went to bed aching to hold Raymond in her arms. She thought that these memories might soften him, too, but he was so obsessed with treasure fever that there was little room in his mind for anything else.

For weeks the *Success* and the *Star* cruised the Bahama Bank, with no results. At night Susanna frequently paced on the deck, too restless and filled with longing to sleep. Often she saw light under the door to Raymond's cabin and knew that he was poring over his maps, deciding where to go next. He had no thoughts of quitting, but as week followed week with no success there was muttering among his crew, and Susanna could see black looks following him wherever he went.

One day a sailor named Mullen approached Raymond. "Cap'n," he said bluntly, "I've been selected to talk to you on behalf of the crew. You're driving us too hard. If you don't listen to us there'll be the devil to pay."

"Are you threatening me?" Raymond said shortly. "You could be hanged for your insolence."

"No, sir, I didn't mean any disrespect. It's just that we're all mightily discontent, and you could easily remedy the situation if you'd only listen. We don't think our request is unreasonable."

"Very well. Out with it, man—what is it you want?"

"We want leave to go ashore."

"You know what I've told you. There will be no shore leave until we find treasure. I won't have you getting drunk and lolling around all day with island girls until you've earned it. Discipline will go to hell."

"Begging pardon, sir, we were thinking of putting in at one of these islands that seem to be uninhabited. All the boys want is a chance to stretch their legs and do a bit of hunting and fishing. We're down to salt pork, biscuit, and a tot of rum a day. Some nice roast pig, fresh fish, and a few coconuts would be mighty tasty. It's hard to be sweating away here on board ship all day, with the sun burning us to a crisp, and a veritable paradise right before us."

"Very well," Raymond conceded reluctantly. "I suppose a bit of fresh food and a day of rest might do us all good."

"We passed a likely island yesterday," Mullen said. "We spotted plenty of game ashore, and there's good anchorage."

"We'll kill two birds with one stone," Raymond said.

"I'll give you one day to hunt and fish and amuse yourselves. Then, while we're in shallow waters, we'll beach the *Success* and scrape the ship's hull clear of barnacles."

Raymond gave the order to reverse the ship's direction, and by the next morning they were again within sight of a heavily wooded island that did seem to promise good hunting. At his instructions the crew ran the *Success* into the shoals at high tide, where the water was just deep enough to float her. The heavy cannon were all shifted to the starboard side of the gun deck, heeling the ship over. Then, to lighten her, the smaller culverins, known as murdering-pieces, were hoisted out and carried to the beach, as well as stores, cannonballs, and powder from the magazine. Raymond, Susanna, and the officers moved to the smaller vessel, the *Star*, which was light enough to float in shallow water close to shore.

The next day when the tide was out the *Success* would be beached on the sand. When this happened Raymond planned to give orders for the crew to wade out, carrying lines secured to the ship's side. Once ashore his men would pull the listing vessel over on her starboard side so that the other side could be scraped. After that she would be heeled to starboard in the same fashion and the other half scraped.

"For one day you can all go ashore and enjoy yourselves," Raymond said when the crew were assembled. "But woe be unto you if the men who are to have first scraping duty aren't back here at low tide."

"Thank you, sir. We'll need supplies," Mullen continued. "Water and canvas for tents, and guns for hunting—muskets, fowling pieces, and pistols."

The flesh crawled on the back of Susanna's neck as she thought of turning those cutthroats loose with lethal weapons.

"Cast lots among yourselves for a few men to stay aboard for an anchor watch," Raymond ordered after he had overseen the provisioning. "You can send others back to relieve them for the next watch."

The crew prepared to go ashore in longboats, whooping with delight at the prospect of a bit of hunting and swimming. Susanna's uneasiness mounted as preparation continued. "Do you really think this wise, Raymond?" she said when she could draw him inside for a moment.

"Is what wise?"

"Sending this crowd of armed ruffians ashore. You've removed the culverins and cannon. What is left to defend the ship?"

"So now you know more about running a ship than I do?" he said, his lip curling in scorn. "Mind your own business, Susanna."

She watched uneasily as most of the crew rowed ashore in the ship's boats and disappeared in the dense jungle. Only she, Raymond, his officers, and a handful of sailors on watch remained on board the *Star*, and the *Success* lay on its side like a beached whale, waiting to be grounded completely by the outgoing tide. As time passed Susanna's uneasiness mounted, but there was no point in trying to talk to Raymond again.

Throughout the morning she kept a close watch on the island. It was curiously silent. She wondered why she did not hear the report of pistols if the men were hunting, and why there was no one swimming and fishing in the surf.

Soon enough Susanna's apprehension proved to be well-founded. A few hours after the crew had departed one of the longboats rowed back to the *Star*, with three men on board. One of them was the ship's carpenter, one of the few members of the crew that Susanna regarded as reliable. The two men with the carpenter were ill-visaged scoundrels she would not trust as far as she could throw them.

Susanna was convinced the men were plotting some mischief, but what it might be she did not know. The longboat drew alongside the *Star* and the three men quickly climbed the rope ladder and leaped onto the deck. "I came back to get my box of tools," the carpenter said to one of the men on watch. "We'll be needing them ashore."

"What do you need your tools for?" she heard the sailor ask.

He hesitated. "Oh—some of the boys want a little shelter thrown up."

The man on duty shrugged. "Go ahead. It's no business of mine."

Susanna was sure something was afoot. She wandered out onto the deck and stood casually at the rail a short distance from the men who had returned to the ship.

The carpenter disappeared below and was back in minutes with his tool box. Just as the three men were about to go back over the side of the ship he bent over, clutching his stomach.

"What ails you?" one of his companions growled suspiciously.

"Cramps!" he hissed between clenched teeth. "Ooh!" he grunted as another one hit him. He turned his head to one side and gave Susanna a wink which the others couldn't see.

Susanna ran forward. "Come with me," she said. "I've got something in the medicine chest that should help you out, at least temporarily, so you won't miss your holiday."

As soon as he was out of sight he straightened up and took Susanna aside.

"You're not really sick, are you?" she asked.

"No," he said in a fast, tense whisper. "I've got to get word to the captain at once."

"I don't know where he is at the moment," she said. "Tell me what's going on, and I'll pass the message along."

"Very well. We've not a moment to lose," the carpenter said. "There's a mutiny afoot. I didn't find out about it until I was ashore. I said I'd build a shelter to protect the mutineers' provisions and powder, but I'd have to go for my tool chest first. I was really just looking for an excuse to come back to the ship and warn the captain. The others aren't sure of me, so they sent two of the men who organized the whole thing with me."

"Is everyone in on the plot?" Susanna asked, goose bumps of fear rising on her arms.

"Just about everyone."

"Tell me the plan," Susanna said. "I'll tell Captain Galt."

"The men are going to strike tonight in the dark, when you're asleep," the carpenter continued in a near whisper. "You and the captain and officers will be left on the island. The men plan to take over the ships and become pirates."

"Who's the ringleader?" Susanna whispered.

"Ramon Garcia. He organized the whole thing."

"I knew it," Susanna said. "I never trusted that man for one minute."

"He's been a pirate before," the carpenter continued. "At night he often boasts of it, telling us how much he's stolen, and how many men he's killed. He says he can tell us all how to become rich, and he's got just about everybody convinced. A few are only going along because they're afraid not to."

"Thank you for warning us," Susanna said. "Go ashore now and pretend to be in with the mutineers."

"What will you do, miss? Almost all the weapons are ashore."

"I don't know. Captain Galt will think of something."

As soon as the three men left Susanna hurried off to find Raymond. A frown creased his brow as she told him of the plot. He quickly summoned his officers and got Susanna to tell them exactly what she had heard.

"We're badly outnumbered," he said, "and we can't even be sure the sailors on watch are loyal, so we've got to act as if we know nothing when we're with them. Susanna said most of the crew is in on the plot. The mutineers have most of the small arms ashore, and the culverins too. We've got our cannon, but the ship is aground, and listed so that we can't use any of them. There's no way we can hope to succeed if we attack. Does anyone have any ideas?"

The gloomy expressions on the faces of his officers told Raymond that they were no more sanguine than he about their chances of escaping. The culverins, or murdering-pieces, were loaded with old nails, spikes, and bits of scrap iron. Firing scattering shot from their bulbous muzzles, they alone could mow down half an army with little difficulty.

"Excuse me, sir," Susanna said, raising her hand timidly. "One idea did occur to me while I was looking for you. The only advantage we have is that the mutineers don't know we've discovered their plot. They're not planning to do anything until we're all asleep tonight."

"Yes, yes," Raymond said impatiently. "So?"

"I have a plan," she said. "It's pretty desperate and risky, but it might work. Do you think we could sneak ashore and retrieve the culverins, while the men are off hunting and waiting for night to fall? Look—you can see the weapons plainly from the deck. They've just been left on the beach, with no one to guard them.''

"I don't know," Raymond said, rubbing his chin thoughtfully. "It just might work at that. The crewmen seem to be staying away from the side of the island closest to the ships. We'd just have to pray that no one saw us while we were hauling the culverins away. There aren't many of us and it would take some time, so it's mighty risky.

"But it's worth a try anyway," he said with grudging admiration. "I can't think of a better plan and I don't fancy spending the rest of my life on this godforsaken spot. What do the rest of you say?"

"Let's face it, we've nothing to lose," the second mate said.

"Aye, aye," the other officers murmured assent. A formal vote was taken, and Susanna's proposal was accepted.

Every pair of trustworthy hands was needed for the risky venture. The sailors who had been left on watch were held at gunpoint, trussed, and put in the hold of the ship, as Raymond could not be sure they were trustworthy.

Susanna hastily removed her dress and put on a sailor's blouse and pants. She and the ship's officers took off their shoes, slipped over the side of the *Star*, and waded ashore, their hearts in their mouths. It seemed to Susanna that they made a great deal of noise, although they did their best to splash as little as they could.

Working together they were only able to carry two culverins at a time. It was slow, strenuous work. Throughout the afternoon they toiled, going back and forth from the beach to the ship, until at last all the murdering-pieces were on board. It seemed incredible to Susanna, but apparently they had not been spotted.

"It's possible that the men on watch here aboard the *Star* were part of the plot, and that they were supposed to alert the crew on shore with some kind of signal if we acted suspiciously or anything else went wrong," Raymond said. "That's why no one has been watching us."

The culverins were fastened into place on the deck of the *Star*. Although they were all tired, every reliable person had to man one of the murdering-pieces and stand ready to repulse an attack.

"Do you know how to fire one of these things?" Raymond asked Susanna. He still spoke abruptly, treating her almost as if she were a member of his crew.

"No. You'll have to show me."

For two hours, which seemed like an eternity, the handful of people on board the *Star* waited and watched from the deck, ready to fire their murdering-pieces at a moment's notice. Susanna was about to drop with weariness, but she would rather have died than shown weakness in front of Raymond. At least the air was growing cool as the afternoon wore on. Fatigued as she was Susanna did not think she could have stood for hours on deck with the hot sun beating down on her.

At last, one of the mutineers came around to their side of the island. As soon as he realized that the murdering-pieces were gone he sent up an alarm, and within minutes the beach was swarming with men. Looking out at the *Star*, they could see their captain and his officers, standing behind the loaded culverins with an air of menace.

For several minutes the two groups—the large one on shore and the pitifully small one on board the ship—glared at each other.

"Give yourselves up!" Raymond shouted. "If you do it at once you may not hang."

The men on shore moved about, murmuring among themselves. Ramon Garcia stood in the foreground, his dark, ugly face turned black with rage and disappointment. "It must have been the carpenter!" he shouted. "The carpenter warned the captain!"

In an instant they had all turned toward the carpenter. Rough hand pushed him to his knees.

"If you hurt him I'll see to it personally that you all swing from the gibbet!" Raymond roared.

"Don't be bullied, boys!" Ramon shouted, trying to rally his forces. "There're many of us, and only a few of them! Come along, forward now! We'll storm the ship!"

With a roar he started wading out, brandishing a pistol. One by one the other mutineers ventured cautiously into the water, their muskets, pistols, and fowling-pieces at the ready.

"Stand where you are!" Raymond shouted.

The mutineers hesitated, looking toward Ramon. "We can take them!" he bellowed, beckoning with his pistol for his men to follow him. "It's us or them!" he shouted when his men wavered, hesitating. "Don't trust Cap'n Galt! We'll all swing if we don't succeed! And think of the plunder we'll take as pirates!"

"Throw down your weapons!" Raymond called back. "If you put up your hands and throw down your weapons, I'll be lenient!"

Their leader snarled defiance. "It won't work, Cap'n! We've got all the small arms, and there are only a few of you. You're not a match for the lot of us."

He turned to the other mutineers once again, waving them on to attack, but once more they hesitated. They were conditioned to follow Raymond's orders, and now that their plot was discovered they feared capture and the gibbet. Besides, they were not at all sure they could reach the deck of the ship before they were felled by a blast from the murdering-pieces.

Their doubt and uncertainty gave Raymond a temporary advantage. Deciding to act before he lost it, he leaped over the side of the ship and fearlessly waded ashore.

The men backed away from him. They were all intimidated by Raymond Galt, and had only found strength in numbers.

"Let's fight it out, man to man," Raymond said to Garcia when they faced each other.

"You're on," the man snarled.

The mutinous crew drew around the two men as they began to circle each other slowly, their fists doubled. At first they swung and feinted, each managing to dodge the other's blows and seeking to understand the other's manner of fighting. Garcia struck first, leaping forward and smashing his fist into Raymond's face before he could dodge it.

Raymond dropped to the left and landed in the sand. He came up with his fist in Garcia's belly. The mutineer's breath came out in a low "whoosh!" as he fell to his knees. He rolled over quickly for fear that Raymond might try to kick sand in his eyes, and came up lunging for Raymond with both hands.

For several minutes they exchanged blows. Raymond was the larger man, but Garcia was clearly an experienced fighter, too. Finally the two men closed in on each other. Their two bodies locked, swaying and struggling. Falling to the sand, they rolled over and over, each struggling to sit astride the other man.

Raymond at last succeeded in pinning Garcia under him. When he was sitting firmly astride the other man, he managed to free one of his giant fists long enough to deal Garcia a crushing blow to the face. The mutineer shook his head, dazed, trying to clear his senses. Taking advantage of his opponent's temporary confusion, Raymond pummeled the man mercilessly with his fists, until Garcia lay unconscious on the sand.

When the fight was over Raymond stood up, wiped his bloody nose on his sleeve, and moved toward his crew. The men drew back in alarm, demoralized now that their leader was knocked out. Several fell to their knees, pleading for mercy.

"Throw down your arms!" Raymond said in a quiet but sharp tone of command. "Put up your hands, and keep them up while you come aboard! One false move and our murdering-pieces will make mincement of you."

Now thoroughly cowed, the mutineers lifted their hands and waded out to the ship. The *Success* was put right again, and the two ships made sail, leaving the island deserted once more.

Raymond was not a cruel man, but he would not feel safe in his bed at night knowing that Ramon Garcia was alive. As an example to the crew he reluctantly hanged the instigator of the mutiny from the yardarm.

"And that's what the rest of you will get if there's the slightest hint of insubordination from any one of you," he roared, as the assembled crew watched Garcia's heels twitching in the final death dance. The sailors were like lambs now, jumping to obey orders, in terror of the hangman's noose.

"Surely you don't plan to keep them on?" Susanna asked.

"No, of course not," Raymond said grimly. "We're close to the island of Jamaica. I'm going to throw them off the ship at Port Royal and get a new crew. It's a better place to recruit adventurous sailors than London. And

Susanna,'' he said, speaking slowly if the admission pained him, ''you acted well and thought quickly. Thank you for your help.''

It was the only time he had been more than civil to her since the voyage began. She tried to conceal her pleasure.

''It was nothing,'' she said. ''I had no more eagerness to spend my life on a deserted island than you did.''

He gave a short bitter laugh. ''All of this time I've been busy worrying about pirates, steering clear of anything that remotely resembled a pirate ship, and I didn't see what was going on under my own nose. I never thought that my greatest danger would come from the members of my own crew.''

16

Susanna was fascinated by the town of Port Royal on the island of Jamaica. The port, it is true, was full of bawdy houses and cheap grog shops where sailors got roaring drunk on the local rum, but ports, she had observed, were much the same anywhere. She thought the island was the most beautiful place she had ever seen, full of lush green thickets and dazzling white beaches that ran down to the blue-green water. The town itself was full of excitement and color. Beautiful and inexpensive local goods were sold in outdoor markets. Dark women with huge baskets on their heads hawked their wares in the streets, singing the merits of their products in the local patois which had a lilting rhythm that fell delightfully on the ear. She could sit for hours just listening to the people of Jamaica talk. Their stirring music, too, was unlike anything she had ever heard—with its heavy percussion and syncopated rhythms, it exerted an almost hypnotic pull on her.

While Susanna enjoyed the pleasures of the island Raymond had work to do. He decided to take yet another gamble, and sold the cargo he had brought to divert pirates from his true mission in order to buy new provisions and pay for a better crew.

He was also dissatisfied with his equipment. "I'm worried about what may happen to our longboats in rough water if they're heavily loaded with precious metals, and we can't bring the *Star* in close enough to hoist the treasure aboard her directly."

He met a French sea captain, a local man named Jacques LaBorde whom he thought trustworthy, and explained the problem to him. "You need a pirogue," the man said at once.

"A what?" Raymond had never heard of a pirogue.

"It's a boat made from a single, large, hollowed-out tree. The natives use them in the Sugar Islands. The hollowed tree is split in half lengthwise. Then planks are placed between the two halves to form a flat bottom. It makes a craft that is very light but won't capsize in the heaviest sea."

"That's what I need, all right. Could you arrange to have one made for me—in secrecy?"

Day and night Raymond worked—seeking reliable seamen, sounding out local sea captains, and cautiously seeking advice from the few he trusted.

"You know, if you're in earnest about treasure hunting, there's an odd fellow you might want to talk to," Jacques LaBorde told him one day. "Most people think he's half-cracked, but there may be something to what he says."

"Who's that?"

"His name is Jules Martin. He's a bookish man, a

scholar, which in itself is almost unheard of in these parts. How he wound up here is more than anyone knows. Most seafaring folk have little enough use for people who pore over books and theorize about life instead of living it, so he's never been too popular. But I for one always considered him a smart man. He used to pester seamen with some crackpot theories about where sunken treasure was to be found, but they laughed at him so hard he leaves most of us alone now. Keeps pretty much to himself.''

"Where does Jules Martin live?" Raymond asked.

"He's built himself a little aerie up on a hill, where he can be alone with his thoughts and look out to sea.''

LaBorde gave Raymond directions to Martin's house. "And Galt," LaBorde asked. "Take a bottle of rum when you go visit him. He doesn't take kindly to strangers, but he's right fond of his bottle.''

That very evening Raymond went in search of him, armed with two bottles of rum.

He got lost once, and when he asked a local woman to direct him to Jules Martin's house, he could tell by the smile she gave him that she thought Martin to be daft.

The house itself certainly didn't promise much, being constructed of bits of confiscated lumber, palmetto fronds, and anything else that would keep the crazy-looking structure from falling apart. As he climbed the steep precipice that isolated Martin from his fellow islanders, Raymond wiped his sweating brow, wondering if he had been sent on a fool's errand.

He knocked on the door several times, and had about decided that Martin was not at home when the door opened a crack, a pair of small bright eyes peered out, and a curt voice said, "Who's there?"

"My name is Raymond Galt. I'm looking for Jules Martin.''

"You've found him." The door opened another inch, and a short, bandy-legged man with a bald pate and a wild gray beard peered out at him. He was dressed in a ragged shirt and pants several sizes too large for him which were held up with a piece of rope. "Who told you about me?"

"Jacques LaBorde sent me to you."

"State your business," Jules Martin said abruptly.

"LaBorde told me you have some interesting theories about where treasure might be found in these waters."

A feverish light kindled in the strange man's eyes. "He said that, did he?"

The door opened a little wider. Jules Martin looked Raymond up and down. "You're a sea captain?"

"Yes."

"English?"

"An English colonial. I'm from Massachusetts."

"Hah!" the man yelled, pointing his finger in Raymond's face. "A man who had the sense enough to leave. I hate the English. Well, don't just stand there, man—come inside."

At first sight the interior of Jules Martin's house looked completely disorganized. Piles of books and papers lay everywhere, amidst plates and cups and bits of sea tackle, but Raymond had the impression that Martin could lay his hand on anything he wanted at once.

"So it's a-treasuring you'd go, eh?" Martin's small bright eyes darted about in his face in a peculiar way as he talked.

"I've thought on it," Raymond said casually, pulling one of the bottles of rum out of his coat pocket. "Would you care to join me in a drink?"

Jules's eyes lit up when he saw the liquor. He picked up a tankard, poured an indeterminate brown liquid out of it through a crack in the floor, and handed it to Raymond.

He took another one for himself which was no cleaner, swabbed feebly at it once with a dingy rag, and held it out.

Raymond poured them both a generous tot of rum and sat back. At first he drank along with Jules, but soon he only pretended to drink while he refilled the other man's tankard.

Once he had gained a small measure of Jules Martin's confidence, and kept him well plied with liquor, Raymond had no problem getting information out of him. Behind his crusty manner the man was obviously lonely and eager to talk to anyone who would take him seriously.

"Where have you been searching?" Jules asked.

"I didn't say I'd been hunting for treasure. I said I'd been thinking about it," Raymond said cautiously.

"Come man, don't lie to me. You've got the treasure fever in your eyes. It's written on you plain as day."

"Very well," Raymond conceded. "I have been looking on the Bahama Bank."

"Hah!" Raymond was to find that Jules punctuated his speech with strange little grunts and explosions of sound. "Find anything?"

"One chest of treasure, but the rest was irretrievable."

"Hah! Looking in the wrong place," Jules said emphatically. "The Silver Shoals, that's where you should be."

"Silver Shoals?"

Jules leaped out of a chair, found a volume, and pointed to it. "The Silver Shoals. That's where the *Plata Flota* sank in 1643. Humph!"

Raymond drank his rum in silence, knowing he would get his story in due time.

"*Plata Flota*," Jules repeated. "The Silver Fleet." He thumped his book. "It's all written right here."

He told Raymond that every year a fleet of galleons arrived to load treasure at the storehouse of Porto Bello on the Isthmus of Panama. In 1643 the Silver Fleet left Porto Bello as usual, bound for Cadiz, bearing treasure worth many millions in its holds.

"The Silver Fleet made its way through the Windward Passage between the islands of Cuba and Hispaniola," Jules continued, indicating its route on a foolscap map. "Every year it put in at the town of Porto Plata to buy supplies and refill its water barrels before setting out on the long voyage across the Atlantic."

Jules told Raymond that in 1643 the Silver Fleet headed for home as usual after leaving Porto Bello, but a terrible hurricane roaring out of the southeast scattered the galleons and drove them to the northwest. As he talked he got out various books and ships' manifestos, gesticulating wildly and pointing to his documents as he talked.

"At last the ships were blown up onto the reefs." Jules stopped, looking at Raymond in triumph.

"And where are these reefs?" Raymond prodded patiently.

"Rocks jutting out of the sea, northwest of Porto Bello, man, as I told you. Hah! *Los Abrojos*, the Spaniards called them—the Silver Shoals."

He rummaged among his papers, and pulled out another book. "In 1650 a sailor claimed he'd seen a galleon that was sunk on the Silver Shoals. Humph!" He thumped the page before him. "One Esteban Ortega. He said that the galleon foundered near a high flat rock rising out of the sea."

"A high flat rock rising out of the sea on the Silver Shoals," Raymond said, trying to stifle his excitement. "Could you draw me a map?"

"I've already done it."

"I'd be willing to pay you generously for it."

"No, man, take it—it's yours. I have no need of money."

Raymond looked around, thinking that Jules seemed to him to need money. A chicken flapped up through a large hole in the floor and began strutting along a rickety table that had one leg shorter than the others. Jules had put a book under the short leg to balance it.

"Shoo, Gussie, there's a good girl," the eccentric said, flapping his hand ineffectually at the chicken, which ignored him.

"No, man, I don't want your money. I've got my books, and an island woman to take care of me. Hah! But when you're rich, send a case of rum back to me!"

"I'll do that," Raymond said, rising and holding out his hand.

Jules ignored the hand, giving him instead the rolled-up map. Raymond took the other bottle of rum out of his pocket and set it on the table.

The eccentric scholar shuffled to the door of his shack and bade Raymond good night.

Within the month the *Success* and the *Star* were threading in and out of the small keys of the Silver Shoals. The shoals were shaped like a half-moon, punctuated here and there by low-lying islets. Scattered clumps of swaying palm trees rose over the small islands' jungle thickets, and the exotic birds Susanna loved so were much in evidence.

The waters were much more treacherous than those of the Bahama Bank. Jagged rocks jutted out of the aquamarine water, and many more lurked beneath the surface, ready to rip wide open the hull of any ship unfortunate enough to strike them. To add to the danger the waters were rough and choppy, frequently churning into a wild, white fury as they broke against the submerged rocks. The patches of seething white water were called boilers, and every sailor dreaded them.

Raymond found not one but a number of flat rocks rising out of the sea, and the area around each of them had to be investigated. Usually he had to anchor both of his ships far away from the rocks to avoid the treacherous boilers, and send out men in longboats to look for wrecked galleons beneath the rock. After they had searched a small area thoroughly, both ships would move to another area and drop anchor.

Susanna was heartsore as she watched Raymond struggle with the elements and his ambition. He had changed. No longer the lusty braggart she had first met in Boston, Raymond had matured, grown accustomed to command. But he had also become silent. His eyes had a hard, flinty cast, and his mouth was set in a thin line of determination, as, day after day, he sent out his longboats in the cool, sweet, early mornings.

As the sun rose it turned the sea into a boiling cauldron. The backs of the crew, burned dark as teak, glistened with perspiration as their eyes searched the waters below. At the end of the day they would return, disheartened and exhausted, as the sun sank, turning blood-red as it neared the shimmering, distant line of the horizon.

As worried as Susanna was for Raymond, she never tired of watching the spectacular sunsets, or the great banks of white clouds rearranging themselves in an infinite variety of patterns, or the brilliant colors and intricate shapes of the coral reefs in the blue-green water. In the clouds and coral reefs she liked to imagine that she saw the shapes of animals and trees, flowers and castles.

On one night, when Raymond seemed particularly disheartened, she approached him after supper. She was still dressing for dinner every night, in the hopes that the sight of a pretty, stylish woman would cheer him up.

Raymond stood on the upper deck, staring disconsolately out to sea. The moon had risen, and was tracing a beautiful, silvery path across the water, but he seemed not to notice. Instead of looking at the moon, he was staring at the latest high flat rock he had found.

"Raymond," Susanna began tentatively. Lately they hardly exchanged a word, and she really did not know what she would talk to him about.

"Yes?" he said curtly, drawing his brows together in a frown of irritation.

"In Jamaica there were talking birds in the markets. They had brilliant plumage—green and scarlet and yellow."

He looked at her as if she were crazy. "You came up here to tell me that you saw parrots in the markets in Jamaica?"

"Well," she went on, "in Boston you used to tell me that there were talking birds down here, and I didn't believe you."

He snorted. "I know. You didn't believe that it was warm here in the winter either. And you always told me that my treasure hunting schemes were ridiculous and would come to nothing. Well, Susanna, I'm sure you're delighted that at least one of your predictions is coming true."

"No, Raymond, I'm not glad at all—not that I think it is coming true. You're not defeated yet, not by a long shot."

"I don't know. Perhaps I am crazy. When I was growing up I was able to do anything I set my mind to. Everything came to me easily. I suppose I thought life would always be that way. My father told me time and again my expectations were unrealistic."

"No, Raymond, I'm sure they're not." It frightened her to hear him talk that way.

"That's why you rejected me, isn't it? You thought I was a blustering fool, a jovial bag of wind."

"Don't be ridiculous. It wasn't that way at all. Why do you think I came away with you this time?"

"I really have no idea. You should have married a rich man while you had the chance. Lansdown isn't a bad sort—a bit too proud for his own good, but not hard to live with. You'd have been a rich, titled widow in no time at all."

"That's not what I want," Susanna said desperately. "I told you repeatedly I would have been perfectly willing to marry you if you had remained a carpenter. I still would," she blurted out.

"Then why?" He turned and seized her, grasping her by the shoulders and shaking her so violently that she almost cried out. "Why, Susanna? Why in God's name did you leave me?"

"Because . . . oh Raymond, I've made a dreadful mess of everything! It's hard to explain. I wanted you to have everything I thought you deserved. An elegant lady for a wife, someone who could walk beside you in that other world you seemed destined to inhabit. I didn't think I was like those people. I didn't think I belonged in that world. But I was wrong. The only difference between me and them was that they have been taught a set of manners and acquired a few accomplishments anyone can learn, and they wear beautiful clothes and jewels. I'm just as good as they are, I know that now."

"You're a damn sight better than most of them." His hands were still digging into her shoulders painfully, but she could not ask him to let her go. It had been so long since he touched her, even the pain was welcome.

"That's exactly what Lucinda said. Oh, Raymond, why didn't you come after me, when I left you in Bristol and went to Chippenham? It would have been easy enough to find me.''

''Because I thought you wanted to leave. I had begun to reflect on what my father always said—that I simply couldn't reach out and grab everything I wanted from life. I decided to let you be free if that's what you really wanted.''

''I was so lonely,'' she whispered. ''I thought I would die from missing you. But I loved you so much, I couldn't bear the thought of holding you back in any way.''

''Loved me?'' He spoke the words with wonder, as if he had never heard them before. ''Why didn't you tell me? Why didn't you ever tell me?'' At last he was looking at her, really looking, his eyes searching her face. He had dropped his stiff mask of false pride and was trying to understand.

''Because I was shy. And there was something else. I knew you wanted to go back to Boston, and I thought I could never go back there with you. After all those terrible things happened to me, I felt so defiled, so dirty. . . . I know it's stupid. I had done no wrong, but somehow I felt guilty for everything that had happened to me, as if I were somehow to blame.''

The horror of her last months in Boston came back, and flooded over her. She choked back a single sob that seemed to rise from somewhere deep within her, some dark place close to hysteria.

Raymond drew her to him, locking her in an embrace with arms as strong as steel. ''Oh Susanna, hush, my love. The things they did to you and said to you were terrible. I thought you had shaken them off. I should have encouraged you to talk about them, to get rid of your rage and frustration and grief. Instead, like a fool, I let you bottle it all up inside.''

''I don't care—it doesn't matter now. Oh, Raymond,

nothing matters now that you're talking to me again. That dreadful silence—it was worse than any kind of abuse."

He lifted her chin and kissed her then, gently at first, then with increasing passion. "Susanna," he cried hoarsely, "how I've missed you. God alone knows how much I missed you."

In a single easy motion he lifted her and strode to his cabin, almost kicking the door down in his impatience. They undressed each other with trembling fingers. "God, you're so damn beautiful," he said in a husky voice. "I never thought it possible to miss anyone the way I've missed you."

He went abruptly still and inhaled sharply as his eyes fixed on her full perfect breasts. The hard, haunted look had vanished from his face as all the sorrow had fled from hers.

He drew her to him, and groaned as her taut nipples teased the thick mat of hair on his chest. She could feel his hard maleness against her. Then, his sun-bronzed face beautifully tense, he lifted her onto the spartan berth in his cabin. His head bent slowly to one breast, and his tongue began a teasing arousal of the nipple, sending a hot shudder of need surging through her body. She clutched him, suddenly impatient, and drew him to her.

"No," he said, pushing her away. "I have to look at you first." His eyes searched her features. "How I missed that look of passionate abandonment," he said. "It transforms your face."

As he spoke his hands were busy, still slightly shaky as they traveled down her silky belly and rubbed the soft skin of her gently-curving hips and inner thighs.

"God, I can't stop now," he said in a low growl. "I'd like to take my time but I've wanted you too long, been tortured by dreams of you too long." His hands were moving over her feverishly, kneading and caressing her body, leaving trails of fire on her sensitive skin.

Immersed in a whirlpool of sensation, Susanna lay helpless, prey to a fiery torment of the senses. "Don't hold back on my account," she managed to gasp.

Seconds later he took her, pressing deep and hard into her flesh with his own. She gave a sharp gasp of pleasure as he thrust deeper, and then with another moan she let herself go in the ecstasy he brought her to again and again and again. For hours they made love like brute beasts, with a hunger and violence of which Susanna thought herself incapable.

Afterward they lay in each other's arms, looking through the porthole at the moonlight on the water. "Raymond," she said, "I never want to spend another night apart from you, never again for the rest of my life."

He stroked her hair and kissed each of her eyelids. "You'll not, if I have anything to say about it. The last months have been sheer torture without you. We're getting married at the next port we come to. This time you'll not have a chance to escape!"

The next morning the longboats went out as usual and searched all day in the area of the high flat rock. Toward evening they began once again to head back to the *Star*.

The youngest sailor in the crew, a boy named Jerry, asked the man in charge of his boat to stop for a minute.

"What for?"

"There's a piece of coral down there I want." Some of the sailors had small collections of coral, seashells, and other interesting and curious objects they found in their travels.

"All right, lad, but be quick about it."

The boy dived over the side of the boat. "Where in

tarnation is he?'' the captain of his boat said after more than a minute passed and the lad had not come up. ''He'll drown if he stays down any longer.''

Just then Jerry's head broke the surface of the water. ''Green guns!'' he shouted.

''What?''

''Green guns—I saw green guns down there!''

Hastily the sailors pulled the boy back over the side of the boat. He collapsed in the bottom, winded, trying to catch his breath. ''It's down there!'' he said between gasps. ''A great galleon!''

''Why haven't we spotted her before?'' one of his mates growled. ''We've been cruising these waters for days.''

''It's wedged in between two giant rocks. The shadows from the rocks hide the vessel when you look at it from above.''

''It will be dark in a few minutes,'' the boss of the boat said. ''Can you remember the spot and find it again tomorrow morning?''

''Aye—I'm sure of it!''

The sailors hastened back to tell Raymond of their find. In her cabin Susanna heard a great shout go up from the deck. She ran out to see the sailors jumping about and laughing.

''A double tot of rum for every man Jack tonight!'' Raymond roared in his old voice. He already looked ten years younger.

Susanna hastened to join him. In front of the entire crew Raymond grabbed her and gave her a kiss. ''You've brought me luck, lass!'' he shouted. ''If I'd known this would happen I'd have mended our quarrel weeks ago!''

The next morning Raymond went out in the largest of his longboats, taking Jerry, his native divers, and as much equipment as he could get on the boat. He was worried that Jerry might not be able to find the spot again. The men rowed for some time, bending their backs well into their oars, and the longboat sped across the water.

"That's the place!" Jerry cried at last.

"Are you sure?" Raymond had suffered so much disappointment he couldn't bear to have it happen once again.

"Yes sir, I'm sure."

Raymond was so excited he stripped off his clothes and went down with the divers. He swam down past darting fish and waving fronds of coral. Sure enough, the guns of a Spanish galleon, turned green by the sea, were jutting out of a wrecked hulk which was wedged firmly between two large rocks. There was a gaping hole where the ship's belly had been ripped open when she foundered.

Raymond and the divers swam through the opening. Inside, in the murky gloom, they could see bars of silver and a few gold ingots gleaming dully. Raymond could dimly discern the outlines of great casks and chests, too, before he had to swim back to the surface.

"It's there all right!" he said when he had been pulled into the boat.

When the divers returned Raymond ordered the crew to mark the spot with a buoy so they would be sure not to lose sight of it. Then, despite the desire of the men on board to go down and explore the galleon, he insisted on going back to the ships and launching the pirogue. "This time we're going to do it right," he said.

Back at the spot marked by the buoy the men rigged the grapples to the drag cables and sent the divers down with them. Now there was nothing to do but wait, while the experts did their work.

Raymond thought he would die with impatience. Cables were fastened to the larger objects, while the smaller ones were loaded in diving tubs. When the divers were ready for an object to be hauled to the surface, they signalled the crew with three short jerks on the line.

The first things brought to the surface were a tub filled with broken pieces of plate, assorted coins the divers had scooped up from smashed chests, and some silver and gold bars encrusted with coral.

During their first day, they removed from the wreck a sizable number of silver and gold bars and several thousand pieces of eight.

"This is only the beginning," Raymond said to Susanna that evening. The sun had turned into a shimmering red ball on the horizon, and Raymond and the longboat's crew were displaying the day's find for the other officers and sailors.

"There's a lot more down there, all right," one of the divers said. "We'll have to work at least one more day just filling tubs with the light stuff. Then we'll begin on the chests."

For two weeks the crew worked from dawn till dark, stopping only when the wind made the water too choppy. The position of the ship, turned on one side and wedged between two rocks, made the task of reclaiming her bounty a difficult one.

After the initial excitement of seeing his treasure being brought up at last, Raymond and the officers stayed on board the *Success* and began the laborious task of itemizing and describing the contents of the galleon and attempting to estimate their value. The ship had been heavily laden. In the hold of the *Success* Raymond sat surrounded by pieces of eight, doubloons, and pistoles, arranged in gleaming piles on tables. Bars of gold and silver were counted and stacked on the floor.

Every day Raymond watched as his treasure grew, and every night he made passionate, abandoned love to Susanna, who had moved into his cabin. She was glad, secretly, that they had mended their quarrel before he discovered his treasure. It was clear to everyone as the sunken galleon yielded more and more gold and silver that Raymond was going to be a very wealthy man, and now he need never think that she loved him only for his money.

The most exciting of the ship's treasures were the last to be brought up—two large chests holding a king's ransom in precious gems. Raymond opened the chests with a crowbar, and as soon as he got a glimpse of what lay inside he sent a sailor to fetch Susanna.

"I wanted you to be one of the first to see this," he said when she arrived. Susanna gasped as Raymond drew out caskets full of diamonds, many of them uncut, and other precious jewels—rubies and sapphires, emeralds and pearls.

The first chest was filled to the brim with unset gems. "I can't wait to see what the other one holds," Susanna said as Raymond pried it open. Inside lay the most exquisite jewelry she had ever seen, more splendid even than anything she had seen at the court of King Charles. An egg fashioned of gold filigree twisted open in the middle to reveal a dozen flawless pearls. A diamond tiara that belonged on the head of a queen followed. Next she pulled out a casket of rings—square-cut emeralds, huge flawless diamonds, blood-red rubies—all set in cunningly fashioned bands of gold.

Raymond lifted out a magnificent ruby necklace. "This is for you," he said. "I was looking for something perfect, something that I thought would be just right for you, and this is it."

"Raymond." Susanna gasped when he had put it around her neck and she saw herself in a mirror. Even though the setting needed cleaning the stones were incomparable.

There followed ropes of pearls, pins, brooches, and

pendants. A gold pin in the shape of a dragon caught Susanna's fancy. "May I have this for Lucinda?" she asked.

"Of course," Raymond laughed. "You may have anything you want, anything in the world. Do you realize that after I give the king his cut and pay off Samuel Coffin I'll still have an enormous fortune?"

He waved his hand. The entire hold of the ship was filled with plunder. "We're going to be the richest people in New England."

As soon as they were quite sure everything had been retrieved from the wreck Raymond gave the order to lift anchor. Now that they had their treasure their greatest problem was to protect themselves from pirates. They steered clear of any approaching vessel, no matter how innocent it seemed, and Raymond was thankful, after the mutiny of his first crew, that he had no more fighting on his hands.

They stopped only once, in Porto Plata. The town was nothing more than a ramshackle collection of limestone structures with palmetto roofs. "But never fear—I'll find someone here to marry us, just as I promised," Raymond said.

"No," Susanna said.

"No? Did you say no? I thought we'd settled all that, woman. Don't think you're going to escape from me a second time!"

"Of course I want to marry you, Raymond. I just don't want to do it here. I want to be married in a magnificent church, a cathedral perhaps, in a beautiful gown, wearing my new jewels. I want Lord Lansdown to give me away, and I want Lucinda to attend me. And who knows? Maybe the king himself will stand up with you."

"The devil take you, girl," Raymond sighed in exasperation. "What will you think of next? First you tell me that you're just plain Susanna Collins from Boston, whose proper place in life is to be married to some indentured servant. And the next thing I know, you insist on being married in a cathedral, with a king and lord in attendance, bedecked with jewels. I can't wait to see what you'll be wanting next."

"Don't worry, Raymond," Susanna said serenely. "When I think of what it is I next desire, you'll be the second one to know."

17

Within the walls of Windsor Castle the sun shone through the stained-glass windows of St. George's chapel, throwing brilliant colors of red and blue and purple on the impressive ceremony being carried out below. Beneath the ancient vaulted roof, below the altar hung with crimson and gold velvet, sat King Charles II. Before him knelt a man dressed in a robe of crimson taffeta lined with white, sporting a white hat with a feather, and white boots and gloves. At his side stood a page bearing a sword, hilt upward, with a pair of spurs fastened to it.

Rows of noblemen flanked the king on either side. The Lord Chamberlain was in the process of adminstering an oath. "I solemnly swear to honor my God, maintain true religion, love my sovereign, serve my country, and help maidens, widows, and orphans," the kneeling man promised.

The Lord Chamberlain stepped forward, took the sword from the page, and handed it to the king. After King

Charles had put its belt around the man's neck so that the sword hung over his left arm, two other noblemen came forward and fastened the spurs to his heels.

King Charles raised his own sword and struck the kneeling man lightly on the shoulder with the flat of his blade. "Arise, Sir Raymond," the king commanded.

The new knight arose, fastened his sword at his side, and, turning, lead a solemn procession down the aisle of the chapel and into the brilliant sunlight.

"And congratulations to you, too, Susanna. You'll be Lady Galt soon enough," the king said when they were outside, kissing the cheek of the beautiful woman who came forward to stand beside the newly created knight.

"Lady Galt!" she said, savoring the words. "I suppose I can learn to live with that."

"I've just made your intended the new governor of Massachusetts," the king said. "While we're in a benevolent mood, is there anything you would like?"

"Yes," she said. "I'd like to send for my cousin in Chippenham, Sarah Cheever. I'd like to take her home with us, now that we can provide her with a good dowry. It's too bad she won't be able to get here in time for the wedding tomorrow."

"Don't you ever ask for anything for yourself?" the king asked, laughing.

"But I've already got everything I want," Susanna said, taking Raymond's arm and letting her other hand fall to rest on her slightly swollen belly.

"You'd better send for your cousin in a hurry," Raymond said. "We'll have to leave right away if we want our first child to be born in Boston."

"He'll be an English subject wherever he's born," said the king.

"But he'll belong to the New World, too," Raymond added.

The next day, in the same chapel, Susanna Collins became Lady Galt. The king himself and half his court were in attendance as Susanna walked down the aisle on the arm of Lord Lansdown. She was wearing a gown of white brocade sewn with raised roses of gold thread. The dress was low-cut in the current fashion, and had puffed sleeves and a long train. Around her neck she wore a necklace of priceless pearls, Raymond's wedding gift to her from his treasure chest.

Raymond looked unbearably handsome in a velvet suit of deepest blue-that matched the color of his eyes. Lucinda stood to one side of the altar, crying into a lace handkerchief.

Two days later Sarah Cheever arrived from Chippenham. The girl looked thinner and more worn than ever. "We'll fatten you up soon enough in Boston," Susanna said.

"Will there be someone to teach me Latin in Boston?" Sarah asked wistfully.

"Sarah, you can learn all the dead languages you want to, and some live ones too," Raymond said, laughing. "Although why you want to waste your time on that nonsense is beyond me."

"Are you really rich now?" Sarah said, looking at the well dressed couple.

"Of course we're rich, Sarah," replied Susanna. "Why do you think the king knighted Raymond and made him the governor of Massachusetts? He was so grateful for his share of the treasure Raymond found he almost danced a most unregal jig when he heard of it!"

"We're still not sure exactly what we're worth, but it's at least three hundred thousand pounds," Raymond interjected.

Sarah's eyes almost popped out of her head. "Three hundred thousand pounds! You'll be the richest people in the world! I've never heard of so much money!"

"And guess what?" Raymond added. "I hear that ships are flocking to the Silver Shoals in numbers that you wouldn't believe! I'll bet fortune hunters will be down there cruising those waters as thick as pickpockets at a hanging!" He laughed good-naturedly. "Well, I wish 'em all the luck in the world."

"How about you, Raymond? Do you think about going back and trying again?" Sarah asked.

"Whatever, for child? I've got more money than I ever dreamed of possessing. I'll never be able to spend a tenth of it. No, my wanderlust is spent. I'm looking forward to settling down and having some babies to bounce on my knee. Besides, I'll have my hands full running Massachusetts."

"I still can't believe all that money," Sarah said, shaking her head in dazed wonderment. "Does this mean that when we get to Boston I can buy all the books I want?"

"You can buy all the books in the world," Susanna said. "Tell her about Jules Martin, Raymond."

Raymond had already told the story of the eccentric scholar who had led him to his treasure to the king and before several other audiences, and he had perfected it by now. He even had the man's peculiarities of speech down pat.

After they had all laughed over the story, Sarah asked, "Surely there must be something he wants in return for telling you about the Silver Shoals!"

"He asked for a case of rum," Raymond said. "I'm sending orders for him to be supplied with as much of the finest Island rum he wants for the rest of his life. And, of course, he's to contact me if he ever wants anything else. But I imagine his greatest pleasure will now be swaggering down to the docks and thumbing his nose at all the captains who've been calling him a fool all these years! And of course I've sent an appropriate token of my gratitude to Jacques LaBorde, who sent me to Jules Martin in the first place.''

When Susanna and Sarah had a moment alone she inquired about affairs in the Cheever household in Chippenham.

''Well, after I wrote you I felt terribly guilty about wanting to leave the children, even though I'm not very good with them and they drive me to distraction,'' Sarah confessed. ''But while you were away a miracle happened. My father has actually found a woman who pleases him and is a good housekeeper too! They're getting married as soon as he's out of mourning. She's already made a world of difference at home. That's the big news. And I guess you'd like to know that John Carver died.''

''I'm sorry I couldn't have known him when his mind was still good. I'm sure he could have passed on many stories Mary told him about my mother.''

''I'm so glad to be with you I don't know what to do,'' Sarah said. ''Thank you for rescuing me.''

It was on a glorious spring day in 1677 that the *Golden Rose* sailed into Boston Harbor carrying Sir Raymond Galt, the new Governor of Massachusetts, his beautiful twenty-year-old bride, and their young cousin, Sarah Cheever. Raymond could not conceal his excitement at going home. For days he had paced the deck restlessly, straining his eyes for his first glimpse of his beloved Massachusetts on the horizon.

''Susanna!'' he roared, bursting into their cabin as they neared their destination. ''I can see it! Come out on the deck!''

Sure enough, through his spyglass she could dimly make out the outline of the Massachusetts shore.

When they finally sailed into Boston Harbor Raymond was like a child in his enthusiasm. "Calm down," Susanna said, smiling at her new husband. "You're an important personage now, remember? You've got to act dignified."

He took a deep breath and squeezed her shoulder. "I know. But it's good to be back, isn't it?"

He took a deep breath, inhaling the scent of fresh-sawed lumber mingled with the smells of tar, wood-smoke, and drying fish. "It even smells like home."

"All harbors smell alike to me."

"Oh no. I swear Boston harbor smells like none other in the world."

Raymond wore a suit made especially for the occasion, a magnificent affair of scarlet, white, and gold, which stood in bold contrast to the homespun and old-fashioned finery of Boston's citizens. After the ship landed he mounted a handsome black stallion and led a parade to the newly built Town House, where important meetings were now held. Behind him walked long columns of militiamen. All along the parade route constables had to push back the crowds. People had come from all over the colony, and neighboring colonies as well, to look at the new governor who was also probably the richest man in the New World. Cheers went up on all sides as he rode past, with Susanna and Sarah following close behind on more docile mounts.

At the Town House a delegation led by the mayor and other important citizens was waiting to meet them. After the mayor had read a proclamation of welcome, Dr. Griggs, who was one of the delegation, stepped forward. After bowing and congratulating Sir Raymond on his new appointment, he said, "And may I present my wife?"

Raymond suppressed a smile as out of the crowd stepped none other than Elizabeth Harden! Wreathed in smiles, she sank to the ground in a deep curtsy, and greeted Raymond and Susanna as though she had never seen them before in her life.

"My goodness, Lady Galt," she said, her eyes sweeping Susanna's gown of rose velvet, "is that the way ladies are dressing in London? So . . . revealing."

"Yes, Mrs. Griggs," Susanna said sweetly, with a pointed look at the other woman's out-of-date finery. "Only country folk in England have worn ruffs for these many years now."

The town had not changed much. Sheep still grazed on the common, looking placidly at the malefactors locked in the stocks. Boys still played stool-ball and blindman's bluff on Boston's cobbled streets. To Raymond the harbor might mean home, but to Susanna home was the clustered, gray-timbered houses and the steepled churches on the long slope down to the water from the tall hill with its beacon pole.

The biggest event during their absence had been what had come to be called the Great War of King Philip in 1675-76. Metacom had finally succeeded in pulling most of the New England tribes together in an alliance against the white man, and in a number of bitterly fought contests the Indians had at first triumphed, then slowly been pushed back.

For over a year Metacom had succeeded in evading capture, slipping from one Indian camp to another. An Indian fighter named Colonel Benjamin Church was finally responsible for King Philip's downfall. Using friendly Indians as scouts, he'd finally managed to pick up Metacom's trail and track him to his stronghold, which the Indians called Mount Hope. There the Indian chief who had terrorized New England for a year and a half was seized and slain. His ornaments and treasures were seized by soldiers, and his crown and belts of gold and silver were sent as a present to King Charles II.

Before King Philip was caught more than six hundred whites had been killed or captured. Hundreds of houses and a score of villages had been burned or pillaged. Crops had been destroyed, cattle driven off, and in some places agriculture had been brought to a temporary standstill. Susanna knew that her kidnapper had wrought great havoc among her people, but she could not help being saddened by news of Metacom's death.

Raymond paid Samuel Coffin for the *Golden Plover* with interest, and gave him a generous piece of his treasure, much more than half of the original treasure chest Raymond had found, which was all Coffin was strictly owed.

Raymond, Susanna, and Sarah were soon installed in the recently built governor's mansion. "Later we'll build our own home," Raymond said. "It will have to be bigger than this for all the children I plan to have!" It was there, in the governor's mansion, that Susanna gave birth to her first children, boy and girl twins, about three months after their arrival in Boston.

"Nicolas and Abigail," she said sleepily when the midwife allowed Raymond into their room. They had agreed to name the child for Susanna's father if it was a boy and for her mother if it was a girl.

"My parents are still alive, so there's time enough to name one for them," Raymond said.

"And Lucinda," Susanna murmured. "I'd like to name a girl for her. And then of course there's the king. He's done so much for us, I think we should name one of our sons Charles, don't you?"

"Heaven sakes, woman, we'll be busy making babies for years to come with that list!"

"I'm up to it," she said, and then yawned. "Just give me a few weeks to rest."

Not long after the babies were born the housekeeper told Susanna one day that there was a man to see her in the kitchen. "He's only a tradesman, but he insists that his business is with you and nobody else. I tried to get him to wait in the parlor, but he said the kitchen was good enough for him," Mrs. Boughton said with a sniff of disdain.

In the kitchen she found Michael Hale waiting for her, dressed in a tradesman's baggy leather breeches, his round-brimmed, high-crowned hat in his hand.

"Michael!" she said, holding out her hand. "It's so good to see you. Come into the parlor, we'll have tea."

Susanna had introduced tea to Boston, and now people of fashion often offered it when they had guests.

"Tea! I've heard of it, but never tasted it." In her parlor he looked anxiously around, twisting his hat, clearly ill-at-ease.

"You can have ale if you prefer."

"That will do very well."

After they were settled and had exchanged greetings Michael said, "I'm sure you're busy, so I'll come right to the point. I wrestled with my conscience over coming to see you for many a day. There were times when I thought it unnecessary, but finally I decided I'd never sleep easy until I said my piece."

He took a deep breath. "We were wrong, all of us. I mean, about what we did to you. I never did believe the charges they brought against you. I was just angry and hurt and wanted to lash out at you. And I was strongly encouraged to throw in my lot with your other accusers."

"Really, Michael, this isn't necessary," Susanna said gently.

"Yes, it is. It's necessary for me. Anyway, I wanted you to know that after your hearing, before you . . . left Boston, while you were still in jail awaiting trial, I went to the magistrate and to Reverend Gilchrist and retracted my statements. I said they were all false. Of course events were moving along on their own accord by then, and there was nothing I could do to stop them. But I did try. I just wanted you to know that."

"I'm glad you told me. I never did hold anything against you." Susanna looked at the timid tradesman's assistant before her and wondered how she could ever have dreamed of marrying the man.

"Are you happy now, Michael? I mean, is everything all right?" she asked.

"Oh, yes, Sus . . . I mean, Lady Galt, as right as rain. I married Hannah Warren. But I suppose you know that."

"Yes, I'd heard."

"Not everyone knows yet, but we're going to have a baby next winter."

"Oh, that's wonderful! Please accept my congratulations." She made a mental note to send a gift when the baby came. "And you're still with George Burroughs, I hear."

"Oh, yes. I suppose you might say that I'm his right hand man."

"I'm so glad everything turned out well for you."

"And I'm happy for you, too. Well, I'd best be getting back to the shop." The young man finished off his ale, rose and bowed awkwardly, and left.

That evening Susanna told Raymond of Michael's visit. "I suppose that ties up all the loose ends from the past," she said. "Now we need to decide on a suitable dowry for

Sarah, and start looking about for a good husband for her."

"Give the girl time," Raymond said. "You women are always miserable until you find a man for every young girl approaching marriageable age. Besides, it seems to me young Sarah is perfectly capable of catching her own husband. Have you seen the eyes she's been making at Makepeace Proctor in church?"

"I didn't think men noticed those things," Susanna said, laughing. "Yes, I've noticed, but I put it down to a young girl's foolishness."

Raymond drew her to him and gave her a long, lingering kiss. "It wasn't foolishness with us, was it? You wove a lovespell to bind me to you forever. Why not let young Sarah weave one of her own?"

Susanna was delighted to have the babies, for to tell the truth now that she was a lady of leisure with servants to dance attendance on her, time occasionally hung heavy on her hands. Not long after Michael's visit Susanna decided one day to walk out to her old cottage. She had been very saddened to learn upon arriving in Boston that both Hannah and Ebenezer Akin had been killed in King Philip's War and that their cottage had been burned to the ground, but Susanna's old home was intact.

Inside it looked as if she might have just stepped out for a few minutes, except that everything was covered with dust. Her furniture, linens, and cooking utensils lay exactly where she had left them on the Sunday she had been put in jail. She imagined that people must have thought she had put a curse on the place and were afraid to loot it. The furniture her father had made, the homely household utensils she and her mother had scrubbed a thousand times—

all lay unaltered. She had grown accustomed to fine things, and her cottage seemed very small and dark to her now.

She climbed the stairs in a reflective mood, thinking of her parents and the Akins, the friends she had made in England and all the adventures she had had since that brilliant October day when Raymond Galt had burst into her life. No one had whispered a word about witchcraft since her return, and from the reddened faces and averted glances she imagined that many were hoping she would soon forget the whole incident. It had all happened less than two years ago, but it seemed more like a lifetime.

Upstairs her loom lay where she had put it, with the wool thread she had been using to make a new cloak for herself still on it. She sat down at the loom and stepped on the pedal. Up went one frame of heddles, lifting half the lengthwise threads. Between the two sets of warp threads she passed the shuttle, then lowered the heddles and brought the batten forward with a thump, so that its reeds pushed the new crosswide thread into place. Then she pushed down the other pedal, raising the other frame of heddles. Back the other way she passed the shuttle, and then lowered the frame of heddles. Again she pulled the batten forward. She would have repeated this procedure until she had enough material for her cloak.

She looked up from her loom. In the gathering dusk she saw dim, wavering figures gather in her attic—her father and mother, Hannah and Ebenezer Akins and people she somehow knew to be her cousin, Mary Cheever Carver, and Mary's parents, Samuel and Elizabeth Cheever. Standing beside Cousin Mary was her husband John Carver. Dressed in quaint old clothes were other folk she did not recognize but knew to be her ancestors. They were all smiling at her.

"I have children," she said to her parents. "Twins—a boy and a girl. I named them for you. Raymond is very busy with his official duties now that he's the governor of the colony. He says we will build a new society here, unlike anything else the world has ever known.

"It's all right," she said to her mother. "I went through a difficult time, but now everything is all right." The dim, smiling figures did not change. "You know all this, don't you? You can see me, can see what's happening to me."

The figures faded slowly, until once again she was quite alone in the attic. Long after she could no longer see them she could still feel their presence. She sat for a while in the companionable silence, knowing that they would always be with her, and that she would never be alone again, no matter what happened to her. One day she would join them, and she hoped that someday when she was gone her children would also feel their presence, so that they too need never be alone.

She was letting the afternoon get away from her. By the time she walked home it would be approaching dusk. She had the babies to feed, and Raymond would be coming home, wanting his supper.

About the Author

A former professor of philosophy, Katherine Sargent is now a full-time writer of fiction. She lives in New Iberia, Louisiana, with her husband and three cats—Douglas Furbanks, J.T., and Tuffy. *Lovespell* is her fifth Fawcett historical romance. She enjoys hearing from her readers at P. O. Box 1431, New Iberia, LA 70561.